BLINDING JUSTICE

Also by Debby Meltzer Quick

Anomaly Series
Don't Say a Word
Blinding Justice

McKinney Class of 1986
May I Have Your Attention Please
I Just Can't Say I Love You
Absolutely and Totally Smitten
The Stories That Must Be Told

Blinding Justice

Anomaly: Book 2

Debby Meltzer Quick

ISBN: 979-8-9871874-8-7

Cover design by: Jai Design
Cover illustration by: Vivian McKay
Author photograph: Milana Gilligan Photography
Copy editing and Typesetting: Nicole Frail Edits

*To everyone who deserves a second chance . . .
and those who allow it.*

1

PETER STOOD BEHIND THE HEDGE surrounding the courtyard to watch the ceremony. He knew he wouldn't be welcomed by the family. His family. What used to be his family. True, it had been his choice to walk away all those years ago. But he had never walked away completely. He had been watching them, from afar, for years. Not in the ways of a stalker. The world had been invaded by the internet. Information could be found online.

He'd seen when his daughter made the cheerleading team in high school, and then when she was voted team captain during her senior year. He had found the yearly honor roll from his son's school every year on the digital version of the town's newspaper and the list of names of the graduates when he finally finished school. His daughter was three years behind her brother, and then they were both at State University. Lucky for Peter, who was adept in the ways of modern technology, social media was becoming easier and easier to access. He was able to see pictures and stories on MySpace, and then Facebook. He could see his children's activities and thoughts, at least the ones they made public. When he finally decided to make contact, he would have to urge them to be more private with who could see their information. But for now, he was glad it was available to him so he could track their progress in life.

He'd found it harder to find information on his wife. She was now his ex-wife, he knew. He could see her progress at work as she'd been promoted through the years, making great strides even after she was left to raise their two children on her own without financial assistance except the balance of their joint savings account. But the news that hit him the hardest had been the announcement in the *Wisteria Weekly News.* Janice had gotten engaged. And the man she was engaged to was the dentist he used to bring his children to see when they were small. The man who provided the children with a new toothbrush every six months. Maybe Janice liked the perks. Maybe Dr. Flagg polished her teeth for free. What hurt the most was thinking about what else of Janice's he was polishing.

Peter hadn't left because he'd stopped loving his wife. He'd left because he *did* love her, and their kids. He hadn't felt like he'd had a choice. And he didn't really regret his choice. The children were doing great. Janice was happy. And today, on this beautiful spring day in Wisteria, his daughter was getting married.

He watched as his son walked down the aisle, escorting his mother to her seat in front, and then went back to walk his grandmothers to their seats with their husbands. The bridesmaids started their trek, and Peter shook his head in disbelief. His daughter's friends had all grown up so much. He'd felt as though no time had passed, but this was proof that it had. As if to mock him, his left knee started to ache again. He shifted his position to take some weight off it. Soon, his son walked back down the aisle, this time on the arm of a woman he'd never met, but he knew she was his daughter-in-law. They took their places at the altar. A tear rolled down Peter's face as he realized that his daughter-in-law was obviously very pregnant. He was going to be a grandfather soon. He had missed so much.

The music stopped. Peter looked to the back of the aisle, and he saw his daughter. She was a vision of absolute beauty, an angel, with her chestnut hair wrapped around the back of her head, wavy tendrils framing her face, her fragile features, her beaming smile. He wasn't close enough to see them, but he remembered her shining blue eyes. She was radiant. She was holding on to the arm of an older man whose face he couldn't see. He braced himself to see the dentist walking his daughter down the aisle on her wedding day. It was a job that should have gone to Peter, and it would have, if only he had made a different choice . . . but if he had made a different choice, this wedding might not have ever happened.

The music started. The Wedding March. Everyone stood as the bride made her way toward her true love. Peter tried to get a good look at the face of the dentist, only to find . . . it wasn't the dentist at all. It was a man he'd never seen before. He was a man of average height with a deeply receded hairline. What was left on his head was a tufty gray fringe, and he wore a pair of lopsided, round spectacles that appeared to be sliding down toward the tip of his bulbous nose. His black tux matched all of the other men in the wedding, but on this man, the suit looked frumpy, as if he had slept in it the night before. The man stumbled slightly, and Peter's daughter caught his arm. They looked at each other and giggled before continuing their walk. When they made it to the altar, the groom stepped forward to meet them. His daughter kissed the older man on the cheek, took the groom's hand, and went the last few steps to stand in front of the justice of peace, to be finally joined in holy matrimony. The ceremony progressed and then came to its conclusion. The bride and groom kissed, everyone applauded, and the wedding party receded back up the aisle. Peter wiped the tears from his eyes. They were tears of joy, and tears of loss.

Peter Reed had lost years with his family. They were years that he spent searching, trying to discover the truth about himself, and by extension, his family. He did what he felt he had to, to protect them, and to be completely honest, to protect himself. It made sense that they had all moved on. They'd had to. He'd wanted that for them. They were not obligated to stay in stasis until he returned. He wasn't even sure he was ready to return. He only wanted to watch, and maybe establish some sort of brief contact, but—

"Hey, you, what are you doing back there?"

Peter turned to look behind him. A man in the formal clothing of a catering staff stood close by, holding a sealed trash bag in each hand, apparently bringing them out to the dumpster nearby. "I—uh, I'm just—"

"I told the other guy that came by earlier the family said we could leave any leftovers out on the south side of the venue after everyone leaves. But in the meantime, you need to clear out." He turned to leave but then turned back quickly. "Oh, will you all be needing utensils? I can make sure we leave you some plastic forks and knives. And maybe some disposable napkins if you want."

"I don't—I guess—"

The man shook his head. "Listen," he said apologetically. "I understand. I've been through some hard times myself. It's hard to believe that our country has come to this, especially in a place like Wisteria. I'm sorry they don't let you guys stay in the shelter during the daytime hours. I can't imagine it's easy to have to wander around all day. At least there are some shady trees at the park. If it gets too hot, I think the community center has an air-conditioned area where you can go and rest and get something cold to drink. And then come back later for the food. Probably around six?"

Peter stared at the man, and then he nodded. "Okay," he said. "Yeah, thank you. You've been very generous. I-I'll just go."

He turned back toward the courtyard for one more look. He saw her, his daughter. Kaya. She was standing on the lawn, talking to the dentist. The dentist had his hand on her elbow. On her right was the groom. His name was Grayson Pike. His son-in-law. Peter swallowed. He took one more sweeping glance over the group of guests at the reception. There was Janice, his ex-wife, talking to Peter's own parents, Tom and Candice. They all laughed. It made him happy to see them still being friendly with each other. Janice had never done anything wrong. She deserved to have their love and support. Maybe they had even befriended the dentist. And there, sitting at another table, was Graham, his first-born child. Graham had become a man. He was sitting next to his wife. Her name was Gina. She had her hand on her protruding belly, and she was smiling. The older man, the one who had walked his daughter down the aisle, was sitting at the same table, and he was talking. He was also looking around, as if he had lost something. Then he bent down and looked under the table. He came back up and shrugged. Graham and Gina laughed. Peter turned away. He was intruding here. He had to leave. If he didn't leave now . . .

He took a few steps forward.

"Hey!"

Peter stopped, but he didn't turn around.

"Hey! You! Stop."

Peter took another step toward the street, praying his face had been shielded well enough by his baseball cap.

"I said stop! Come on! I can't run in these heels. Give me a break."

Peter took a breath and closed his eyes. Then he opened them again and turned around. And there she stood, about twenty feet away. He took off his hat.

She ran up to the edge of the courtyard, looking over the hedge at the sidewalk. When he looked at her, she stopped in her tracks, her mouth agape, eyes focused on the sight before her. A full minute passed as they stared at each other. Just as she went to take a step toward him, her new husband was at her side. "Kaya, what is it?" he asked, putting his hand on her arm.

She looked at him, and then back at Peter. She pointed. "Him," she said.

"That's the guy I saw behind the bushes during the ceremony," Grayson said. "I'll go talk to him." He took a few steps toward the sidewalk, but Kaya grabbed his arm.

"Grayson," she said softly. "No." She held his arm tightly. "I-*I* need to go. Grayson, I thought he was just some creepy guy, gawking at us, but . . . that's—I think that's—"

"I'm her father," Peter said, taking a step toward her.

Kaya continued to stare, and then a sly smile spread across her face. "I knew you'd come," she said. "I told Graham, years ago. I told him you'd come to my wedding, and you'd watch me get married, and then we'd talk—" She reached out toward him.

Peter quickly took a step back. "No, Kaya," he said. "No. Not yet."

Kaya jerked back, her arm still outstretched. She looked at her hand. "I . . . oh my God." She dropped her arm to her side. "So it's true," she whispered.

"What's true?" Grayson asked. He looked up and glared at Peter. "This is the absolute worst time that you could have shown up, Mr. Reed. This is our wedding day."

Kaya nodded slowly, looking at her feet. "It's the happiest day of my life."

Grayson looked at her. "Kaya, what do you want me to do?" he asked, obviously desperate to act. "How can I help you?"

Kaya looked at him gratefully. "Go get Graham, babe," she said. "But don't tell him why. Just tell him I need him right now."

Grayson nodded. He looked at Peter one more time, shooting him a warning look. "I'll be right back," he said, and he jogged away.

"He's great," Peter said. "I can tell. He really loves you."

Kaya laughed bitterly. "So you don't even need to touch him to tell, huh? I guess your skills are really advanced."

Peter smiled at his daughter, although confused by her words. "You don't need any special skills," he told her, "to be able to see when a man is madly in love with your daughter. I could see it in every part of him. You did great, Kaya."

"And you remember my name."

That statement ripped at Peter's heart. "Your name," he said. "I chose it, you know. Your mother had no idea what to name you. She was reading out loud from this baby name book she had taken out of the library. When she read off Kaya, I suddenly remembered a trip I had taken to Jamaica during spring break in college. These local guys were walking around the beach, trying to sell pot to tourists. They called it kaya. So when your mother said the name, it hit me funny, and I told her that was the name I wanted. I didn't tell her why at first. She just thought it was pretty."

"Everyone thinks it's pretty," Kaya said. "Some people ask me if it's Hawaiian. I looked it up. It actually is a Hawaiian word. It means 'the sea.' I think I like that better than meaning 'pot' in Jamaican."

Peter laughed. "Do you like the sea? Have you ever been?"

"No," she said, rubbing her arms with her hands, as if she were cold. "I plan to, though, someday."

Peter nodded. "We have so much to catch up on."

Grayson ran back over. "Graham is coming," he said. "He didn't want to leave Gina alone, so he was bringing her over to your mom." He turned to Peter. "She's almost at full term."

Peter could tell that Grayson was trying to convey a message to him: *This is my territory. These are my people. You don't belong here. Watch your step.*

Peter nodded. "I could see her earlier. She looks beautiful."

Kaya looked toward the courtyard as her brother walked calmly over to the small group.

"What's up, Ky?" he asked. "Are those homeless guys from before bothering you again?" He looked toward the man on the sidewalk. At first, it appeared that he hadn't made the connection. Then he looked back again and nodded. "Hello, Dad," he said, remaining calm.

"Hello, Graham," he said. "Congratulations on the wife and baby."

Graham nodded. "Thank you." He turned to Kaya. "Do you want me to . . . do anything right now?"

Kaya looked back and forth between her brother and her father. "He doesn't want me to touch him."

Graham thought for a moment. "So we were right then."

Peter watched his son's face. "What were you right about?" he asked quizzically.

"You have the skill," Graham said.

"What skill?" Peter asked.

"Oh, for God's sake, Dad," Kaya exclaimed. "You know very well what skill."

"Maybe I do," Peter answered. "But maybe what some people call a skill, others call a curse."

"And that's why you left me to deal with 'the curse' all by myself?" Kaya snapped.

Grayson stepped up. "I really don't think this is the right time to get into this." He turned to Graham for support.

Graham nodded. "Dad, I'm not sure what to do or say right now. Kaya suspected a long time ago that you would appear at her wedding, behind the bushes. You did exactly that. I also remember her telling me that when you did show up at her wedding, she wouldn't be angry, and she wouldn't turn you away." He looked at Kaya. "Remember that, Kaya? You said that you would listen to what he had to say."

Kaya's face softened. "I did say that."

"Kaya!" a female voice called out. "The photographer needs you."

Kaya looked back at Peter. "This is my wedding day," she said. "I-I guess I'm glad you showed up. It's like you fulfilled a prophecy. But like Grayson said, this is not the time or place to get into this conversation. I do want to talk to you. We do have a lot to catch up on." She reached for Grayson's hand.

"Wait!" Peter called out quickly. He didn't want the moment to end. He wanted to gaze at his daughter in her wedding dress for just a little bit longer. "Who was that guy, the one that walked you down the aisle? I know it wasn't Steve Flagg."

Graham shook his head. "You know about Steve? Well, I guess if you know about Kaya and Grayson getting married, you'd know about Mom and Steve's engagement."

"That's Dr. Blake," Kaya said. "He's a close family friend. Graham and I met him at State. He's . . . helped us a lot over the past few years. He's been, well, like a father to me. I couldn't think of anyone else I'd want to walk me down the aisle. And Dr. Blake knows things. About me. About us." She motioned to her brother. "And I guess, by association, about you, too."

Peter winced. "About me? What about me? What does this man know?"

Grayson spoke up. "Listen, Mr. Reed—"

"Peter, please."

Grayson nodded. "Peter. We have pictures to take, and people to greet. Graham, can you . . ."

Graham nodded. "You two go back. I'll be there in a few minutes."

Kaya gave Peter one last faint smile and then walked away with her husband, hand in hand.

Peter looked at Graham. There was so much he wanted to know, including what this Dr. Blake knew about his family, but right now, his son was standing right in front of him, all grown up. His face relaxed. "You must be close to six feet tall," he said.

Graham laughed awkwardly. "Five-ten," he said. "I think these shoes give me a little bit of extra height. I never got as tall as you, or even Grandpa." He looked more carefully at his father. "I guess it's a good thing for me that male pattern baldness comes from the mother's side of the family, huh?"

Peter's hand went straight to the top of his head. "It's not that," he said. "It's just some thinning on top. Most of it has grown back." He chuckled. "It started during a stressful period in my life, soon after I left . . . Wisteria. I started to pull some of it out methodically, when I was anxious. There's actually a name for it. Trichotrillomania."

"Huh," Graham said. "Is it hereditary?"

"I don't think so." Peter took a step onto the lawn, closer to his son. "Some things are just learned."

Graham nodded. "I'm in school to become a psychologist. I've been working in research for a few years, but now I'm back in grad school. It's a bit different than that path you took."

"To say the least," Peter said. "I guess advertising isn't for the faint of heart. But you've done well, Graham. I've followed your progress since high school."

Graham looked at the ground. "I always wondered if you knew what we were up to." He looked back up. "Internet?"

Peter nodded. "Internet. Son, I have to say I'm very proud of you. Of both you and Kaya. You've really done well. I was a bit skeptical when I saw that Kaya had been working for the police and was planning on attending the police academy. I'm both proud and scared for her. She's a brave girl."

"Woman," Graham corrected. "She's easily the bravest person I've ever known." He turned back to look at the crowd at the reception. He caught sight of Gina, still talking to his mother and her husband. "So do you want to wait, or do you want to talk about the elephant in the courtyard right now?"

Peter felt a palpitation in his chest. "The elephant?" he asked. "What elephant are you referring to?"

Graham smiled in amusement. "I might still be young, Dad," he said, "but I'm not stupid. It might have taken us a long time to figure out what was going on with Kaya, and most likely with you, but we did figure it out eventually, and the hard way. Dad, Dr. Blake has found out that Kaya has the anomaly. I've been tested, and I have it, too, but it doesn't express itself the way Kaya's does. We're assuming we got the anomaly from your side of the family, but we'd have to do some testing to know for certain. We'd probably want to consider bringing in Grandma and Grandpa, too."

Peter looked at Graham, his eyes wide. "Son," he said, shaking his head. "You're gonna have to enlighten me. Because you're saying a lot of things here. A lot of confusing things. And to be honest with you, I have no idea what in the hell you're going on about."

2

"I HAVE ABOUT AN HOUR," Kaya said, grasping her coffee and bringing it to her mouth. "Oh, that's good. I'm so tired. I can't believe I have to get on a plane in three hours."

Graham laughed. "I find it hard to pity you," he said. "It must be so hard for you, to have to face ten days in Italy on your honeymoon."

Peter smiled, watching the banter between his children as he stirred the sugar into his coffee. "I went to Italy once," he said. "I was about nineteen. I'll never forget that trip. I wish we had time." He looked down at his drink. "I know we don't, though, and it means a lot to me that you were both willing to meet with me to talk. What—what did your mother say when you told her about me?"

Graham's smile fell away. "I waited until we got back to the house last night to say anything," he said. "I didn't want her to have to react in front of all of her friends and family. She was shocked, of course. In a way, she was glad you were able to see your daughter get married. Mostly happy for Kaya, but she was definitely shocked. She had questions. She still does. I asked if she wanted me to arrange a meeting." He shook his head. "She wasn't sure. She said she had to think about it. Steve told her that he supported whatever she decided to do."

"I'm not a threat to him," Peter said quickly. "I mean, I'm not going to make any trouble for them. I made my bed a long time ago. But I don't know how she feels, so I'll stay clear if that's what she needs." He continued to stir his coffee without drinking any. He looked up. "There are a lot of questions that I have for you, though."

Kaya nodded. "Same for us. I-I guess I made a lot of assumptions yesterday when I saw you, but Graham said that maybe you didn't know what we were talking about. I think . . . I think I wanted to think you knew. It would make it easier for me to accept that you left." She squinted at him. "Why *did* you leave? And don't say you needed space to find yourself. You were there all along. Something happened. It had to have. I have to believe that it did."

Graham reached for her hand. Kaya was quiet for several seconds, and then she smiled and laughed. She looked at Graham and nodded. Peter was not sure what was going on between the two of them. He didn't know them anymore.

"I guess I can try to explain," he said. He hesitated, biding his time. He had no idea why he was procrastinating with the story. He would still be expected to tell it, even if he didn't tell it right then. And it would have to be the truth. "I left because I got scared."

"Scared of what?" Graham asked.

"Of myself," Peter continued. "There were some things about me that no one knew, and I felt that they were getting out of control. I had to leave before I hurt someone. I don't mean physically, but maybe physically. But definitely mentally."

"When you say hurt someone," Kaya said carefully, "do you mean us?"

Peter closed his eyes. He nodded slowly. Then he opened them. "I mean you, Kaya, specifically. I saw it starting, and I had to make it stop."

Kaya looked at him in confusion. "You never, ever did anything to hurt me. What was it you thought you were doing?"

Peter started at the table in front of Kaya. "I don't know how to say it, really," he said. "I guess I just have to ask you to keep an open mind, and not reject what I'm going to say to you right away. I'm not making any of this up. This is my real experience. And I've learned over the years that I'm not all that unique. But when I tell you, I know you'll question my sanity." He could swear he could see the corner of Kaya's mouth turn up when he said that. "What?" he asked. "Why are you smiling?"

Kaya's smile fell away. "I-I'm not smiling," she said. "It's just, well, I think that maybe I might be a little more openminded than you'd expect."

Peter's eyes went wide. "Okay," he said. "I-I guess I'll just talk then. You see, when I was about seventeen, I started to have some, uh, experiences that I couldn't explain. It seemed that I just knew things. Strange things. Sometimes, I knew things that were going to happen before they happened. It was as if I could see what someone was going to do. Not all the time. Just sometimes. And I wasn't always right. It seemed that if I was in close proximity to someone, close enough to touch them, I could sense what they were going to do."

Kaya and Graham looked at each other. They looked baffled. "How so?" Kaya asked. "I mean, how did it present itself? Did you hear what was going to happen?"

Peter shook his head. "No, I couldn't hear it. I could feel it. In my brain, I guess. Like someone had put thoughts in my head. I didn't need words to understand. You probably know what I mean. Most of the time when we think, we don't use words. It would be too confusing. We don't even realize how our thinking works. Images, sounds, feelings . . . all sorts of senses affect the way we think. So that's what it's like. Like thoughts injected directly into my mind. As time went on, I started to realize that I wasn't seeing the future. What was happening was that I was picking up on the thoughts of people moments before they did something. Say, for example, I'm sitting here with Kaya." He put his hand on Kaya's hand, hoping she wouldn't pull away. "And Kaya starts to think that maybe she *did* want that scone that she passed up when she ordered her coffee. I can feel that thought in my brain, and then, moments later, Kaya gets up, walks to the counter, and orders a scone. Can you see how I thought I could see the future?"

Kaya nodded. "Yes, of course," she said. "And I do want that scone. But I'm gonna have some really great pastries once I arrive in Rome in less than one day, and I want to save some room for them."

Peter shook his head. "You don't seem to be too disturbed by the things I'm telling you," he said. "I mean, I was expecting the two of you to be sneaking looks at each other, rolling your eyes."

"Well, you told us to keep an open mind," Graham said, shrugging. "So you could tell what people were thinking. Why did you think that would hurt us? I mean, I could see us being skeptical if you told us about this back then, but we'd probably get over it eventually. There has to be more to it."

Peter looked at his son. There was something behind his eyes. Something he didn't recognize. He had to remind himself that it had been about nine years since he'd last seen him. He had changed a lot. He had been through a lot, including being abandoned by his father. He probably had some strengths that Peter didn't understand.

"There's more," he said. "It's . . . I mean, it's hard to talk about all this, so just bear with me. So I lived with the fact that I can sense thoughts for years. I found ways to work around it. If I didn't want to know the truth, I didn't get too close, if you know what I mean. No touching. There were times when I was younger, when I was out with a woman, and I would feel her thoughts, and I would end the date right then. Then there were other times . . . well, I can't talk about this with my children." He chuckled. "Then I met your mother. I promised myself that I wouldn't abuse my, well, power with her. I swore I would come clean with her. I meant to. I had the best intentions. But somehow, something always got in the way. Mostly my fear. There never seemed to be the perfect time to tell your fiancé, and then wife, that you secretly read minds. Am I right? I mean, what would you do if someone dropped that on you? Probably run away, fast. So, the years went by. And I tried my best to push the whole thing aside, to ignore it. I was doing quite well. There were times with both of you when I thought you might be lying to me about something, like kids do, and I resisted probing to find out if I was right. You had the right to be kids. You had the right to lie to your parents, and then get in trouble if we found out. But only if we found out the right way. It was a struggle. The pull to use my, um, skills . . ." He looked at Kaya. "You used that word, too. Skills. When you started to get older, I thought about it a lot. I thought about what would happen when you finally had your first date. And then your first boyfriend, and your first . . . And then, one day, something very unexpected happened."

"I heard something," Kaya said softly.

Peter felt the blood drain from his face. "You knew?"

Kaya shook her head. "Knew what?" she asked. "What would I have known, Dad?" The way she looked at him made Peter know that she did, indeed, know something. She was holding it back, waiting to hear his truth first.

"I—that one day. We were talking, and you told me about something your friend said to you. Something that hurt your feelings. I can't recall what it was, but that's not important. I hugged you. That was my first mistake. But what else could I do? You were upset, and I wanted to comfort you. I was thinking about how hard it was to be your age, to feel the pain of betrayal. How ironic, huh, since I was going to be the next one to betray you. But at the time, I was thinking that I wanted to take away your pain, but I couldn't. I couldn't control things. And then, well, then something happened that changed my life."

"I heard your thoughts," Kaya said quietly.

Peter was startled. "You remember."

Kaya nodded. "I do remember," she said. "I thought it was strange that you said that. So I asked you what it was that you couldn't control. You freaked out and said you had to go."

Peter closed his eyes, guilty. "I did," he said. "I had no idea that I could do that. It was overwhelming. I had to get away."

"Do what?" Graham said. "You knew you could read thoughts already. Why did this surprise you so much?"

Peter's hand went to his neck and he looked at Graham blankly. "There you go again," he said, "talking in riddles. No, Graham. I had no idea that I could move my own thoughts into other people's minds. It was a total mind blow. It was enough to make me question everything. I mean, I had no idea how to control my own thoughts. What kinds of things would I project onto others? To you, or your mother, or anyone else for that matter? My mind could not be trusted anymore. The more time I took to think about it, the more I knew I had to come clean to all of you, or I had to go, to figure it all out. To figure out how to control it."

Kaya stared at her father. "You really don't know, do you?" she asked. "I mean, you thought it was all about you. I don't know if that was totally selfless or totally selfish of you."

"I've wondered the same things many, many times," Peter said. "I'm still not sure. I think maybe that's why I finally came back—wait, what do you mean I really don't know? Don't know what?"

Kaya looked quickly at her brother. Graham nodded solemnly.

"Dad," Kaya said. "That day, when I heard your thoughts." She sighed. "I-I don't think you put those thoughts in my head. I mean, maybe you did, but I really don't think so. That was just one of the times, maybe even the first time, that I started to hear the voices."

Peter grimaced. "Hear the voices?" he asked. "You need to give me more, Kaya. What voices?"

Kaya smiled. "Dad, when I was young, people used to tell me all the time that I looked just like Mom. We have the same hair, and the same eyes. Grandma always says we have the same laugh. I remember, one time, you pretended that you were upset about it. You said you wished that people would be able to see you in me, as well. Well, guess what, Dad? Surprise! I hear peoples' thoughts. I have, ever since I was fourteen years old."

Peter felt faint. Graham looked concerned. "Do you want me to get you some water?" he asked, starting to stand.

Peter shook his head. "No," he said. "No. I'll be okay." He picked up his cold coffee and took a sip of the bitter brew. "I-I just . . . I never . . ." He shook his head again. "It never occurred to me that—"

"It's hard to believe it never occurred to you," Graham said. "I mean, didn't you ever wonder where it came from? Your skill? I mean, it didn't just drop out of the sky."

"So you know where it comes from?" Peter turned to look at Kaya. "I want to know everything. Everything. From the moment you started to read the thoughts, up until now. Kaya, if I had known—if I had realized—"

Kaya gave him a warm smile. "What would you have done, Dad?" she asked. "Told me that I had superpowers? Taken me to the superhero doctor to get the diagnosis confirmed? Or maybe you would have done what Mom ended up having to do. Take me to the regular doctor."

Peter felt a wave of nausea. "Oh my God."

"Well, it started with the regular doctor, but then—"

Peter put up his hand. "Stop."

Kaya stiffened noticeably. "You got to tell your story," she said. "Now it's my turn."

"No," Peter said, waving his hand. "No. I'm sorry. I didn't mean that you didn't get to tell your story, Kaya. But we don't have a lot of time, and I imagine it's hard for you to tell the whole thing. I suspect that you've had to tell it before, more than once. I have another suggestion." He put out his hands. "I have learned over the years that I can, indeed, share thoughts with people. It's not as accurate or predictable as hearing other peoples' thoughts, but it is part of my package of skills. What I'm thinking we can do is join hands here and open our minds. Clear them of all thoughts, or any many as we can. And then we concentrate on each other. We reach out to feel each other's minds. We welcome each other's thoughts. We project our own thoughts to each other. We can limit the thoughts to only the ones we want to share. The rest stay in deep hiding for the moment. And then we share. It's not voices, Kaya. It's waves of thoughts, of memories we send each other. In my travels, I've gotten better at including emotion, but I'm not a pro. Don't try too hard to share emotions if it doesn't feel natural." He stopped. "Oh. I guess I forgot. I need to ask if you'd be willing to try this. What do you think?"

Kaya looked as if she was considering his suggestion. She looked at Graham. "What do you think?" she asked. "It sure would take a lot less time than explaining it all. I mean, there's high school, my accident, college, Dr. Blake, the hospital—"

"Hospital?" Peter interrupted. "You were in the hospital?"

Kaya took a deep breath, blew it out, and held out her hands. "Let's do it," she said. "Then you'll know everything, right? How long will this take?"

"Not long at all," Peter said. "It's like a zip file on the computer. The thoughts enter your brain quickly, and then expand as you utilize them. Just don't let them flood you. Let them out as slow as you can. But after a short time, they'll feel like your own memories of what happened. Are you ready to know about my time away? Nine years, in exchange for nine years?"

Kaya looked into her father's eyes. "I have no idea," she said. "I mean, I don't know what to expect, but I won't know until I try, right?" She turned to Graham. "Watch us closely," she said. "If anything seems off, pull our hands apart, okay? I mean, I guess I trust Dad. I don't think he would hurt me deliberately. But I still don't trust all of this one hundred percent."

Graham gave her a look of concern. "You don't have to do this, Kaya."

Kaya smiled at her brother. "You would do it in a minute, Graham. I know you."

Graham tried not to, but then he laughed. "I would," he said, "if only for the research value."

Kaya nodded. Then she looked back at her father. She held out her hands. "I'm ready."

Peter nodded back and then reached out to take his daughter's hands in his own.

3

PETER CAME OUT OF IT first. He pulled his hands away from Kaya and turned to look at Graham. Graham could not narrow down his father's expression. It seemed to contain horror, sorrow, gratefulness, love, and confusion all at the same time.

"Are you okay?" Graham asked.

Peter nodded. "It's just a lot, you know, to take in at once." He looked at Kaya, who still sat up straight with her eyes closed. "What she's been through . . . I can't believe it. If I had known . . . Graham, you have to believe that I didn't know. If I had, I would have stayed. I would have helped her. I would have explained, but I didn't have anything to explain at the time. Now I know what you meant yesterday by the anomaly. Seriously, a genetic connection to primitive man. I would not have guessed that in a million years. That means that there were others in our family."

"Yes," Graham said. "I would imagine that, over the centuries, a lot of really confused people ended up in institutions or burned at the stake for witchcraft. And basically, they were just being human. Maybe ancient humans, but still. I have the anomaly. We call it the knob."

Peter laughed. "Yeah, I know," he said. "That was in there in Kaya's thoughts. And the psychiatric hospital . . ." He shivered. "I don't even know what to say about that. All I can say really is that I'm so grateful for you and Dr. Blake, for getting her out of there before she became too institutionalized to be able to make it in the outside world. I can't even imagine what kind of medicines they would have tried on her, had she been committed. You saved her future. I owe Dr. Blake so much. I'm so glad that he was there for her at the wedding. If anyone was going to walk her down the aisle besides me—"

"Steve's a good guy, Dad," Graham said softly. "He's really been there for Mom. You have no idea how hard it was for her, for years."

"I do," Peter said. "Kaya just showed me." His head bowed. "I never wanted to hurt Janice, Graham. I loved her." He paused. "I still do. But I knew that someday she would find someone. She's a wonderful woman. It was just a matter of time."

Kaya's eyes started to flutter. Then they opened. "Graham," she said, reaching to touch him. "It was amazing. I saw everything." She looked at her father, and she laughed. Then she turned back to Graham. "He spent three years in a cell. A monk's cell, in a monastery! All by himself, isolated. Can you believe it?" She turned back to her father. "I'm not laughing at you. I promise. I'm just so amazed. All that quiet! It must have been such a relief, things being so quiet."

Peter nodded. "It was," he admitted. "I didn't speak to anyone the whole time. I didn't touch a soul. It wasn't a silent order. I just chose to be silent. I needed to be truly alone. And I was."

"That must have changed you," Graham said.

"It did. While I welcomed the quiet, I also missed the thoughts. I missed the connections. But one thing I came to know very clearly was that I was not mentally ill. If I had been, the isolation would have driven me off the edge. During the time I was there, I learned how to quiet my own mind. I meditated. I read books. I learned to have lucid dreams. But there came a time when I knew I had to go back to the outside world. When I went to say goodbye to the abbot, he shook my hand, and in that moment, I heard all the news of the world. I didn't even have to read a newspaper. He had it all in his head. It was rather biased, of course, so later I did catch up on my own. But that was the moment I learned that I was able to encapsulate thoughts. That's what I call it anyway. It's similar to what Kaya and I just did."

Kaya nodded. "Graham, we have to try it together later. If I can put my thoughts into your head, it changes everything. We can have whole conversations that no one can hear." She giggled. "I can try it with Grayson in Italy, too."

Peter grinned. "It takes a lot of practice, Kaya," he said. "You'll have to learn to quiet your brain. I can tell from your thoughts that your brain is not quiet. But with you and me, we can listen to each other's thoughts, so we don't have to project to each other."

"But why do we have different experiences with our thoughts?" Kaya wondered. "I mean, I hear them as voices, but you just get a bunch of thoughts in your head. Do you think our skills are different?"

"I don't think they are," Graham said. "I mean, we're talking about brain impulses. Your brain gets information, and then has to interpret it. I'm guessing you have the same anomaly, but your brain tells you things differently. Kaya, your brain turns the impulses into voices you can understand, and Dad, yours works them into your thoughts. Over time, you both have probably built new neural pathways that have strengthened the way you interpret the data, so that's probably what you're stuck with, unless you work really hard to change it. But why would you? You can still take in new information, though. You can build new pathways."

Kaya looked at Graham and smiled. "I was right," she said. "He did spend time in a yurt."

Peter laughed. "You two talked about what I was doing while I was gone? Kaya, you didn't share those thoughts with me. Yes, I spent a year in a yurt, in a campground. It was my hiking and exploring nature phase, after I left Japan. I was trying to incorporate myself back into society slowly. I saw people from time to time, and I spoke with them, and sometimes shook hands with them. I let it all come back to me slowly."

"What about the desert?" Graham asked.

Kaya shook her head. "No desert," she said. "But he did explore holy places, mystical places."

"I thought I might learn something," Peter said. "I had no idea why I was the way I was, and I thought I could find out. I never did, of course. Until right now"

"That leaves a bunch of years unaccounted for still," Graham said.

Kaya looked at Peter. "I'm going to share everything I learned about you with Graham," she said. "He deserves to know just as much as I do. Just because his knob doesn't work, doesn't mean he gets excluded." She grinned mischievously at her brother.

"Don't you be making fun of my knob," Graham said. He caught a wistful look on his father's face. "What is it?" he asked.

Peter shook his head. "It's just the two of you together," he said. "It's . . . it's amazing. You've developed such a wonderful relationship. I could see it, through Kaya's thoughts. Graham, you've devoted yourself to your sister, to making sure she was okay. That was a lot for a young man to take on. Your education, your career—all because of Kaya. I-I just respect you so much." He turned to Kaya. "And you, Kaya," he said. "Your poise, your grace, and your amazingly endless optimism. It's astounding, considering what you've been through. All of the drama in cheerleading, and your fall . . . and your time in the hospital. How scared you must have been." His expression went dark. "I'm just so glad that that rapist finally got caught, before anyone got killed. But what he did to his victims . . . I am so grateful that nothing happened to you, Kaya. I mean, you ended up admitted to a psychiatric hospital. At least you were safe there. Well, as safe as you could be under the circumstances. And then to take such an interest in law enforcement. When I saw that you were accepted to the police academy, I was skeptical. But I can see it now. Everything's going to change for you. How are you going to—"

"No," Kaya said quickly. "No, Dad."

Peter looked at Kaya and nodded. Graham looked back and forth between the two of them. "Okay," he said firmly. "What is it? Kaya, you said you were going to share everything Dad thought to you with me. I should also be able to know what you shared with him."

"I didn't mean to share something with him," she said. "I-I guess it just slipped out."

"Spill it, Kaya," Graham insisted. "If you're keeping something from me, I swear, I'll get it out of you. I'll follow you to Italy and haunt you through your honeymoon. I swear, Kaya—"

Kaya put up her hand. "Okay," she said. "Fine. You broke me. I'll tell you. But this stays between the three of us, okay? No sharing with Gina, or Mom, or anyone else. Not even Grayson."

Graham raised his brows. "What the hell could be so secret that you haven't even told Grayson?"

Kaya stared into his eyes. "I'm going to tell him when we get to Italy and get settled in." She turned to her father. "Should I try to project my thoughts to him?"

Peter smiled. "Go ahead," he said. "But first, take a deep breath. Blow it out slowly, over the count of six. Then do it again. Focus on that one thought. Push all of your other thoughts to the back of your brain. Imagine that the thought is flowing from your brain, into your arm, and down into your hand. Then through your fingers, and penetrating Graham's skin. Imagine it flowing up his arm, and then into his head, and then releasing. Are you ready?"

Kaya nodded. She closed her eyes and breathed. She concentrated. She reached out her hand, her eyes still closed. Graham reached out and took her hand. He concentrated on the touch of her skin, imagining her thoughts moving through his bloodstream, to his brain. And suddenly, it was there, as clear as day. He dropped her hand, his hand going to his head.

"Wow," he whispered. "Oh my God. That was intense. Kaya. Oh my God. Is that what it's like for you all the time?"

Kaya shrugged. "I have no idea," she said. "As you said, everyone experiences it differently." She looked at him timidly. "Did you hear what I told you?"

Graham nodded. "I did," he said. "But I don't understand. You were drinking champagne at the wedding last night."

Kaya blushed. "It was sparkling cider."

"But your coffee."

"It's decaf."

Graham shook his head. "Wow," he said. "Kaya, congratulations! I had no idea! H-how far along are you?"

Kaya smiled. "About six weeks," she said. "I found out for sure the day before the wedding. I didn't want to tell Grayson yet. I wanted to tell him later, so he could focus on just enjoying the day for what it was, our wedding. *Our* day. We didn't plan this. I mean, I'm happy about it, but I wouldn't have done this on purpose, not yet. I wanted to have some time, you know, to get to know each other as a married couple, not as expectant parents. But it is what it is, I guess. And I know he'll be happy. I want to tell him when the stress is off, and not before we travel. I just hope I don't vomit on the plane."

Graham laughed. He still wasn't over the euphoria of hearing his sister's thoughts in his head. He looked at his father. "What do you think?"

Peter smiled. "I'm happy," he said. "Not only have I reunited with my children, but I'm getting two grandchildren out of the package, as well."

Kaya bit her bottom lip, a gesture she had picked up from her mother. "Dad, I still don't know . . ."

Peter nodded. "I know," he said quickly. "You aren't sure about me yet, and how I'll fit into your life. Your life is so full right now, and you'll need time to think about things. I get that. Graham, I'd understand if you felt the same way. But from now on, you'll always know where I am, in case you want to contact me. I'll be there. I know you'll have to learn to trust me. I expected that, and I hope you're able to."

"And then there's Mom," Kaya said.

"I know," Peter said. "You have your loyalty to your mother. That's why I'm so honored that you let me in on your thoughts. So we can have something, some base to grow from. I would love to have a chance to talk to your mother, to explain everything. Maybe someday she can forgive me for what I did. But I'm not even gonna ask for that right now."

Graham listened to the exchange between his long-lost father and his sister. He understood where they were coming from, both of them. But he didn't feel the same way. He felt as if a gift had just been left on his doorstep, and he was not going to send it back. His father was there, in front of him, and he was going to do the best he could to understand what he had done, and what he had been through. Maybe he would even ask him to share his thoughts with him, like he did with Kaya. But not yet. For now, he just wanted to hear things the conventional way, with his own ears.

"Kaya, it's getting late," he said. "You need to get home. Grayson's probably pacing around, thinking you're ditching him right before your honeymoon." He stood, and Kaya and Peter stood up with him. "Congratulations, Kaya," he said, hugging her tight. "For everything. For your marriage, and for your baby." He touched her stomach lightly. "And I can't wait to see what skills your child has."

Kaya gave him a lopsided grin. "In a way, I hope it has a useless knob, like my brother," she kidded. "No, I mean, this will be the first child who will grow up with the knowledge of the gifts of its family, and I intend to be honest. Maybe my baby will have the skills, and maybe not, but either way, it will be a special baby." She put her hand on Graham's cheek. "And you call me immediately if my sister-in-law goes into labor, okay? Any time of day or night."

Graham smiled. "My baby will probably have a knob too," he teased.

"Gross," Kaya mumbled. She turned to Peter. "Dad," she said. "I-I'm not sure how to say goodbye to you right now. I mean, I know now that I'll see you again, but it could be a while."

Peter shrugged. "I'm open for a hug if you want one, but I understand if you don't—"

Kaya propelled herself into his arms, her face pressed firmly against his chest. "We shared thoughts," she whispered. "You heard everything there is to know about me since you left. I think a hug is the least we can share. Thank you, Dad."

Peter pulled away and held Kaya at arm's length. "For what?"

"For showing up at my wedding even though I didn't know where to send the invitation. For making yourself seen. For telling us your truth. For . . . for the gifts you've given me. At first, they may have been a curse, but now, now they're part of me, and part of us." She thought for a second. "I guess that's all." She laughed.

Pete smiled. "You're welcome," he said. "And thank you for hearing me out."

Kaya grabbed her purse, kissed her brother on the cheek, called out goodbye, and left.

Graham was left standing face to face with his father. "What now?"

Peter shook his head. "I don't know," he said. "What do you think?"

Graham shrugged. "Do you want to see my house? I mean, I'll have to check with Gina first. You know, pregnant wife and all. She probably wants to deep clean before we have guests. But we have a basketball hoop over the garage, just like we had when I was growing up. Maybe we can play a game of HORSE or something. You could stay for dinner. Where *are* you staying, anyway?"

"The Rodeway Motel," Peter said. "I paid for the week, just until I figured out what I'd be doing next. If I want to stick around, I'll have to find a job. I haven't worked in my field for nine years. Most of the work I've done during that time is drudge work. You know, washing dishes, janitorial. Enough to pay for a room somewhere. I know they're always looking for custodial work in town. You still shoot hoops?"

Graham gave a lopsided grin. "From time to time," he said. "I'm no Lebron James or anything." He picked up his cup and lid and crumpled them in his hand as he walked toward the trash can.

"Oh, God, you're not a Lakers fan, are you?" Peter said, lifting his own cup, still full of cold coffee. "I mean, if you are . . ."

"Well, they're pretty good, Dad, you have to admit."

Peter shook his head. "C'mon, Graham, have some loyalty here. You were raised a Pistons fan." He carefully deposited his cup in the trash.

"I never understood that," Graham said, heading for the door. "I mean, we don't live anywhere near Detroit, or Michigan for that matter. You've never lived there. What's the draw?"

Peter pushed the door open. "Well, there was this girl once . . ."

Graham laughed as he walked through the door into the heat of the July morning. "Of course there was," he said. "There's always a girl behind everything, isn't there?"

He and his father headed toward Graham's car.

4

ALICE STOOD IN FRONT OF the medicine cabinet, holding the bottle in her hand. She moved it closer to her eyes. The words were blurry. She moved it away. Still blurry. This was even with her glasses on. "Dang," she said under her breath. "I'm gonna have to ask the pharmacist to make the labels bigger."

She looked down at the large white Samoyed curled up by the open door. "They told me it would get worse, Pony-Boy," she said. "But I guess part of me didn't believe them. I thought I had more time."

She took out her cell phone and snapped a picture of the bottle. She fumbled with the screen and sent the photo to her email address. She went into her bedroom and started up her oversized desktop computer. She opened the email and downloaded the photo. Next, she opened the downloaded file and enlarged it. "Oh," she told Pony, who had followed her into the room. "It says two pills once a day, not one pill twice a day. You would think I would have remembered that. Well, no harm, no foul."

Back in the bathroom, she shook two pills into her palm and swallowed them with a Dixie cup of water. The pills were chalky. She made a face. Then she splashed water on her face. "Do you want to go for a walk now, Pony?" she asked. The dog stretched into the downward dog position and yawned. Then he walked out of the room, coming back with his leash in his mouth. Alice laughed. "Good boy." She attached the leash to the four-year-old dog's collar, and he led her to the door.

It was a warm July day. Alice didn't mind walking Pony in any weather, but the walks in the summer were the most gratifying. Pony would lead her to the park, where they would walk on the sidewalk around the periphery of the wide expanse of grass. Pony would stop to sniff every tree or bench. Alice found that the more her vision faded, the more she could smell the odors and aromas around her. Flowers smelled more fragrant, but conversely, dog shit smelled horrendous. It was Pony's way of letting her know it was time for her to pick up his waste in a green plastic bag. Her least favorite part of having a pet. But Pony was worth every tiny bag of poo. He seemed to be gifted with the ability to know where Alice needed to go. He had never been trained to be an assistance dog; it came to him naturally.

Alice had started her descent into blindness when she had first taken in the pup about four years earlier, but her sight was much more intact at the time. She had bonded tightly with her dog, as if they were of one mind. Pony, named after the character Pony-Boy from *The Outsiders*, would most likely throw himself in front of a bus to save Alice's life. And Alice would do the same for him.

"Good afternoon, Alice," a voice called out from in front of her. "It's a nice day, isn't it?"

Alice smiled. "Hello, Brad. It is a nice day." She waited for Brad's sob story.

Brad sighed. "Well, sometimes it's hard to tell if it's a nice day in my apartment," he said sadly. "I've gotten a warning that they're gonna turn off my electricity. And my water. I have to pay the bills by the end of the week if I want to keep them on for the next month."

"That's too bad, Brad," Alice said. She reached out, and Brad took her hand. She smiled. "It's too bad that it's not true, though. You want the money so you can buy a new game for your gaming system or something, Brad, don't you? You know I can tell when you lie to me. It's not okay to lie to people to get the things you want. Some day, you'll tell a lie to someone who hasn't known you since you were ten, and they won't be as nice as I'm being to you right now." She pulled her hand away. "You can get by with the games you have. Or you could go to the library and borrow one. Just make sure to bring it back when it's due." She patted Brad's arm. "I'll see you tomorrow, Brad. And no more sad stories, okay?"

Brad's head was bowed. "Okay," he said softly. "Sorry, Alice." He started to walk in the other direction.

Alice shook her head and continued on her way. Living in a small town had its merits. Everyone knew everyone else. But that was also the downside of living in a small town, knowing everyone and never being able to be anonymous. Sometimes, anonymity sounded like a luxury. Alice had lived in Florence her whole life. She'd attended Florence Elementary School, Florence Middle School, and Florence High. She had left to go to college in Maine, but she had been back now for two years. It was as if no one had changed. Sure, they were all a few years older, and Alice was in her twenties. Her parents were both gone now. Her mother had succumbed to cancer five years earlier, and her father had not handled the loss well. He fell into the false comfort of his good friend alcohol, and it was his downfall. He was dead two years later. Alice had no family to watch her graduate from college. She came back home alone, just a girl and her dog. The house was paid off, and, as their only survivor, it now belonged to her. And it still looked like her parents' house. At least, a fuzzy version of her parents' house.

After she brought Pony back to the house, and had her breakfast of toast and jam, she headed off to work. It was a ten-minute walk, her second walk of the day, but this one was on the main streets of Florence. People rushed down the sidewalks to their offices, as cars zoomed down the roads to add to the traffic downtown. If it could be called downtown. It was a six-block radius, with no buildings taller than six stories high. The only other hub of activity was the hospital complex, on the border of Florence and Wisteria, the even smaller neighboring town. But even so, the hospital was called Wisteria Memorial Hospital. Alice had spent a lot of time at the hospital complex, with ophthalmologists and retinal specialists, trying to nail down an exact diagnosis and treatment plan. So far, all that was known was that she had a rare degenerative disease of the retina, and that it could not be reversed. Now, they were just trying to slow down the rate of progress.

Alice arrived at work ten minutes early. She had never anticipated as a child that she would turn out to be a morning person, but being a dog owner had turned her around. Pony was a morning dog, and he enjoyed the taste of the dew drops on the blades of grass. Alice had learned to appreciate the smell of the dew. That, and the smell of the coffee brewing at the Arista Coffee shop located on the first floor of her office building. She started each workday with a large mocha latte, with fluffy whipped cream and a squirt of chocolate sauce to top it all off. Since she was the first one there, she unlocked the door to the office and made her way to her desk. She laid her drink down on the blotter and hit the button to turn on her computer. She took a seat and waited as she sipped her hot drink. She had an extra-large monitor as an accommodation for her sight. Her employers were doing the best they could to keep her around. They would never be able to find someone like her, no matter how hard they tried. She was their secret weapon.

She was a law clerk, but she was so much more. She was one of the most important members of the team at the prosecutor's office, and they knew it. Without her, their prosecution rate would most likely be much lower. Alice had a gift for knowing when people were lying. No one knew why, but when they later found evidence to back up her hunch, her track record was nearly one hundred percent. She was a true purveyor of the truth. Even her name, Alice, meant "truth."

Her boss, Assistant District Attorney Carla Poppet, found that hysterical. "Truth is your superpower," Carla had told her once after winning a big case. "Alice Talman, keeper of the truth. Truth pulling out the threads of truth. It's as if your parents knew what you could do and they chose the perfect name."

Alice just smiled. Her parents had no idea that her name meant "truth." She had been named after her mother's grandmother.

It had been a quiet week so far. Sometimes, there would be weeks between cases. The population of this rural town did not allow for tons of heinous crimes. This gave Alice time to do research for upcoming cases. Research was the job she was actually paid for. She had access to volumes upon volumes of legal reference books, and she intended to make the most of them. There were some big appeal cases approaching, and she had to find case history regarding precedence. She enjoyed the research. She opened the huge reference tome on her desk and then took the magnifying instrument from her drawer. She spent the next four hours studying and making notes, briefly looking up from time to time to greet and gossip with her officemates. When lunchtime arrived, she and Carla walked to the park and ate takeout food from the small café down the street. It was an idyllic afternoon in small-town America.

"You have your appointment at the medical complex at three today, right?" Carla asked.

Alice nodded as she swallowed her bite of tuna wrap. "Yes," she said. "My friend Tony's coming to pick me up. Otherwise, I would have had to take a cab. Even in a small town, cab fares can add up after a while, even with my huge salary from the county."

Carla shook her head. "It doesn't seem right," she said. "I mean, you have a car, and you could drive up until last year. You would think there would be a foundation or something that could help with transportation for people with vision impairments."

"You would think," Alice said. "They have things like that in the city, but not in places like this. It would be easy if we had a bus system. But at least I have Tony."

Carla smiled. Alice might be losing her vision, but she could still see a smile that big. "I've heard you mention Tony before," Carla said. "You went to high school with him, right?"

"That's right," Alice said, unscrewing the lid of her Snapple peach iced tea. "We were together in high school. We're still friends." She squinted at Carla. "Just because you met your mate at Florence High School doesn't mean that everyone else did."

Carla laughed. "Not everyone is so lucky to have someone like Kaylie. But this guy takes time off from work to bring you to doctor's appointments. That's gotta mean something."

"Yes," Alice said, rolling her eyes. Her eyes were still good for rolling. "It means he's been working some nights. He's a lab technician down at Milner Labs. They all take turns on the night shift. He has to watch the samples. Apparently, they get up to mischief if you leave them alone for too long. That's why I made the late afternoon appointment, so I know he'll have gotten a good day's rest."

Carla chuckled. "Good day's rest. Alice, we are so lucky to have you working with us. If I didn't have you, I'd have already gone to work for my father's firm, Kraft, Simon, Williams, and Poppet."

"Didn't your father tell you if you came to work with him, he'd make you a partner, too?" Alice asked. "Kraft, Simon, Williams, Poppet, and Poppet. A regular Poppet show."

Carla groaned. "Oh, that never gets old, Miss Telman. Yes, and it doesn't help that my great-grandfather was famous in Florence for being the mastermind behind the Poppet Puppet Theater, or that it's still open seventy-five years later, and every child in Florence was forced to, I mean *privileged* to see dozens of shows there when they were young. No, I was never teased. No wonder my father became a lawyer and then recruited me to do the same."

"Most likely to be the next D.A. in Charleston County," Alice pointed out.

"Only because Arthur's retiring," Carla said, "and no one else will run against me. Alice, I wish you would just suck it up and go to law school already. When I become D.A., I would kill to have an assistant like you. I would win every case, or at least know when to drop a case. Our office has avoided so much embarrassment that we would have otherwise had by taking innocent people to court. I'm sure it happens to all D.A. offices, but we're special. We have the one and only Alice Telman."

Alice felt her cheeks get hot. "I'm just lucky, that's all." She took the last bite of her wrap, and the last sip of her Dr. Pepper. "I think we're due back about now. I'm trying to get ahead of the McHale appeal. I want to make sure I don't miss anything. You worked really hard on prosecuting that guy, and I don't want to see him walk on some stupid technicality."

"Yeah, that guy deserves every year he was sentenced to," Carla said. "No one messes with the elderly in Florence. They're sacred. You mess with my grandparents, or anyone like them, I'll cut you down. Me and Alice, the finder of truth."

Alice laughed as she stood. "The finder of truth needs to get back to the office to find the girl's room. I've gotta pee."

Tony arrived at two thirty. "Are you ready?" He sat on the edge of Alice's desk. "Oh, it's me, Tony, by the way."

Alice chuckled. "Tony, I'm not totally blind yet. And plus, I've known you since we were five. I know your voice. And your smell. Is that the Calvin Klein cologne? The one that you got for Christmas from your parents? It smells really good."

"I only dabbed it behind my ear," Tony said. "I can't believe you can smell it from there." He sniffed the air. "I can't smell anything at all."

Alice smiled. "My other senses are growing heightened. Now give me your hand." Tony reached out and grabbed Alice's outstretched hand. "Did you get enough sleep after work this morning?"

Tony nodded. "I did. Seven hours."

Alice shook her head. "Why do you even bother? You know I know when you're lying."

"I was testing your powers," Tony said. Then he laughed. "Your superpowers. I stayed up playing my new video game."

"Is it the baseball one? If it is, you should loan it to Brad. He's trying to collect money in the park to buy it."

"That guy," Tony said. He stood up. "It's amazing that he was able to get emancipated from his sorry excuse of a father. Seventeen-year-old boys should not be able to live alone in a small town. Every mother and grandmother leaves food at his door. I have no idea who pays his bills. I'm just glad he's still in school."

"His father is the worst," Alice said. She stood up. "Let's get this over with. They're doing that test where they shine the lasers in my eyes so they can see the backs of my eyes where the retinas are. I see lights in my eyes for hours after. Ugh. And then they tell me what they see. The only good news I get is that nothing's changed. That's what I'm hoping for today."

"But it's gotten worse in the last six months, right?" Tony asked. He sounded concerned. "I mean, you've had more trouble with reading and stuff."

Alice nodded. "Yeah, I guess." She followed Tony out of the building and to his car. "I guess that even if there's no change, I might still see some differences. You know, like things shifting and stuff."

Alice got in the car, and Tony closed the door. Then he got in on his side. "You know, Alice," he said, "maybe if things get any worse, I could help more. I could move in with you."

Alice's mouth dropped open. "Move in with me? Tony, you know we're just friends." Her heart started to pound, waiting to hear his response.

Tony laughed. "You know that's not what I mean. I could pay you rent. I could help you out. I could make sure you get where you need to go, and I can help with the cooking and cleaning."

Alice reached out and touched Tony's arm. "You're being honest with me," she said. "In some ways, but not in others. You really want to do that, to help me. I don't know, Tony. I mean, I can do stuff on my own. I don't want to lose my independence. It means a lot to me. It always has."

"I know that about you," Tony said softly. "I don't think I'd get in the way of your independence. But it would be the best of both worlds, for both of us. We would save money by living together, and we could share responsibilities, and we both wouldn't have to be alone anymore, right?"

Alice felt her heart clench. "I'll think about it, Tony," she said. "I mean, I worry, though. Wouldn't that make it harder for you, you know, with dating?"

Tony was silent for a moment. "I don't think so," he said, forcing a smile as if trying to hide some sadness. "I think it wouldn't affect anything. I think I would still be able to meet women. You know, we'd just have to both be okay with it. I mean, you're a good-looking woman, Alice. Really attractive. I mean, really. I'm sure you'll meet someone at some point, and I would be okay with that, too."

Alice reached out and rubbed Tony's shoulder. "You're so great, Tony," she said. "I appreciate you so much, and your friendship. Seriously, I'll think about it. It's good to have options."

She took her hand away and turned toward the windshield. Tony had just lied to her. He would *not* be okay with her meeting someone. Tony was not okay with that at all. He was in love with her. Still in love with her. His feelings still came across strongly. She wanted to think about it more, to explore it more, but she had to let it go. She didn't have time to deal with Tony's tender feelings. There was too much going on in her life right now to deal with this. It would take too much energy to think about it. No matter how it made her feel.

The blue lights were still glowing in her eyes as Alice sat in the specialist's examination chair. The overhead light was low, making it hard for Alice to make out the features of the room. She tried to read the eye chart on the back of the door. The first line contained only an I. That was it. She sighed. She squinted. Under the I, there was a P, Q, and something that looked like an N, but could be an M.

The door opened, and Dr. Lumis walked in. "Hello, Alice," he said pleasantly. "Good to see you again."

"Yeah," Alice said. "Good to 'see' you, too." She tried not to sound too bitter. She liked Dr. Lumis but not what he represented. "What's the good news this time? Anything new?"

Dr. Lumis brought up the test results on his computer and turned it optimistically toward Alice. "I can see a little more progress in the degeneration," he said. "Not much. Probably not enough to make a difference. It does seem like the progress has slowed down in the past year, so perhaps the vitamins are helping some. Have you had any new symptoms?"

Alice thought about it. "Same symptoms, only worse," she said. "I have to magnify any print. I have to enlarge prescription bottles. My eyes are sensitive to light. I can't drive. You know, the new normal."

Dr. Lumis came closer and touched Alice's arm lightly. He knew that touch was important to visually impaired patients. "You've been coping very well, Alice," he said. "Sometimes too well. Have you found a support group yet?"

Alice shook her head. "Too busy," she lied. "I haven't had the time. Maybe I'll look into it later."

Dr. Lumis nodded. "Good. Not much to discuss now, so I'll let you go. Make an appointment for six months and call me if you notice any changes before then."

Alice got out of the chair. "Thanks," she said. "See you in half a year." She found Tony in the waiting room and grabbed his arm. "Let's go."

Tony looked at her. "Everything okay?" he asked.

Alice shrugged. "Same old, same old," she said. "You know, a twenty-four-year-old woman losing her vision for no particular reason. No big deal."

Tony took her hand. "I'm so sorry, Al," he said softly. "This shouldn't be happening to you. I want so much to do something to make it better for you."

He was telling the truth. Alice squeezed his hand. "I know you do," she said softly. "Come on, let's go back to my house, and then I'll take you out for dinner tonight. That might help a bit."

Tony smiled. "Couscous Grill?"

"Yes," Alice said, smiling also. "Your favorite restaurant." They started toward the elevator. "Let's take the stairs instead, okay? I could use the exercise to burn off a bit of my frustration."

Tony led her to the stairs, and they started down, Tony still grasping Alice's arm tightly.

"I'm not gonna fall down the stairs, Tony," she told him. "I can still see the edge of each step. And I'm holding the railing."

"You can never be too careful," Tony said, still holding her elbow. They reached the bottom of the steps. "Damn it, I can't remember. Did I park in lot A or B this time?"

Alice thought about it. "I can't remember either," she said. "Let's check lot B first."

She started to turn left but found herself walking right into what felt like a squishy wall. She stumbled and fell over backward.

"Oh my God!" a woman's voice called out. "I'm so sorry! Are you okay? I'm so clumsy these days. Oh God, let me help you up."

The woman reached down. Alice could see she was a pretty young woman with pale skin and long brown hair.

"I'm running late for my OB appointment," she went on as Alice grabbed her hand. "I'm having my first ultrasound. My husband's already there. I didn't want to keep him waiting too long."

She pulled Alice to her feet. Then she stopped. The woman's face went flat. She was still holding Alice's hand. Alice was still holding her hand. She felt a current run through her. Some strange electricity that ran up her arm. She pulled her hand away.

"Did I shock you?" Alice asked. "I'm sorry. I don't know what that was."

"That's okay, Alice," the woman said. "It didn't hurt. Look, again, sorry. I have to go." She turned quickly and ran up the stairs. Alice watched her blurry form as it approached the top of the steps. The woman turned around to look at her.

"What's your name?" Alice called out on a whim.

"You don't know?" she called back, her voice sounding confused.

"I don't," Alice said.

"It's Kaya," the woman yelled out. "Kaya Pike. What's your last name?"

"Telman," Alice said. "Alice Telman."

The woman smiled. "Nice to meet you, Alice Telman," she said. "Bye."

"Bye," Alice said.

Tony turned to look at her. "What was that all about?" he asked. "Did you know her from somewhere? I don't think she was in our class at Florence. I would have remembered her."

Alice shook her head. "I've never seen her before in my life."

"Then you were both acting weird," Tony said. He grimaced. "And how did she know your name?"

Alice felt dizzy, but she didn't know why. "You know what, Tony?" she asked, looking up at him. "I have absolutely no idea."

5

THE FIRST THING ALICE DID when Tony dropped her off after dinner was take Pony out for a walk. Pony was very happy to be outside, and Alice had to restrain him from jumping up on her neighbors in pure joy. His joy made her happy. She kept him out longer than usual, feeling bad for having left him alone for so long. No one should abandon their best friend, even for a little while.

With that in mind, when she returned home, Alice decided to call her human best friend, Emilie, who was in graduate school near Chicago. Emilie had returned home briefly after college but then decided that she wasn't quite ready to go back to being a small-town girl. She gave Alice a big, loving smile when she delivered the news that she would be going to Northwestern University in Evanston, Illinois, to study Information Technology.

"You could get a master's degree in IT anywhere," Alice had protested. "Why Chicago, of all places?"

"The bigger the better," Emilie had told her. "I went to college in a small town, and I grew up in a small town."

"And you'll probably die in a small town, John Mellencamp. I know the song as well as you do." Alice sighed. "I don't want to live here without you."

Emilie had touched Alice's hand. "I'm coming back," she said firmly.

Alice closed her eyes. "I know you're telling me the truth," she said. "But it's your truth right now. Even you know that your truth can change in two years. Please don't make me promises you don't know you can keep."

"I don't know why you think I won't come back," Emilie said. "I just need to get this out of my system. That's all."

"You'll meet someone there," Alice said.

"Oh, you can see the future now, too?"

Alice's face had felt cold. "You'll meet someone, and you'll tell him you want to come back to Florence, and he'll think he can go with you, but at the last minute, he'll realize that he can't leave his whole family, and you won't want to lose him, so you'll stay. I mean, you're already there, and all of your stuff is there. It will be easier for you both."

"That's a great story," Emilie had said. "Even if it isn't bedtime. We have no way of knowing what will happen, that's true. But I love Florence. I just need to make sure that I've experienced something else. You have to try to understand. You have your house, your job, and your dog. You're settled. You don't want to have adventures."

"Or maybe I just can't have adventures," Alice said, working on her friend's guilt.

"That's a load of crap, Al," Emilie said. "You can do anything you want. And we'll do things together when I come back. And Tony will do anything you want, if you ask him."

Alice's shoulders had slumped. "That would be really cruel. I broke up with Tony after high school for a reason, Em. It wasn't working for us anymore. I wanted to go away for college, and he didn't want to leave Florence. I couldn't go for four years away from home with him here in town and us not being together. It would have been too hard. He knew that. He understood."

"I don't think Tony has ever stopped loving you," Emilie had said softly. "Don't you think you might just keep an open mind, and see if maybe there's still a spark there for you? What do you have to lose? You don't have anyone else right now. And who would you even meet here in Florence? If a new guy moves to town, he'll most likely move here with his lovely wife. Or if he's single, he's either gay, or there will be a long line to his front door filled with single women desperate for new blood."

"Tony and I are friends," Alice had insisted. "I like being friends with him. We have a history. We share a lot of the same memories. Yes, I loved him, and yes, there's a part of me that will always love him. But for now, Em, I just need him to be my friend. Okay?"

Emilie crossed her arms in front of her and huffed. "Fine."

It didn't help that Tony was Emilie's twin brother.

One year had passed since that conversation. Alice picked up her landline and punched in Emilie's number. "Hey, Em," she said when her best friend answered.

"Al!" Emilie exclaimed. "How are things going?"

"Why do you sound so happy?" Alice asked instead of answering. "Too happy."

"I'm not too happy," Emilie said. "I'm happy. I'm always happy. Plus, I'm talking to you. That makes me happy."

"Did you just talk to Tony?" Alice asked, hoping she was wrong.

"He's my brother, Alice," Emilie said. "We talk a lot."

"He told you we went to dinner."

"He did say something about that."

"It was just dinner."

"He said that his entree was really good."

Alice sighed. "He must have called you the second he got home. I didn't do anything to lead him on, Em."

"Why not?"

"Oh for God's sake." Alice was tempted to slam the phone down. "He helped me today by driving me around. I thanked him by taking him to dinner. Let's talk about something else."

"If we have to," Emilie said. "I would rather talk about being the best friend of the bride and sister of the groom at your wedding, and us becoming sisters—"

"I had a weird experience today," Alice said. "I met someone, and—"

"You *met* someone? Al! You spent the afternoon and evening with Tony. When did you meet someone today? It's not someone you're prosecuting, is it? I've heard about things like this. They never work out well. You'd have to get conjugal visits at the prison if he's convicted, and you'd have to perform under pressure. You'd never have an orgasm, and then things would start to unravel because he'd think it would have something to do with him, and then you'd think about it, and you'd wonder if it was something with him, and maybe you're not okay with being with a convicted felon, and then you'd call me, and I'd have to talk you down, and remind you that Tony's still there for you . . ."

"Nice bedtime story," Alice said. "But no, it's not someone we're prosecuting."

"Then why did you let me go on for so long with my story?"

"I wanted to see how you would end the story," Alice admitted. "But no. It wasn't a guy. It was a girl, and Tony was with me at the time."

"Threesome?"

"Would you cut it out?" Alice yelled. "This story is taking much longer than it would if you would just shut up. No, I literally ran into a woman at the medical center. She helped me up. But there was something strange about her."

"Did she go to Florence High?"

"I don't think so," Alice said, thinking back. "She was kind of a blur, but she didn't look familiar at all, and her voice wasn't familiar. Tony didn't say anything about recognizing her. Her name is Kaya Pike, but that might be her married name. She was going to get a fetal ultrasound."

"How did you end up finding out so much about someone you just ran into?" Emilie wondered.

"That's the weird thing," Alice said. "She helped me up off the ground, and once I was standing, she called me by my name. My first name. I had never said it, and neither had Tony."

"Maybe she did go to Florence," Emilie said. "Or maybe she went to Wisteria. We played them in a lot of sports and stuff."

"I have no idea," Alice said. "But when she touched my hand, something happened. I got a weird tingle up my hand and arm. Like an electric shock."

"That is weird," Emily said. "Was it static or something?"

"In the middle of summer? I don't think so. It felt like some sort of . . . connection."

"Do you think it was some sort of love at first sight?"

Alice laughed. "Actually, no," she said. "I've considered everything else but that. But no, it's not that. It's something more."

There was a pause. "You think she's like you?"

"I think she might be," Alice said. "She said my name and then went up the stairs. I watched her go, and then she turned around. I asked her name, and she told me. Then she asked me my last name. I could tell she was curious, too. She felt it, too. She has some ability. She was surprised that I didn't know her name. At least her first name."

"I'm not convinced that you haven't just met somewhere before," Emilie said, "and you both don't remember where, but somehow you recognized each other. She probably remembered your name. You know how that is. Sometimes things just pop into your head even if you're not thinking about them."

Alice considered that. "You could be right," she said. "I guess that part of me really wants it to be something else. I've never met anyone else like me. And no one else knows about me, except you and Tony. My parents knew, of course, but they never really bought into it too much. They just thought I was really intuitive. They couldn't even imagine that I might have the ability to see things that others couldn't see."

"So this Kaya. You think she can tell if someone's lying, too?"

"I prefer to think of it as sensing whether they're telling the truth," Alice said. "It just seems like a nicer power. I don't know. I didn't really get that feeling. I got the feeling that she knew something. And that she knew that I knew something."

"You should look her up," Emilie said. "You have her name. Kaya Pike. That's not a really common name. Look up her number, and then call her."

"She might think I'm attracted to her," Alice said. "That I want to go out with her."

"So tell her you're not," Emilie said. She sounded as if she were rolling her eyes. "Just call her and tell her that you noticed something strange when you ran into each other. See if she says she did, too. If not, just let it go and figure you met somewhere once. You can play the geography game with her. You know, see if you used to live near her, or know the same people. At least maybe you'll solve the mystery."

Alice absently chewed on the side of her tongue, a nervous habit she developed after the first time she was forced to throw away her gum at school. "I could do that," she said. "At least I can see if I can find her number. I don't have to call right away. But I can if I want."

"Good girl," Emilie said. "Listen, I need to go. I have a coding exam in the morning, and I need to get ready for it. They actually expect you to show them you know how to do this stuff in grad school. I'll call you this weekend, okay?"

"Thanks, Emilie. I love you. I miss you. Don't forget you promised me you'd come home next year."

"I'll be there," Emilie said. "My two favorite people live in Florence. And I have to come back to make sure they don't lose sight of each other."

Alice hung up the phone and then laughed. "Pony," she said. "Best friends are funny. Sometimes they drive you crazy, but the best thing is, they stick with you once you're crazy." She patted the large dog behind his ears. "C'mon," she said. "Let's go to the bedroom and see if we can find a phone number so we can stalk a stranger."

The next day at work, Alice spent the majority of the day continuing the research on the McHale case. The whole town would be invested in how this appeal worked out. She couldn't make any mistakes. Carla was counting on her. But her mind wasn't in the right place. She took the piece of notebook paper out of her purse and unfolded it. She looked at the large numbers she had written in thick Sharpie so she could see them more clearly. They started with a Wisteria exchange.

Kaya Pike lived on Congress Road in Wisteria, with her husband, Grayson. The site where she got the information also listed close relatives: Graham and Gina Reed, and Janice Reed. Reed must have been Kaya's maiden name. She had searched Yahoo for more information and found a wedding announcement for Kaya and Grayson from three weeks earlier. They had just gotten married, and already they were going for their first fetal sonogram. Things were moving quickly for Mr. and Mrs. Pike. Alice stared at the paper for several minutes, so long that the images started to blur. She heard someone walking toward her, and she quickly folded it up and put it back in her purse.

"You look like you're ready for a break," Carla said, sitting on the edge of Alice's desk. "Melody and I are heading down to the coffee shop for a midday snack. You know, after lunch, pre-dinner. Power food. Do you want to come? We've been discussing McHale all morning, and we need a change of scenery. And maybe you've found something we can use in case history?"

Alice smiled. "It's my turn to treat you guys," she said, standing up. "I hope there's some scones left. Have you tried the almond one recently? I think they're using a new filling."

They purchased their drinks and pastries and found a table by the window. Alice found herself gazing out the window, watching familiar strangers walk by as her coworkers talked about legal technicalities.

"Alice?" Melody said. "Are you in there somewhere?"

Alice turned abruptly to look at her coworkers. "Oh. I'm sorry. What?"

"I was asking what you found out about the whole jurisdiction issue. Do you think it's legit?"

Alice tried to regain her focus. "I haven't gotten through all of that yet," she said, "but it doesn't sound like something they can build their case on. It's kind of flimsy."

Carla looked at Alice with concern. "Are you okay?" she asked. "You seem kind of distracted. That's not like you. You're usually so focused."

"I'm sorry," Alice said.

Carla shook her head. "I wasn't admonishing you, Alice," she said. "I'm just concerned. Did you get bad news at your appointment yesterday? You haven't mentioned what the doctor said."

"No, not really," Alice said. "Just more of the same. Small changes, no answers. I guess I'm just tired today. I have some stuff on my mind. I promise, when I get back to the office, I'll find that information."

"We have time," Carla said, reaching for Alice's hand. *No, we don't,* Alice thought. *You're not being honest. You're just a good friend.*

Alice smiled. "Thanks for your support," she said. "I promise, tomorrow, I'll be more present."

Melody laughed. "It's actually a relief to see you distracted," she teased. "I mean, sometimes, I feel like we're living in *Groundhog Day*. Every day, the same thing. I welcome anything that's different. Is there anything we can do to help you? Seriously, let me do something."

Alice grinned. "No, really, I'm okay," she said. "I talked to my best friend last night. I've got this. But I'm really lucky to have such great people in my life. I might take you up on your help sometime. You know, when I need my bathroom cleaned or something."

Carla laughed. "We'd even pick up your horse poo for you," she said. "That's how much you mean to us."

"It's Pony poo," Alice corrected. "He's just a tiny horse. But definitely big for a dog."

Alice forced herself to stay focused for the rest of the afternoon, but when she got home, she allowed herself to space out on her couch.

She stared straight ahead, Pony at her feet, as she considered what to do. When dinner time came, she made herself some mac and cheese from a box and ate the whole package. Then she felt sick. She wasn't sure if it was from the food, or from what she was considering doing. She sat still again, this time watching rerun sitcoms on her large screen TV.

On impulse, she grabbed the phone. She pulled the piece of paper with the phone number out of her purse and dialed the number before she could think too hard about what she was doing. She heard the ringing coming from the receiver, only slightly louder than the sound of her pounding heart.

"Hello?" It was a man's voice.

"Hello," Alice said. "Is Kaya there?"

"Just a minute."

She was there. Alice was about to talk to her. She had no idea what she was going to say. Something like, *Hi, I have a strange ability to detect the truth. What's your secret power?*

"Hello?"

Alice panicked but then quickly pulled herself together. "Hi, Kaya? This is Alice. Alice Telman. We bumped into each other at the medical center yesterday?"

There was a pause. "Alice," Kaya said. "I was hoping you'd call. No, I knew you would call. You called. I'm so glad you called."

Alice felt her whole body relax. She had been right. Somehow, Kaya was like her, and somehow, Kaya knew it, too. For the first time since she was in high school, Alice felt like she wasn't completely alone in the world anymore.

6

"I HOPE IT'S OKAY THAT my brother came along," Kaya said as she sat down next to Alice on the bench. "He's been on this ride with me for a long time. I feel better if he knows what's going on."

Alice looked at Graham. "Graham, do you have, you know, abilities, too?"

Graham shook his head, "No, just Kaya," he said. "Ours seems to be hereditary. Our father has them, and I have the component of the brain that makes it possible, but mine doesn't work."

"How do you know all this?" Alice asked. She glanced around her to make sure no one at the park was close enough to hear their conversation. It was a quiet Saturday morning. One of the local kids was having a giant swim party at the community pool for his birthday, so that explained the absence of children. She did see Brad on the other side of the park, talking to a man selling hot dogs from a cart.

"Graham had a psychology professor who was interested in my case," Kaya said. "He did some tests on me. The general understanding is that my ability to understand thoughts was an ancient ability that helped our ancestors survive. Most people have evolved out of it. I guess whoever controls evolution didn't see how it could be helpful going into human future times. I mean, I guess I don't need my skills, but they can be helpful at times. They've gotten me out of a few jams."

"So explain to me exactly what your skills are?" Alice asked.

Kaya nodded. "If I touch someone, in any way, I can read their current thoughts. For a long time, I thought I was hearing voices, and so did everyone else. But it turns out that I pick up thoughts, and I convert them to voices in my brain so they make sense to me. My father, who went away for a long time, came back recently, and he reads thoughts kind of as a lump that dissolves into his memories. He can also project his thoughts into other people's brains. He just started teaching me how to do that."

"So you always have to be touching someone to read their thoughts?" Alice asked.

"Yeah," Kaya said, looking at her hands. "That's how it's always been. It can be with my hands, my feet, my arms . . . anything, actually."

"Oh," Alice said. "I use my hands a lot to help focus me, but I don't need to touch."

Graham's eyes went wide. "You don't?" he asked. "Wow. So how does it work for you? You're just near someone and you hear their thoughts?"

"No," Alice said. "I don't hear thoughts. My gift, I guess you'd call it, is different. I can tell if people are telling the truth. But yes, I do need to be near them. Touching helps. But in my job, touching isn't always an option."

"What do you do?" Kaya asked.

"I work for the county D.A.'s office as a law clerk," Alice said. "I do research and write briefs and stuff. But I also do some other things for them. That started when they figured out I was never wrong."

Graham smiled. "You're their secret lie detector test."

Alice nodded. "I used to go to depositions with my boss, Carla. She's the A.D.A. She does all the real work in the department, and the D.A. takes all the credit. Especially since he's a man and she's a woman. But she'll get to be in charge when he retires. I know it. Anyway, I would be in a deposition, and I'd listen to what the witness would say, and after, I'd tell Carla that the person was lying. That they would make a poor witness."

"I didn't think they did depositions in criminal cases," Kaya said.

Alice smiled at her. "You know your stuff," she said. "They usually don't. It's only in special circumstances, when there's an issue with the witness. Like, maybe they won't be able to go to the trial for some reason."

Kaya grinned. "I'm going into law enforcement," she said. "I studied it in college. I got into the police academy, the class starting in September, but now I'll have to defer, since I'm pregnant. Little peanut had bad timing in the grand scheme of things, but we'll figure it out."

Alice nodded. "So yeah, I don't spend much time with Carla in depositions, but I do attend all meetings with her now. Every time I've given her feedback, she's figured out later that I was right."

"How do you know?" Graham asked. "Does a voice tell you that the person's lying?"

Kaya shoved him. "Obviously not, Graham," she said. "That's my thing. I think Alice will have her own."

Alice laughed. "No, I don't hear a voice," she said. "Thank God. That would be freaky." She gasped. "Oh, I'm sorry, Kaya, I'm not saying it would be freaky like weird."

"No, it's weird," Kaya assured her. "I started hearing the voices at fourteen. I didn't even know they were disembodied until Graham started noticing me talking about them."

"I get a sensation when someone's lying," Alice explained. "Like nausea, but not nausea that makes you sick. Kind of like when you know that someone is lying to you directly, you know? Like personally. Like, if someone says they didn't do something, and you know they did?"

"Like a stirring in your stomach," Kaya said. She touched her own stomach. "I have those now, but I just call them morning sickness." She smiled at Alice.

"So you were fourteen when you started to notice you had this skill?" Alice asked. "I was seventeen when mine started. At least when I noticed it."

"Do you remember the first time?" Kaya asked. "I remember my first time, although I only realized it in retrospect."

"I do," Alice said. "It was my senior year here at Florence High. My boyfriend at the time, Tony, and I were talking about going to college. I was planning on leaving the state, getting as far away as I could. I was tired of all of it. I had a lot going on in my family, and I needed a break. Tony told me that he would come with me, wherever I went. It was the first time he had ever lied to me."

Kaya cocked her head. "Why would he lie about something like that? I mean, you'd find out eventually."

"I know," Alice said. "It didn't make any sense at the moment. But what was really going on was that he didn't want to lose me. He didn't even know he was lying, but he was never going to leave this area. He's a small-town boy. He would never feel comfortable so far from home. I had wanted to believe him, that he would follow me wherever I went. I did believe for a split second. But then the feeling came over me. At first, I didn't know what it meant, but then suddenly, I did. I knew Tony wouldn't go to college with me. And it hit me like a ton of bricks. I told him that I knew he wouldn't go, and he got mad. He thought I was calling him a liar, and I guess I was. It was really hard."

"What ended up happening?" Graham asked.

"We stayed together for a few more months," Alice said. "But I knew that we wouldn't be able to stay together after I left. He kept saying things he thought I wanted to hear, but every time, I knew. I knew other things, too. Like when my mother had a lump under her arm, and I went to the doctor with her to get it checked out. The doctor ordered some tests, but as we left, he told my mother she had nothing to worry about. It was just a precaution. But he was lying. I knew he was lying. My mother felt such a sense of relief to hear the doctor say that, because she trusted him. But it was a lie. So when the results of the test came back, and it turned out she had stage four cancer, she was pretty shocked. So was my father. But I was just angry at that doctor for giving her false hope. Why did he do that? But that solidified it for me. I knew right then that I could tell when someone was telling the truth. And when they weren't."

Kaya reached out and touched Alice's arm. "I'm so sorry."

Alice pulled her arm away. "Oh, sorry," she said, embarrassed. "I didn't mean to do that. I guess I just didn't want you to know what I was thinking. You know, about that doctor."

Kaya gave her a gentle smile. "I'm learning to control my gift. My father's helping me. He has good control of his. If I don't focus on your thoughts when I touch you, I don't hear your thoughts. I used to get assaulted by thoughts all the time, and it was exhausting. I learned to ignore them a lot, but now I'm learning to shut them off unless I need or want them." She looked at Graham. "We should see if Dr. Blake can do some tests on Alice." She turned to look at Alice. "Our friend, the professor, he did functional MRIs on us, and he just did one on our father, too. That's how we found the brain anomaly that causes me to hear thoughts. Maybe you have something like that, too. It's not bad, the testing. It does take some time, but it's interesting."

Alice felt slightly queasy. "I don't know. I mean, I'd love to know what causes me to be able to read the truth, but I'm not too keen on the idea of testing. You see, I have some vision issues, and I've had to have a ton of tests. The other day when I saw you at the medical center, I was just coming from the retina specialist and having tests done. I've had so many tests done over the years, that even the word *test* makes me feel like running. Maybe we can wait on any testing. Maybe when things slow down a bit."

"I'm so sorry," Kaya said softly. "When did all of that start?"

"When I was seventeen," Alice said. "So my senior year. They found something in a routine test when I was sixteen, but it wasn't until about a year later that my vision started to go downhill. It's been a slow progression, and they don't know why."

"So you have a vision impairment?" Graham asked.

Alice nodded. "I can't read regular-sized print anymore, so I have to have magnifying equipment at home and at work. I can't read books anymore, really, so I have recorded books from the library. I'm planning to go to the city to meet with the Commission for the Blind to get some more stuff. They can send me books and equipment and stuff, but I've been putting it off. I guess there's a part of me that thinks I don't need it yet. But I really do."

Graham snickered. Kaya turned to him quickly and smacked him in the arm. "Why are you laughing?" she asked, sounding horrified. "I might not have the best sense of humor, but I do know that going blind is *not* funny, Graham."

"First of all," Graham started. "Don't downplay your sense of humor, Kaya. You're hysterical. Second, I'm not laughing about Alice's vision loss. Alice, I hope you can sense that that's true. But something just came to me. You said that you started to lose your vision at seventeen, which is around the same time that your skill of being able to tell if someone was lying began, also. Then you went to work for the D.A.'s office. And what does the D.A. department do? They seek justice. And what is justice?"

Alice smiled slyly. "Justice is blind," she said. "Yes, I'm aware. But I've never actually witnessed anyone else come up with it, and definitely not so quickly. I'm not sure if this whole thing is literal or ironic.

The specialists can't find what's causing my disease, and they have no idea how to stop it. So yes, by all accounts, I'll end up blind, probably before I'm out of my twenties. If I do go blind, I wonder if my talent for detecting bullshit will become more acute."

"That's a huge tradeoff," Kaya said. "Alice, I can't for the life of me believe that your skill is related to your vision loss. But I guess there's a lot I don't understand. I mean, how could we understand? If what I can do, and my father can do, was something that people could do thousands of years ago, then why is it expressing itself so clearly with me, and in exactly the way it does? I wonder if your skill comes from a different part of the brain. Maybe for some reason, it *does* come from the visual cortex or something." She paused. "But we don't have to know that yet. When you're ready, you can have the fMRI. Or even if you're never ready, that's okay. All right. Let's stop all of this depressing talk and play a little."

"Play?" Alice asked. "What, like in the playground? There's a hopscotch grid over there on the sidewalk."

"No, not like that," Kaya said, waving her hand in front of her. "I mean, with our abilities. Let's show each other what we can do."

Alice chewed her tongue for a moment. "Okay," she said. "I'll go first. Tell me something, and I'll tell you if you're lying. You have to try to say it like you believe it, though, okay?"

Kaya nodded. "Graham and I have a younger sister named Katie."

"Not the truth."

"Okay," Kaya said. "One out of one. My mother's marrying my childhood dentist in the fall."

"Truth," Alice said.

"I spent time in a psychiatric hospital four years ago," Kaya said.

Alice gasped. "That's the truth. Oh, Kaya."

Kaya shrugged. "I got pushed off of a cheerleading pyramid in high school by another cheerleader who wanted to kill me."

Alice paused. "This is a tough one. I'm getting a mixed message."

"I either did or I didn't," Kaya said. "Which one?"

Graham leaned in closer to hear her answer.

"No, you did fall off the pyramid," Alice explained. "And you did think you were pushed. But there's a tiny bit of doubt in your mind about that part. You're not sure you were pushed."

"But I was!" Kaya demanded. "She said she was going to push me!"

Alice nodded. "That's the truth," she said. "But there's something about what came after that's not. I think that you're not convinced, Kaya. I think you might be conflicted about it. Is it possible that she wanted to push you, and thought she would, but then before it happened, you fell? I mean, I can't read thoughts like you do, but something is telling me that even you don't believe you were pushed. Or maybe you don't want to believe you were pushed?"

Graham spoke up. "I didn't see her do anything to push you, Kaya," he said. "I was watching closely. I always watched you on the pyramid because of what you heard Jill say all the time. I always wondered if maybe you heard her trying to talk herself into knocking you off, but then, you heard her thoughts, freaked out, yelled at her, and then fell."

Kaya opened her mouth to protest. Then she closed it. "I-I don't know," she admitted. "It was a long time ago. I was so convinced that she did it. Wasn't I? I mean, no one believed me when I told them that I heard Jill's thoughts. Was I so busy worrying about being believed that I didn't even remember that I might have lost my balance on my own?" She looked at Alice.

"You're telling the truth right now," Alice told her with a shrug. "But what does it really matter now, anyway? That was a long time ago."

Kaya sighed. "You're not an awful person if you think about something," she said. "But if you act on that thought, and someone gets hurt, that's a whole different story. I can't hold Jill responsible for her thoughts. It's possible she might have had those thoughts long before I heard them, and maybe she would have had them long after if I hadn't heard her thoughts and fallen." She paused. "Maybe I was unfair, at least in my mind, to Jill. She had no idea I could read her mind. She was innocent at that point. Well, just until the point when she tried to put laxatives in my friend Bailey's water."

Alice laughed. "Oh my God!" she said. "That's horrible! Maybe she *does* deserve your wrath." She thought for a moment. "I think I heard about your accident back then. I was a junior at the time. I didn't go to basketball games, but I heard about a cheerleading accident during a Florence-Wisteria game. Was that you?"

Kaya smiled. "God, you can't get away with anything around here, can you?" she protested. "So you must be two years older than me. I'm always the baby in every situation. Let's not talk about my horrible past anymore. Let me have a turn." She reached out her hand. "Take my hand," she said. "I'm gonna try at some point to use my skill without using touch, but for now, that's what it takes. Okay. Now, you can control what you tell me with your mind, and you can hide things that you don't want me to know. Oh, wait. Tony? Is that the guy you were talking about, your boyfriend in high school? He was the guy with you at the medical center the other day? You're still with him? I thought you broke up. Oh, never mind. Sorry. You did. But you have a lot of thoughts about him circling around your brain. Okay, okay. I'll focus on something else. You don't have to yell at me. Yes, I am hungry, and I would like to go get a burger with you. No, Graham can't come. He has to get back to his wife and baby. Well, how about instead of me telling you the baby's name, I think it to you? Would you be okay with that? No, it doesn't hurt. Right, Graham? He knows. It's just like a thought popping into your mind. Ready?"

"Mason!" Alice blurted out. "Mason *Raxton*?"

Graham shrugged. "It's one of my wife's family names. She likes it."

Kaya grinned. "I can't believe your middle name is Florence, Alice!" she exclaimed.

"Stop reading my mind without my consent!" Alice demanded, pulling her hand away from Kaya. Then she laughed. "I never tell anyone my middle name, but hearing Raxton made me think about mine."

"Your parents named you after the town you lived in when you were born?" Graham asked.

Alice shook her head. "No, I had a great aunt named Florence. I was named after her. My first name comes from my great-grandmother."

Kaya turned to Graham. "Alice means 'truth,'" she told him.

Alice let out an exasperated sigh. "How do you know that?"

"I didn't," Kaya said. She looked into Alice's eyes. "Either you told me that when I was holding your hand, or I got what my father calls a zip file from you when we had contact. That's when I get a capsule of information from someone, and it expands in my brain after. Or, I could have picked it up after you pulled your hand away. It's amazing what thoughts people have when they don't know they're thinking them. We were talking about names and where they come from. Here, if it makes you feel any better, I'll give you something about my name." She grabbed Alice's hand again and sent her a thought.

Alice laughed loudly. "Marijuana?" she asked. "Your dad . . . really? Oh my God, that's funny. Okay, Kaya, I know enough now. Don't worry about it. We're totally even."

7

KAYA WAVED AS SHE WATCHED Graham get into his car and drive away. Then she turned to Alice. "Okay. I have to say it. Alice, you have some weird thoughts going on around your head about this Tony guy. But you can't talk about it with your best friend. I know we just met, but I'm a good listener."

Alice squinted at Kaya to try to get a better look. "It's weird," she said. "I feel a couple of different things about you right now. I feel like I was violated since you were somehow in my mind, roaming around, but then I also feel like we're close, both because we were in each other's minds, and because we share a sort of secret."

They walked in silence for a few moments.

"It's complicated with Tony. I loved him back in high school. He was my first real boyfriend, and we were, well, we were each other's firsts, you know? I mean, in every way. So when it ended, it was a big deal. And then I left." She sighed. "And then I came back, and he was here. And he was single. And I was single." She stopped and faced Kaya. "But I hadn't been single the whole time. That's the thing. And he had."

"Oh," Kaya said. "Oh. I can see how that would be awkward."

Alice nodded. "It was awkward. I came back alone, but with a new history. And Tony had hopes. I wasn't ready to fulfill them."

"You had someone special at school?"

"You could say that," Alice said. "My first college boyfriend was amazing. His name was Cody. He was a junior, and when he graduated, he joined the Peace Corps. That was the end of that for me. And then I met Jackson my senior year, and we really hit it off, in all ways. I thought I was falling in love with him, and I thought he was falling in love with me, until one day I knew he was lying."

"What was he lying about?"

"I was never one hundred percent sure," Alice admitted. "I'm pretty sure he was seeing other women. Probably not seriously, but enough to let me know that he wasn't going to settle down. But the worst thing is that he just kept lying. He said he wanted it to be just me and him. And if I didn't have my gift, well, at that time it didn't feel like a gift. I guess it just saved me some time, and a lot more heartache. I would have found out eventually."

Kaya sighed. "Guys are creepy, huh? I figured that out in high school. I was a cheerleader, remember, and guys were always touching me in the hallways at school, especially on game days when we would wear our uniforms to school. You know, to pep everyone up. I read a lot of thoughts that were really gross. But nothing beats the rape guy."

She told Alice about the experience in college that led to her being put in the psychiatric hospital against her will.

"Everyone thought I had lost my mind and I was paranoid. But the good news, if you can even call it that, is that he got arrested two years ago. He went after a woman in a dark area and tried to pull her into an alley. That was his MO. But he chose the wrong woman. She was an expert in martial arts and self-defense. She was patrolling the area on her own, hoping to attract someone like him. And she did. And the campus police, who were keeping their eyes on him, were only too happy to arrest him for attempted assault. Then, a few girls on campus came forward with their stories about him, which was bound to happen, and his fate was sealed. He was expelled before his case even went to trial. And if I had never heard his thoughts that day, it's possible he could still be out there. Yeah, it really is a gift, Alice."

"Hey Alice," a male voice called out.

Alice turned to her right. "Hey, Brad."

"You got a minute?"

Alice turned to Kaya. "This is Brad," she said. "Brad, this is my new friend, Kaya. She lives in Wisteria."

Brad stuck out his hand and shook Kaya's. "Nice to meet you," he said. He turned back to Alice. "I don't suppose you have a few bucks I can borrow, do you? I need to get some groceries. I'm low. I only have enough for like, another day."

Alice shook her head. "Brad, you're not being truthful with me again," she said. "I can tell. What's going on? Is there something you need that you don't have? I know that Mrs. Katz makes meals for you every week. And Mr. Duncan from the grocery store brings you your essentials on Fridays. Have you checked out the library yet for the games? I know they have them. They have lots of them."

Brad lowered his eyes. "I haven't checked yet, Alice. Sorry to have bothered you."

Alice gave him a kind smile. "Brad, you just have to let people know what you need. Tell us the truth, okay? Maybe we can help. Everyone in Florence is on your side."

Brad nodded. "Thanks Alice. I'll see you later." He looked up at Kaya. "Nice to meet you, Kaya."

When Brad had walked far enough away, Kaya turned to Alice. "What's up with that guy? How old is he?"

"Brad is seventeen," Alice said. "He kind of belongs to all of us in town. It's a really sad story. His dad is horrible. He went to prison. His mom took off before that even happened. The family court judge gave Brad the option of going into foster care for a year in the city, or seeking emancipation and staying in Florence. He wanted to stay in Florence to finish high school, and the judge approved the emancipation. He gets some money from the state, and he has a studio apartment in Mrs. Katz's building. Everyone looks out for him. They give him food, make sure he has clothes and that his utility bills are paid. I'm not sure what's going on with him lately, but he's been coming down to the park, trying to get people to give him money. This is the second time this week that he's lied to me. Last time, it was about the water and electric bills. Now it's about food. He knows he can get video games from the library. Maybe he needs a new pair of sneakers, or something else all the other kids from school have."

Kaya shook her head. "No, that's not it," she said.

Alice's brows went up. "What? Did you hear his thoughts?"

Kaya nodded. "A bit," she said. "He wanted you to give him some money. He felt bad. Like really guilty. He didn't want you to know what it's for, but he's desperate. And no one will give him money, except a few people roaming around town who don't know him. Alice, he's scared. What could he be scared of?"

Alice felt her blood turn cold. "Oh," she said, almost in a whisper. "Oh no. He didn't say anything else?"

Kaya looked around. "We can get him back here if you want. I'm sure I can get him to say more."

Alice shook her head. "No, I think I have an idea what he's scared of. Come on, let's get to the pub and order some food, and then I'll tell you all about it."

Twenty minutes later, they were seated in a corner booth, away from prying ears, having ordered their lunches. "I get so hungry these days," Kaya said, rubbing her hands together. "I want to eat every-thing, and then, like, an hour later, I just want to puke it all up." She laughed. "You know *that's* the truth! But sorry I shared that informa-tion. I've actually been here before, when I was in high school. It was after a basketball game at your school. You know, big rivalries and all. We all came here after for burgers and shakes. We don't have a place like this in Wisteria."

"Well, we *are* the bigger town," Alice bragged. She leaned in closer. "Are you excited about the baby? It must have been such a shock to find out you were pregnant right before your wedding."

Kaya smiled. "I am excited," she shared. "The timing was bad, but when is the timing really any good? I'm sad about not being able to go to the police academy, though. That was a letdown."

Alice raised one brow. "Is it, though?"

Kaya's shoulders slumped. "Yeah, I guess I can't get anything by you like that, can I?" She sighed. "I do want to go to the academy," she said. "I really do. But I'm just not ready yet. Once I go, the ex-pectation will be that I get a job as a cop. I really don't want to be a cop. I mean, I do, but not a patrol cop. I want to be an investigator, like a detective. I want to talk to witnesses, kind of like you do. I want to help flush out the truth, like you do, but differently, you know? I mean, I can ask questions, and then get the real answers, whether they say them out loud or not. But a beat cop?" She shook her head. "From what I understand, you spend the majority of your time being bored, and the rest being scared. That's not the life for me. I need more. But I don't know how to get it yet. I need time to think about it."

Alice nodded. "Thanks for being so honest with me, Kaya," she said. "I think you and I are gonna be friends, and we need to be able to talk to each other, and be honest." She bit the corner of her bottom lip. "That being said, I have to tell you something." She paused, not making eye contact with Kaya. "I think that maybe Tony and I do have a future, but I'm not ready for it yet."

Kaya smiled. "I thought I sensed something like that in your thoughts," she said, "but I wasn't sure, because you had so many thoughts going on at the same time. What's holding you back?"

Alice shrugged. "I don't know if it makes sense," she said. "It's just that I don't know what's gonna happen with my sight. It's a slow process, and it could take years for it to get to the point where I'll need a lot more help."

Kaya nodded. "Tony wants to help you," she said. "I sensed that. It's because he loves you."

"I know he does," Alice said. "But I don't want that to be the basis of who we are as a couple. I want it to be a partnership. I want us to be equals, and I don't know if we'll be able to be. Even now, he's already making offers to move in with me and help take care of me. When I protest, he backs off a bit and says it would be a good deal for both of us, but I just don't trust that yet."

The waitress came to the booth with their drinks. "Thanks, Janie," Alice said as she picked up her ice-cold glass of Sprite and took a sip.

"I know I still love Tony," she went on after Janie left, "but he doesn't know it. Even his sister, my best friend Emilie, she doesn't know. I haven't told her. She wants it to happen so bad. I haven't let anything happen. I feel like if I even kiss him once, it will be all over for me, and I'll lose control."

"I bet it feels like you're losing control already," Kaya said. "I would imagine losing your sight and not knowing what's coming next feels like falling into a deep cavern. In the dark."

Alice nodded. "Exactly," she said. "A bottomless cavern. It would be nice to not be there alone, but on my terms. And I don't know what those are yet. Kaya, I *don't* know what I'll need when my sight gets really bad. I might need the kind of help that Tony's offering. I might be underestimating how difficult my life will be because it's happening so slowly, and I can adjust to each shift. But I will need some help. Even if I can stay independent."

"You mentioned the Commission for the Blind earlier," Kaya said. "Maybe it would make sense to bite the bullet and just go there, and find out what they can do to help you. You know, maybe they have classes. You could learn braille if you haven't already, and learn how to handle money, and sort your clothes. You can find out what types of things you'll still need help with, and you can figure that out before letting Tony know how you feel, so you can set boundaries for him on what he should help you with."

Alice looked at Kaya with astonishment. "Wow," she said. "You said that your brother was the psychology major? What you just said is brilliant, Kaya." She looked back down. "I've been putting it off for so long, since I don't want to think about how it's gonna be. My eye specialist also wants me to find a support group for people with vision loss, but I've been dreading hearing how bad it's been for all of them. I just don't want to know how bad it's gonna be."

"Can you bring someone with you?" Kaya asked. "I'd be willing to go with you if you want. I'm not even working right now. We figured I'd get a temporary job after we got married to last until I started the academy, but we haven't figured out an alternative yet. I could drive you to a meeting and stay with you, and then if you don't like it, you don't have to go back."

Alice thought about it. "I don't know," she said. "Maybe."

"It doesn't hurt to try it," Kaya urged her.

Alice laughed. "Are you always this pushy, or is it just your pregnancy?"

"Just the pregnancy," Kaya said.

"Liar," Alice murmured.

"You told me you were going to tell me about Brad," Kaya said, trying to change the subject.

Janie came back with their food. "Are you guys talking about Brad?" she asked. "Did you know that Mara Thomas really likes him? She actually told him, but he's so shy. She's hoping that he'll take her to senior prom this year. He has gotten really cute in the last year or so. And he's got his own place!" She giggled and then walked away.

"It's just like Wisteria here," Kaya said. "Very small town."

Alice nodded. "So here's the thing with Brad," she said, keeping her voice low. "Brad's dad is a well-known criminal. You may have heard of him over in Wisteria. Chet McHale?"

Kaya gasped. "The Grandma Killer?" she asked in a whisper.

Alice nodded. "That's the one. Well, everyone here has known Chet for a million years. He even went to school with my father. They were drinking buddies. My dad and his drinking, though, are a different story for a different time. So anyways, Chet turned out to be a total lowlife. He knocked up Shari, who was just out of high school, when he was twenty-eight, which didn't make him a lot of fans in town. They ended up getting a place over by the border of Garrison, and they made their little love nest, except there probably wasn't a whole lot of love going on there. Chet was a petty thief, but as time went on, I guess he got into scamming. He kept most of his business out of town, but then he got into something that I guess he thought was going to be his big break. It required investors, of course, for his fake business. He talked it up, and even used his own mother to tell her friends. Mrs. Corrigan was one of his mother's friends. She believed in him, and she supplied him with a great deal of money from her savings. Of course, it was never enough. He kept coming back to her with some story, and some paperwork and multimedia presentations to back it up. Finally, she had to tell him there was no money left to give him, and that's when the visits stopped. Mrs. Corrigan was just sitting around, waiting for the return on her investments, but it never came. It was all a scam. But what no one knew was that Chet had taken more than just Mrs. Corrigan's savings. He had also been swindling her social security. So poor Mrs. Corrigan was destitute. What she ended up having to do was to choose between buying food and buying her prescription medication. And it just so happens that one of those prescriptions was insulin. Mrs. Corrigan was a type-1 diabetic."

"Oh dear lord," Kaya whispered.

Alice nodded. "She didn't tell anyone about this because by then I think she had figured out that she had been swindled out of everything, and she wasn't going to make a penny on Chet's fake business. She was horribly humiliated. No one knew how bad it was until she showed up at the Wisteria Memorial Hospital one day with ketoacidosis. That's something serious you get when you don't take care of your diabetes. Well, they treated her, and sent her home after a few days, but the problem wasn't fixed. And the damage was done. It was probably less than two months later when she was admitted again, and this time, she didn't come out."

Kaya sighed. "I had heard parts of the story before," she said, "but not the details."

"The details were horrible," Alice said. "So anyway, it was some time before the local law enforcement were able to make the connection between Mrs. Corrigan's death and Chet's funny business."

"How did they make the connection?"

Alice stared into her new friend's eyes. "Chet's son told them, that's how."

8

"SHE SELLS SEASHELLS BY THE seashore," Peter said. "But I'm not getting each word. I'm just getting the gist of it, since I know the tongue twister. Kaya, maybe you need to slow down a bit, and do it word for word. You can't be an expert at pushing your thoughts all at once."

Kaya fumed. She was getting impatient. "I want to be able to do it now," she said. "I know I can do it, and I want to be good at it."

"Is that what it was like for you in cheerleading?" Peter asked. "You decided you wanted to do a move, and then you just did it? Or did you have to break it apart, and work on the different steps until you perfected them?"

Kaya rolled her eyes. "God, sometimes you sound so much like a dad," she said, "and I'm not ready for you to be my dad again. But you're not wrong. I'm being too impatient."

"You have a lot on your mind," Peter said. He sat back. "Let's take a break. Tell me more about your meeting with Alice."

Kaya smiled. "It's been a long time since I've made a new friend," she said. "It's nice that we start off by sharing such a big thing in common. It was so fun sitting with her the other day, playing with our skills. We laughed so hard. But she has it rough. She's losing her sight, and she thinks it will be gone before she hits thirty. She has so much to do before then, so much she wants to see. And she needs support. You said you met other people in your journeys that you knew had skills. What was that like for you?"

Peter tipped his head to the side as he thought. "I was pretty guarded," he said, "and for the most part, so were they. There were only three, in the whole nine years. The first was a guy I worked with in Arizona. We were doing construction. He was the one I learned about the ability to send messages from. I mean, he didn't teach me. We never really talked about our skills. One day, something, a brick or something similar, was teetering on a ledge, starting to fall, and I guess he didn't feel he had enough time to yell out a warning, so he sent a quick thought to me. I got it in time and got out of the way. He probably thought that I didn't realize what he had just done, and we didn't talk about it. I left that city soon after. I thought it was too risky to stay near him. I don't know if that guy saved my life, but he sure kept me from injury that day. I say a silent thank-you to him most nights."

"He sent the message without touching you?" Kaya asked.

Peter nodded. "Yeah, I figured it was something he could do that I couldn't. I tried a couple of times, but it didn't work, and plus, I didn't have anyone to practice with. But now that you tell me that Alice can use her skill from afar, it's made me wonder."

"Tell me about the other two people you met."

"Well, one was a woman," Peter said guardedly.

"Oh," Kaya said, her face growing hot. "Maybe I don't want to hear."

"We never spoke of it, but our communication was based mostly on touch, so we never had to say a word."

Kaya's hands went to her ears. "You must stop talking now, Dad. No more words. Gross. I might need to wash my brain out with soap now. God, Dad. You're still my father."

Peter laughed. "So Janice raised a prude," he said. "Yes, I'm your father, but I'm still human. And the last person I met was an older woman in a bookstore. Don't worry. This one is chaste. I was looking at books about meaning in life. I had picked one up, and she came over and handed me a different book. She didn't say a word, but I suddenly knew her message. She felt I would benefit from the book she was handing me. I looked down, and her hand was on mine, and she was looking at me. She hadn't said any of her words out loud."

"How do you know that you weren't just reading her thoughts when she touched you?"

Peter shook his head. "No, it was too precise, what she said. It wasn't just a thought. It was a message. And the way she was looking at me . . . it made me wonder if she could read thoughts from a distance, too, and knew I was like her. I always wondered about that. But I never made an effort to try it myself."

"I want to learn how," Kaya said. "But I'm kind of afraid that if I do, it might be hard for me to tune out the noise. I'm getting better at doing that when I'm touching people. I just have to breathe like you showed me, and focus. But if I was assaulted by everyone's thoughts, it might be a lot." She paused. "But you know what would be cool? Being able to tell what my baby's thinking, if it's capable of that kind of thought."

Peter smiled. "I tried that with you and Graham when you were babies," he said. "I never got anything concrete, just random, wordless thoughts, like instincts. Hunger. Touch. Cold. Hot. Uncomfortable. Loved. But sometimes it was helpful when I didn't know why one of you was crying."

"I should try it with Mason," Kaya said. "But I'd also like to try it in utero. I know it's too early, but closer to the end of the third trimester."

"Are you scared?" Peter asked suddenly.

Kaya looked at him questioningly. "About what?"

"About having a baby," he answered. "I know that you're an adult, and you have a partner, but I still think of you as that fourteen-year-old girl I left behind. She was so confident. I remember how driven you were to make the cheerleading team. You went to four dance classes and one gymnastics class a week, and when you weren't doing homework or gossiping with your friends on the phone, you were out on the deck practicing. You were in such control. But now, with an unexpected pregnancy . . ."

"It may have been unexpected," Kaya said, "but it's not unwelcome. Grayson's happy, and I'm happy. And after talking to Alice about it the other day, I realize that the timing couldn't be better. I wasn't ready to start my police career yet. I might want to take some time to think about what I'm going to do. I never would have had this chance without baby Pike showing up at this perfect time. But yeah, I guess I am scared. A bit. Not terrified, though. I think all first-time mothers are scared."

"Or second time," Peter said. "I remember your mother freaking out when she found out you were on your way. We were always planning on having more than one child, but not at exactly that moment. She never said anything to me, but when I'd hug her, I got all the thoughts. She had just gotten to a point where she was sleeping regularly, and able to shower and put on makeup every morning. She was able to communicate with Graham in full sentences, and she knew what he wanted most of the time. She was happy that she and I had more alone time and could leave Graham for long periods of time with our parents or a babysitter. And then, poof, it was all going to start again."

"I had no idea Mom felt that way," Kaya said. "I'm surprised."

Peter smiled. "Like I said, she never complained. It was all just thoughts. She might not even have realized she was thinking them. But as the months passed, the thoughts changed, and soon, she was excited to meet you. She loved you so much, even before she met you the first time. We both did."

Kaya felt a warmth wash through her. She was half tempted to reach out and embrace her father, but she wasn't ready for that kind of affection with him yet. She wanted to be, but her body would not obey. "Tell me about your meeting with Mom last week."

Peter nodded. "It was awkward," he said. "I won't mince words. I could sense her anger, and even some hatred. But there was also some love there, deep inside."

Kaya gasped. "She let you touch her?"

Peter laughed. "We met in public," he exclaimed. "We were in line at a deli to get sandwiches. Our feet touched. I might have engineered that to happen. I wanted to get an idea of where she was before we started talking."

"That gave you an unfair advantage," Kaya scolded.

Peter snorted. "You're really going to tell me you've never taken advantage of the unfair advantage with Grayson?"

Kaya bowed her head.

"I didn't think so. But I limited what I let myself hear. I'm pretty good at that, remember? I've been dealing with my skills much longer than you. So when we sat down to wait for our orders, I treaded lightly. I asked her to tell me about you and Graham, and I think that made it easier for her. We talked about you two for a long time, and then we ate our sandwiches. And then she asked me, point blank, why I walked out on the three of you."

Kaya stared at her father. "What did you say?"

Peter shrugged. "I knew that she knew about your skills, Kaya, so it wasn't as hard as it was when I was explaining it to you and Graham and I didn't know you knew yet."

"Did she understand?"

"She was upset that I didn't trust her enough to tell her everything, right from the start, even before we got married." Peter sighed. "She's right, you know. I should have. But I never could. I didn't even believe it all myself. I had only been dealing with it for a couple of years when I met her, and I had never met anyone else who had the same, or similar, experiences. I thought she would accuse me of making it up for some reason, although I don't know what reason she would find, and I panicked every time. And then, after a while, it becomes too late. I had a secret I'd kept for several years. And when I decided to leave, I thought I was taking the secret with me."

"So you told her all that?"

"I did," Peter said. "She understood to some degree. I think she's angry, Kaya, but more about you than about her. She thinks that if I had stayed, I could have been there for you, so you wouldn't have gone through so much. You would have had someone to guide you."

"But you didn't know," Kaya protested. "You thought you were protecting us by going away."

Peter gave her a warm smile. "Thank you for saying that, Kaya," he said. "That's the first time I've heard you say something like that since I've been back. That makes me feel like you really understand." He paused. "We talked for an hour, and then your mother had to get back to work. We said we'd keep talking, if only for the sake of you and Graham, and our grandchildren. We're part of each other's lives forever, you know. Children do that to a couple."

He let his shoulders slump and took a sip of his glass of water.

"We should get back to practicing," he said. "We both have to get busy looking for work. Graham has been very generous by letting me stay with him and Gina and the baby, and I'm trying to earn my keep while I'm there, but they're a new family. They need me to find a place of my own so they can do their own thing."

"You can stay with me and Grayson for a while," Kaya offered.

Peter touched her hand. "That's very sweet of you to offer, Ky," he said. "But your apartment is very small. You only have one bedroom, and you'll be busy getting ready for the baby. There's really not enough room for three people, one of them being a strong, bossy pregnant woman."

Kaya laughed. "You're right," she said. "You've got a pretty big personality, too, Dad. And yeah, I really have to find something I can do for the next seven months. Something not too stressful. Okay. Let's focus." She stopped. "I really want to help Alice," she said. "She's really upset about this seventeen-year-old boy who lives in Florence."

"What kind of help does she need?"

Kaya told Peter the story of Chet McHale. "And Brad was the one who connected his father to the death of Mrs. Corrigan. I mean, he didn't kill the woman, but his actions led directly to her death. So Brad's information led to the police finding out about his scam, and it led to finding more victims. They were able to build a case. And they were able to tack on a charge of unintentional manslaughter."

Peter gasped. "You've got to be kidding me," he said. "They got him for her death? I've never heard anything like that before."

Kaya nodded. "A lot of people haven't," she said. "He was found guilty. It was all over the news here for several weeks. He was sentenced in total to fifteen years. He was not happy, and neither was his lawyer. The lawyer instantly told the press there was going to be an appeal."

"Based on what?" Peter asked.

Kaya shrugged. "I guess based on the fact that Chet wasn't responsible for Mrs. Corrigan's diabetes, and he didn't tell her not to buy the insulin. She made her own choices. But other things, too. The defense attorney had requested a change in jurisdiction, since he didn't think the people of Florence, Garrison, and Wisteria would make an impartial jury. The judge denied it. And also, they said that the D.A.'s office had no right to talk to Brad about him, or anything else, without a parent or guardian present. In the first trial, the defense attorney called for a mistrial based on that and the jurisdiction issue. The judge denied both. He said that Brad had the right to present himself to the police to tell his story without a parent present, first because he was specifically giving information about a parent, and second, because he was over sixteen. So they're challenging that."

"So they're not saying that the guy isn't a nasty felon," Peter summed up. "They're just saying that they think there are technicalities that can get this loser off."

Kaya nodded. "And it's Alice's job to research those technicalities, and make sure that the county has every I dotted and T crossed. In the meantime, Brad's been emancipated, and he's living on his own in town. He goes around asking for handouts from his neighbors. Alice said she knew he was lying about why he was asking, but she thought it was for normal high school kid reasons, like wanting to buy stuff like video games. But when I met him, I shook his hand, and I immediately knew there was more than that. That kid is terrified. He's lying about why he wants the money, but I don't know why. But it's for sure not for video games."

Peter thought about it. "Is he afraid of his father?"

"Alice thinks that could be it," Kaya said. "She said that Chet was remanded to custody as a high flight risk after his indictment, so he didn't have access to Brad. Brad stayed with some school friends until the emancipation, and then he got his little studio apartment. He might be afraid that Chet will win his appeal and come after him."

"That sounds like a real possibility," Peter agreed. "Where's the boys' mother?"

"No one knows," Kaya said. "She vanished after Chet was arrested. They went to question her and she was gone, along with a lot of her stuff. Not even her parents know where she is."

"She hasn't even been back to check on the son?"

Kaya shook her head. "No. And she's always been devoted to him. She was only eighteen when he was born. Apparently, her family had wanted her to either relinquish Brad for adoption, or for her to stay with the family and they would help raise him, but instead, she decided to try to be a family with Brad and Chet. I can't imagine she looks back on that as the best decision of her life."

"Kaya," Peter said, "I don't know if this has been covered already, but has anyone investigated as to whether this woman might not have run away? That, maybe, she might be dead?"

Kaya nodded. "That was considered," she said. "But they never found a body, and due to the circumstances, everyone thought she had every right to leave the scum. They just don't understand why she didn't take Brad with her when she left."

"So what is it that you want to do to help Alice?" Peter asked.

"I'm not exactly sure," Kaya admitted. "Right now, Alice knows that Brad is lying and I know he's scared. She was present at the trial, and pretty much everything Chet said was a lie, even when he gave a sob story during sentencing about his concern for his son being out there with no one to take care of him."

"You're not thinking of wanting to meet with Chet, are you?" Peter asked, his voice laced with concern.

Kaya raised her shoulders defensively. "I . . . maybe have been thinking that," she said. "I don't want to try to catch him committing more crimes or anything. I just want to make sure that he's not doing anything to threaten Brad from prison. I mean, this kid might have everyone in town helping him with rent and food and stuff, but in the bigger picture, he's a scared kid who has no one he can trust. I want him to have a fighting chance. And so does Alice. But that means I have to learn a new skill. I have to be able to read thoughts without touching someone. Because to be honest, I don't think I could touch that guy. I think it would be too much, especially with being pregnant. Too much negativity. I remember what it was like when I touched Jonas Clark, that rapist guy at State. It almost made me crazy. I felt so threatened and violated. And it wasn't just his words. It was the vibe that came off of him. Dad, I'm hoping that you'll help me. I know that this is sort of dangerous, and I know you won't want me to do it for my own safety. But what good is a gift like ours if we can't use it to help innocent people like Brad McHale? I mean, there has to be a reason we have our skills. And I want to make the most of them." She looked at her father with pleading eyes. "So will you help me?"

Peter smiled at his daughter. He reached out and touched her hand. "Kaya," he said, "you had me at hello."

9

"SO GRAYSON," ALICE SAID, "YOU took the day off from work to come out with us?"

"No," Grayson said, struggling to keep pace with his wife and Alice. "There's a sewage problem in the office, so they had to close it down. They said it could be toxic. I've been in the bathroom after my boss. I think they could be right."

Alice laughed. Grayson was telling the truth. He hadn't taken the day off, but she could tell he was glad to be there with Kaya so he could keep an eye on her. "What kind of work do you do, anyway?"

"I work at a hardware store," Grayson said. "Right now I'm working the floor, but I'm in a management training program. I'm not sure I want to make a whole career out of it, but at least it's a good place to start. I'm a bit of a wimp when it comes to disciplining people, especially if I have to fire them or something."

Alice didn't think anyone would consider Grayson a wimp, but he did consider himself to be one when it came to his work. Grayson was tall, well over six feet, and his muscles were defined. She would feel safe to have him in the room if she were ever to confront someone. He was just intimidating enough, but he had gentle eyes. They were most gentle when they were looking at his wife. Alice could sense that his love for her was the purest truth he knew. And Kaya felt the same. "You two met in high school?" she asked.

"We met in line for lunch," Kaya said. "His thoughts were some of the first I ever read. The first thing I read from him was the word *wow.*"

"I couldn't help but think that," Grayson said. "Not only was she adorable, but she also liked chocolate pudding. It was the last one. I let her have it. She gets all my pudding now."

Alice and Kaya laughed. "Babe, that sounds more sexual than cute, you know," Kaya said. "But it's still sweet." She reached up and kissed his cheek.

"So this guy Brad's just gonna show up here?" Grayson asked. He sat down on a bench, and the women sat down with him. "He just hangs out in the park every afternoon around this time?"

"He doesn't hang out here," Alice said. "It's lunchtime. He goes and talks to people, like Bengal, the hot dog guy, and then, lately, he's been kind of panhandling. He might try to stay clear from me now since I've turned him down a few times, but he might recognize Kaya and try her. That's why I'm gonna walk away when we see him. He'll see you guys as more vulnerable to his plight."

Grayson nodded. "So then Kaya just has to start talking to him, and try to get him to think about the truth."

Kaya nodded. "We need to get him to sit down with us for a few minutes, maybe between us, so I can find a way to make physical contact. And then I can read his thoughts."

"It sounds like a reasonably safe plan," Grayson said. "But what if he doesn't think what you want him to?"

"I'll ask leading questions," Kaya said. "Remember, I did my internship in the campus police department at State with Sergeant Morris. I learned a thing or two about getting people to talk."

Grayson looked at his watch. "It's twelve thirty," he said. "Do you think we missed him?"

Alice shook her head. "No, he'll be here soon. They have lunch during the school year at twelve fifteen, and he's a creature of habit. Plus, he knows that twelve to one is lunch hour for most businesses in town." She pointed to another bench. "Right over there is my boss Carla and her wife Kaylie, looking adorable. They have a baby, but she's in daycare while they work." She waved, and Carla and Kaylie waved back. "They met in high school."

"Everyone met in high school," Kaya said, looking sideways at Alice.

"Yes," Alice said, her voice strained. "Everyone."

"I'd love to see Tony again," Kaya said. "It would be nice to have more friends in the area, since a lot of my high school friends have moved away."

"Emilie's coming back for a week at the end of the month," Alice said to deflect the conversation away from Tony. "She'll be home for her birthday."

"Oh, that means it's Tony's birthday, too," Kaya said. "Twins," she told Grayson.

Alice reached out and put her hand on Kaya's knee. *Enough*, was the message she sent her. Kaya looked contrite.

"Is that Brad?" Grayson asked, pointing his chin to the left. "The skinny guy over there looking around like he's lost in his own backyard?"

Alice looked up. "That's him." She stood. "I'll make myself scarce. I'll walk back to my office. Come find me there when you're done."

She waved at Brad as she walked down a perpendicular sidewalk, watching him come closer to Kaya and Grayson. As she walked further from her new friends, her vision began to blur, and she couldn't make out what was happening with them. She turned away and walked back toward her building.

She thought about Kaya bringing up Tony. She wondered if maybe it hadn't been wise, telling Kaya her thoughts about still loving her old high school boyfriend. But Kaya had already been inside her head and knew that Tony lived there full time. Plus, she needed a friend to confide in. But now Kaya knew her feelings and would encourage her to explore them more. Alice didn't want to explore her feelings; she wanted to ignore them. When you ignore a plant, it dies. Well, not all plants. Some thrive on neglect. But if she ignored her feelings, they were sure to dissolve. She laughed to herself. She was a seeker of truth. She couldn't lie to herself any more than she could ignore her feelings for Tony. She reached her building and sat down on the concrete steps in front. No sooner did her bottom hit the ground than her cell phone ring.

"Tony," her voice announcer told her. She rolled her eyes. So much for ignoring him.

"Hey, Tony," she said.

"Hey, Al," Tony's voice said back. "What's up?"

"You called me," Alice protested.

"I know I did," Tony said. "I just wanted to see how you were doing. I haven't talked to you since we had dinner last week. Em says you made a new friend."

"Yeah, it was the woman I ran into when you were with me at the medical center," Alice said. "Kaya. I called her, and we've been hanging out."

"Are you shitting me?" Tony asked. He laughed. "Only you would make friends with a frantic woman who knocked you over on the way to her ultrasound. What's she like?"

"Well, she's like me," Alice said. "Remember I suspected that she might be? But she can do other stuff. I can tell if people are telling the truth, but she can actually tell what people are thinking."

Tony paused. "If I didn't know that you can do what you do, I'd think you were losing your mind, Al. But I do know. I can't believe you're not the only one."

"It's a big world, Tony," Alice said. "It would be really egotistic of me to think I could be the only one. Her dad can do it, too, and he's met some other people in his travels. They have a friend who has access to a functional MRI and has ran tests on them."

"That's beyond cool," Tony said. "I've seen some of those pictures in the lab. They're incredible. Can they do yours, too?"

"Maybe someday," Alice said. She felt her brain wander. "Tony, I need to go now, but do you maybe want to meet for lunch tomorrow? Maybe we can go to Gaucho's?" The words were out of her mouth and she couldn't wrench them back. She tried not to wince.

There was a silence on the other end of the phone. "You want to go to Gaucho's with me?" he asked. "I mean, yeah, I'd love to, but could we make it dinner? If we're going to Gaucho's, I think it should be dinner."

Alice closed her eyes. She wondered if she had made a huge mistake. Maybe she should have suggested Couscous instead. Maybe Gaucho's was too much to start with. "Okay," she said. "Why don't you pick me up after work tomorrow, and we can go to Gaucho's for dinner?"

"I'd like that," Tony said softly. "Thanks for asking me."

Alice could see Kaya and Grayson walking toward her from the park. "Listen, Tony," she said. "I'll see you then. Have a good rest of your day, okay?"

"Sure. You, too, Alice. Bye."

Alice hung up her phone and looked at the couple now standing in front of her. "How did it go?"

Kaya sat down next to Alice, and Grayson remained standing. "Well, it was difficult," Kaya said. "I mean, not difficult to read him, but just hard to, you know, listen to his thoughts."

Alice chewed on her tongue briefly and then stopped. "Start from the beginning."

Kaya nodded. "You were right, he did see us as fresh meat. But I give him credit. He remembered my name. This kid's good at what he does. I hate to say it, but he probably inherited conman genes from his father like I got ESP from mine. So I invited him to sit with us, and he did. I asked him how he was doing. He said that he was looking forward to his senior year starting in the fall, but he was worried he wasn't going to be able to get new clothes. He said he'd grown out of his clothes from last year, and his pants were too short. He was kind of passive aggressive. He was talking in a kind of a whiny voice, and he said it would be tough to have to wear flood pants to school, and that the kids would all make fun of him."

"I asked him if anyone was helping him to get new clothes, because I had heard that his neighbors were looking out for him," Grayson said. "He said that he only got a bunch of secondhand clothes that were in bad shape."

Alice shook her head. "That's not true."

"I know," Kaya said. "I mean, he was wearing pristine Air Jordans. I figured the kid has access to nice stuff. People in town feel for him and take care of him. But I played along, and I put my hand on his knee."

Grayson shifted from foot to foot. "Yeah, I wasn't too crazy about that part," he said. "I was seventeen not that long ago, Ky, and you're a hot girl in her twenties. I made a point not to look to see how he responded to that."

Kaya chuckled. "Grayson," she admonished. She turned back to Alice. "Well, I had to talk to him and listen to his thoughts at the same time, and I for sure couldn't try to encapsulate his thoughts without silence and meditative breathing. But here's what I did hear: he hates what he's doing. He's humiliated, asking for money. He feels like he's treating people like his father did. But he doesn't see another way out. He's desperate. He wants to get out. Out of town.

He wants to get away. He feels that he has to get away. That's what keeps swirling around and around in his brain. He wants to get out of the state. He sees himself going to New York City and disappearing into the crowd. He needs money for a bus, but also for a place to stay when he gets there. He's gonna try to sell some stuff in Wisteria, like his game system, his TV, and his computer. He doesn't want to, but he doesn't know what else to do." Kaya shook her head. "Listening to his thoughts was pulling at my heartstrings for sure. I just wanted to hug him, to tell him everything was going to be all right. But, of course, I couldn't."

"Why does he feel like he has to leave?" Alice asked. "He must have a reason to be so desperate. I mean, he's emancipated. He can do anything an adult can. Why is he being so secretive?"

"He's terrified," Kaya said. "But the problem is, he's so terrified that he's blocking some things. I couldn't figure out why he was so scared. But I played stupid with him. I asked him if he could get his mother to help him. You know, surely if he told her how hard things were for him . . ." She sighed. "He said that he didn't know where she was." She paused. She took a breath. "Alice, I'm pretty sure his fear has something to do with his mother. I also have a feeling—I think . . . I could be wrong. But I have a feeling he knows where his mother is."

"And he's trying to get to her?"

Kaya shook her head. "I didn't get that impression. I got the impression that it wasn't possible for him to get to her. Either he felt like he was trying to protect her, or . . . or she's already beyond any protection."

Alice gasped. "Kaya. Are you implying that it's possible that Shari's . . . dead?"

Kaya closed her eyes and nodded. "I'm afraid she might be."

Alice lowered her face into her hand. "Oh my God," she said. "Oh my God. So if she's dead . . . if she's dead then most likely someone killed her."

Grayson nodded. "This is much bigger than some scam and some poor old lady with diabetes, Alice," he said. "Kaya, could you hear anything else from him?"

Kaya shook his head. "You know how some small animals, like mice and moles, are so timid that they seem to be only concerned about staying alive all the time? Like, they're always shaky, like they've been backed into a corner, and they're just waiting for the cat to come up and eat them? Yeah, that's what it's like inside Brad's brain. He's in survival mode. All he can think of is getting out, no matter what he has to do."

Alice shuddered. "I don't know what to do," she said. "I mean, I work for the D.A.'s office. I feel like I need to keep everything aboveboard, you know? I can't really go to my boss and say that my friend read the mind of a guy whose father we put in prison a few months ago, and he's terrified of that father. I need to have some sort of evidence. I mean, I know Carla trusts my instincts. She never questions them. But she doesn't question them because she doesn't want to know. I can't ask her to trust me on this without giving her more to go on. But at the same time, I feel an obligation to protect Brad. And of course, Shari, if she's still alive. If she's not alive, she has the right to be avenged. Someone needs to be held responsible. In the meantime, we have to make Brad feel safe and keep him from leaving. If he wants to get lost in New York, he will, and we'll never be able to find him. But his father might." She shook her head. "If Chet wins this appeal . . ." She looked up at Grayson, and then at Kaya. "We can't let that happen. I have to help Carla to keep that from happening." She stood. "I have to go back to work. I have to do some more research, to make sure he doesn't win. He needs to stay in prison. He belongs there. But what about Brad?"

"He can stay with us," Grayson offered. He looked toward Kaya. "I mean, I know it's not a lot of room, but we could make it work." He and Kaya looked into each other's eyes for a prolonged period of time.

"No," Alice said. "No. We need to get him out of Florence, but Wisteria is too close. We need to find some place where no one would think to look for him. But I don't know of any place. I could ask Emilie, but she lives in student housing. Plus, it would be too hard to keep an eye on him. And she's coming back here in a couple of weeks. I don't know. Do you guys have any ideas?"

Kaya thought about it. Then a smile broke out across her face. "I have an idea," she said. "Oh, God. It's brilliant."

"What?" Grayson asked.

Kaya reached over and grabbed his hand. A few seconds passed. Then Grayson smiled. "Kaya, you're a genius," he said. "If I wasn't already married, I'd propose to you right now."

Kaya smirked. "I'm sorry, but I feel obligated to tell you that I'm expecting a child with the man that I love."

Grayson pulled her to her feet and into his embrace. "I'll love that child like it's my own." He leaned down for a kiss.

"Oh, barf," Alice said, rolling her eyes. But then she smiled. "Tell me your idea, Kaya."

10

TONY CAME FOR ALICE AT five thirty. He got out and walked up to the building, even though Alice had been waiting outside for him. "Hi," he said with a nervous smile. He was dressed in khakis and a short-sleeved polo shirt. He had done something with his hair. It looked nice and neat. As he got close, Alice could smell the cologne. She tried not to inhale the scent too deeply.

"Hi," Alice said back, walking toward him. She let Tony put his hands on her arms and kiss her on the cheek. It was a familiar gesture between two people who had known each other for years, but it was slightly distant, like two lovers who had reconnected after years apart.

"Are you ready to go?" Tony asked awkwardly.

Alice laughed. "I'm standing outside waiting for you," she teased.

Tony closed his eyes and shook his head. "Sorry," he said. "I-I guess I'm just a little nervous. I was kind of surprised that you wanted to go to Gaucho's." He opened the car door, and Alice got in. Tony went around and got in the driver's seat. He put on his seatbelt and started the car. Then he turned to Alice. "Why did you pick Gaucho's?"

"I don't know," Alice said softly. "I didn't mean to. I wanted to have lunch with you. Gaucho's just slipped out of my mouth."

Tony nodded as he put the car into drive. "I'm okay with going somewhere else if you want."

Alice tried not to smile. Tony wasn't being honest with her. He wanted to go to Gaucho's. "No, that's okay," she said. "I haven't been there since, well, senior year prom, and it was always my favorite place."

Tony grinned. "Mine too."

They rode in silence for the five-minute drive. Tony parked on the street in front of the restaurant and went around the car to open Alice's door. She already had her hand on the handle, so the action jerked her arm forward.

"Oh, I'm sorry," Tony said.

Alice smiled this time. "It's okay." She let Tony give her his hand to help her out of the car.

"It looks the same," Tony said as they approached the restaurant. "I haven't been here since prom either, although I have driven by a few times."

Alice felt a sadness flow through her. Tony hadn't done a lot of things since she left for college. Not going to Gaucho's was just a minor one. She knew there were other things, other more serious things.

"I made a reservation," Tony told her once they were inside. "I wasn't sure if it would be crowded. It's Friday night. I'm not sure if it's as popular as it was back then."

"That was prom night," Alice said. "You were smart to make the reservation that night. It does seem crowded tonight. I'm guessing it's still as good as it used to be."

They were seated at a table near the window. As they sat down, Alice felt a sense of deja vu. "This is the same table."

Tony grinned. "I requested it," he told her. "I wasn't sure you'd remember."

Alice laughed. "Of course I remember. You don't forget something like that."

The hostess handed them two menus. "Your server will be Tanya," she said. "She'll be with you in a minute. By the way, it's great to see the two of you together. You might not remember me. I'm Sandy. I was two years behind you two at Florence High. I remember you two breaking up at the end of the year. It was heartbreaking. But seeing you together tonight, well, it gives me hope." She smiled. "I'll let you take a look at the menus. Enjoy your meal."

Alice watched the fuzzy outline of Sandy walk away. "Wow," she said. "That was awkward."

Tony shrugged. "It was kind of nice," he said. "It's nice that people remember us together in high school. And it's nice that we haven't changed enough for people not to recognize us." He picked up his menu and started to peruse his choices.

Alice picked up her menu. The type was small. She was struggling to read the options. She tried to squint, but it didn't help. She cursed herself for not bringing a magnifying glass in her purse. She would have to get an extra one to keep with her at all times. She was reluctant to ask Tony for help. She didn't want him to know how bad it was. She didn't want this night to turn into yet another opportunity for Tony to help her. She wanted to enjoy the evening and not have to think about what she had already lost.

The server, Tanya, arrived at the table. "Welcome. Can I get you some drinks?"

"I'll have an IPA," Tony said. "Whatever's on tap."

"I'll have an iced tea," Alice said.

"I can get those started," Tanya said. "Do you need some more time, or do you know what you want to order?"

Tony looked at Alice. "I know what I want. Are you ready to order?"

Alice made a split-second decision to order her old favorite. That way, she didn't have to let on that she couldn't read the menu. "I think so," she said. "You go first, Tony."

Tony looked up at the server. "I'll have the prime rib with scalloped potatoes, and a caesar salad. Oh, and can we have a basket of garlic bread?" He turned to Alice. "Remember how much we liked the garlic bread?"

Alice smiled. "I do," she said. She turned to Tanya. "I'll start with a garden salad, with honey mustard dressing on the side. And I'll have the mushroom raviolis."

The server looked up from her pad. "I'm so sorry," she said. "We don't have the raviolis anymore. We stopped offering them last year. Is there something else you'd like to try?"

Alice tried not to panic. The menu had changed. She should have expected that. Nothing ever stayed the same. Her ploy to deceive Tony had failed.

"I, uh, I guess I'll need to look at the menu again," she said. "I just remembered that I loved the raviolis. I didn't look very carefully."

The server nodded. "No problem," she said. "You're not the first person to ask for the raviolis. I'll let the manager know that people are still asking for them. Maybe she can see about bringing them back. I'll give you a few minutes. I'll put in the order for your bread and salads." She smiled at them and walked away.

"Well, I guess I'll have to get something else," Alice said. She lifted the menu and put on a charade that she was reviewing her options. She was tempted to just order the prime rib like Tony, although she hated steak, and he knew it. She wasn't sure what her next move would be.

"Hey," Tony said. "You know, the risotto looks really good. You must have passed over it on the menu. I remember you like risotto. And it's mushroom risotto. And I know you'd like the steamed vegetable side. See, it's on the right side of the menu. Like I said, you must have been so focused on the ravioli that you just missed it."

Alice looked at the menu and focused her eyes on the right side. She couldn't differentiate one entree from another, but she smiled. "Oh yeah," she said. "I did miss that. Thanks for pointing that out. I think I will get that." She smiled at Tony with immense gratitude.

Tony nodded. "I know you just missed that."

Alice knew Tony was lying. Tony knew. Tony knew her well enough to know that she was struggling, and he figured out why. She felt a rush of affection go through her body. Without thinking, she reached out and put her hand on top of Tony's hand. Then, she forgot to remove it a moment later as she had intended to. She stared into Tony's eyes, and he stared back. After a few moments, he maneuvered to turn his hand around, and they sat in silence, holding hands, until their server returned and took Alice's amended order.

They were eating their garlic bread and salad when Tony finally and inevitably brought up the prom. "It was the most amazing night of my life."

Alice smiled. She had had more experiences in dating than Tony, but she had to admit, prom night had been pretty spectacular. "Me, too."

"Your plan was brilliant," Tony went on. "I was so nervous, thinking we would be having sex for the first time. I don't think I would have made it through the night."

Alice laughed. "Not just you," she admitted. "I don't think I would have had a minute of fun at the prom thinking about what was coming."

"I remember Chris freaking out about going to the hotel with Shannon after the prom," Tony said.

"And Shannon was so irritable all night, waiting."

"But not us," Tony said. "We probably had a better time than anyone else."

"We had our little secret," Alice said fondly.

Tony laughed. "Who even thinks about having prom sex *before* the prom? I mean, I don't want to say getting it over with, but it kinda was. I bet the people at the motel were amused by us, showing up in our prom finery before prom, renting the room for two hours."

"We only needed a half hour," Alice mused.

"Forty-five minutes," Tony said defensively. "I mean, we did rinse off in the shower after. And we had our reservation to keep."

Alice smiled at the memory. "I remember sitting at this very table," she said. "We were holding hands and looking at each other and trying not to giggle." She giggled. "Yeah, like that!"

Tony laughed. "We were so young," he said wistfully.

"We're still young," Alice said. She tried not to remember that she was losing her vision like an old woman.

Tony put down his fork and reached back out for Alice's hand. "Alice," he said. "Why did you want to come here tonight? You know what this place is to us. What are you trying to say to me?"

Alice let her hand be held. She closed her eyes. When she opened them, she steeled herself to speak. "I don't know," she said, barely above a whisper. "I-I guess I needed to be here with you again. To see, well, what it felt like, to come back to the scene of the crime, to the place, well . . ."

"To the place where we first said we loved each other," Tony said. He looked at their hands, entwined. "And then, one month later, you broke my heart."

Alice felt like her own heart was breaking with that memory. "I did what I had to do," she said quietly. "I didn't see how we could make it work. We were going to be apart for four years, and I didn't see how I could be there for you, to be what you needed. It was a hard choice, Tony. I really did love you. I didn't stop loving you just because I left."

"But you moved on," Tony said. "Em told me. She thought I needed to know, so I could move on, too. In a way, I did. I had to push aside my feelings so I could move forward. I mean, I never met anyone. But it wasn't because I was closed off. Maybe I was closed off. But I came to terms with it being over. And then, two years ago, you came back."

"And we became friends," Alice said. "We had never really been friends, had we? You were my best friend's brother, and then, boom, you were my boyfriend. We kind of skipped a step, didn't we?"

"But we're friends now," Tony said. "I cherish our friendship. It means a lot to me. But Al, I want to be there for you, to be your friend, and to help you, and . . . and maybe to love you again, the way I did before, only now, as an adult, with grown-up experiences. What is it that you want?"

"I-I want . . ." Alice paused. "I'm going away for a couple of days."

Tony looked startled. "Well, that's one way to change the subject."

Alice shook her head. "No, I'm not changing the subject," she said. "I wanted you to know that I was leaving town. I thought it was important for you to know." She squeezed his hand, still in hers.

Tony stared at her and then nodded. "Oh," he said. "Oh. I see. When are you going?"

"Tomorrow," Alice said. "It's for work. I have something I have to do."

"Can you tell me about it?" Tony asked.

Alice shook her head. "No, not yet," she said. "Maybe later. But I can tell you that I'm going with Kaya and her husband, Grayson."

Tony's nose wrinkled. "You're bringing your friends with you for a work trip?" he asked. "That's unusual, isn't it? Where are you going?"

"I can't tell you," Alice said. "We're leaving early tomorrow morning, and we'll be back on Monday afternoon."

Tony nodded. "I guess you needed someone to drive you."

Alice decided that was as good a reason as any, so she didn't contradict Tony's reply. Tanya arrived with their entrees. Alice could smell the aroma of the mushroom risotto wafting from the dish. She knew that Tony had led her in the right direction with her order.

"I'll be back to check on you in a few minutes," Tanya said as she walked away.

Alice and Tony were quiet for a few minutes as they dug into their entrees. Alice savored the flavor on her tongue. She let herself think back to that night, senior year, sneaking glances at Tony as she ate her raviolis, and him sneaking looks back at her. It had been a magical night. It was hard to believe that things had changed so quickly after that night. She tried to imagine how it happened.

"You told me that night that you would be okay with me being away for so long," she blurted out.

Tony looked up from his steak. "I-I don't remember that."

Alice smiled. "Don't lie to me again, Tony," she said. "I knew you were lying then, and I know you're lying now."

Tony nodded. "I knew." He looked down. "I knew right then. After we made love in the motel, I knew I didn't want to live without you. I wanted to go with you, so badly, but I was too scared. I was afraid that I would get lost in the city, and I was afraid that you wouldn't. You were so sure of yourself. I imagined myself watching you pull away from me, going on new adventures. So I knew I had to stay in Florence. But that meant letting you go to follow your own dreams. But I knew it would kill me."

"You told me you would be okay, and I knew you were lying. That was what it was, wasn't it?" Alice reached out and touched Tony's cheek. "We both made sacrifices. You let me go, and then I let you go. We were trying not to hurt each other, but then that's exactly what we did."

Tony pushed his face against Alice's palm. "We loved each other," he said. "That's what you do for the people you love. You let them go if that's the right thing to do."

Alice lowered her hand. She picked up her fork, but she didn't feel that she could eat another bite, no matter how delicious it was. "I . . . I don't want you to take care of me," she said, not making eye contact.

"But when you love someone, you want to take care of them," Tony protested. "It's what you do."

Alice shook her head. "But it's different for us. It's not just the normal everyday taking care of each other, like most people do. There's much more, and you know it. I don't want to be dependent on you. I want to take care of myself. Tony, it's only going to get worse. You've gone to the appointments with me. You know it."

Tony nodded. "I do know it," he said. "I want to help you, but I don't want you to lose yourself. I want you to be able to take care of yourself, but also to be able to ask for help. I want to help you." He paused. "I told you I would move in with you to help you." He closed his eyes. "I'm surprised you didn't sense my lie, Alice. Maybe you were too caught up in worrying about being independent. Yes, I want to help you. But I just want to be with you. I want to be close to you, Alice. It was a ploy. I would take the guest room if it meant I could be with you every day."

Alice cursed eyes that were struggling to see but quick to cry. "I knew you were lying," Alice said. "I-I just ignored the lie. I *am* caught up in the future. Tony, it's going to be hard. I'm going to have to struggle, a lot. And I don't want to drag you into my nightmare. It won't be easy for you."

"You know what's hard for me?" Tony asked. "Not being able to touch you. Not being able to hold you, to comfort you like no one else can. That's what's hard, Alice. Being able to be with you, to be partners with you, to be close to you, and even to help you, that would be easy for me."

"I need to get a box," Alice said. "I . . . I can't eat any more." She smiled. "Thank you for knowing I needed help with the menu."

Tony looked at her with feigned confusion. "I don't know what on Earth you're talking about, Alice Telman," he said, and he grinned.

Once their food was boxed up and the bill paid, they said goodbye to the hostess, Sandy, and headed back to Tony's car. "I have to get up really early in the morning," Alice said.

"So it's a good thing it's not a late night," Tony said, but again he was fibbing.

They arrived at Alice's childhood home. "Here we are again," Alice said. "Back at 45 Baxter Lane. Remember how we used to sit out here in your old beater and make out until my curfew?"

Tony laughed. "I remember. And I also remember that one time that we heard that pounding on the window, and your dad was standing there, fuming. We had no idea how long he was standing there watching us."

"That was horrifying," Alice said. "I was nervous every time after that that he would come out again, so I had to keep checking."

"I remember that," Tony said. "That was when I went out and found that parking lot we could go to instead of parking in front of your house."

Alice smiled at the memory. "The Lutheran church," she said. "I've had a soft spot for Lutherans since that time in my life."

"No one's gonna come out now to see us," Tony said softly. "We're twenty-four-year-old adults, and no one can tell us what to do anymore." He looked at Alice, and she looked back.

What should have happened quickly happened very slowly. They took off their seatbelts. Alice shuffled closer to Tony, only stopped by the console in the middle of the front seat. Tony moved his head toward Alice. Alice moved her head toward Tony. One inch closer. Another inch. Finally, the space closed, and their lips touched. It wasn't like lightning. It was like standing beneath a warm waterfall, face lifted up against the stream. Hands went to shoulders, and then they pulled away.

"You have an early day tomorrow," Tony said. "I'll walk you to the door."

This time, Alice waited for Tony to open her door for her and take her hand. This time, she kept her hand in his as they walked toward the house. They made it to the door. They faced each other, holding both of their hands in the other's, looking into each other's eyes.

"Can you still see my eyes?" Tony asked with apprehension.

Alice smiled. "I can still see them," she confirmed. Then she thought to herself, *I can even see them when I close my eyes. I could be completely blind, and I could still see your eyes. I'll always see your eyes.*

Tony leaned in and kissed her. "The inevitable last kiss by the front door," he mumbled. "And the awkward good night."

Alice grinned and giggled. "Tony," she said. "It's like you said. We're adults now. We're twenty-four years old. There's no one behind these doors to tell us what to do. We make our own choices. And my choice is for you to come inside with me."

Tony's brows shot up. "You want me to come in?" he asked in surprise. "But you yourself said that you needed to leave really early tomorrow."

Alice smiled at him. "Then we'd better get to it quickly, don't you think?" She pulled her keys from her purse, unlocked the door, and they both stepped inside the dark hallway. "But before we do anything else, we have to walk the giant dog."

11

GRAYSON KNOCKED ON THE DOOR—only because he was the stronger knocker, and they wanted the knock to be heard. "Brad, wake up!" Alice shouted through the door. "Brad, it's Alice. We need to talk."

They waited a full minute, and then they heard the pattering of feet across the floor. "Alice?" Brad said sleepily through the door. "What do you want?"

"Open the door," Alice said. "I'll tell you when you let me in."

The chain came off the door, and Alice heard the deadbolt turn. Brad opened wearing cut-off sweatpants and no shirt.

"Let me get a T-shirt," he said. Then he noticed Kaya and Grayson. "What are they doing here?" he asked, backing up cautiously. "You didn't say you weren't alone, Alice."

Kaya took a tentative step forward. "It's okay, Brad," she said softly. "We're not here to hurt you. We're here to help."

"Help with what?" Brad asked, reaching for a shirt on the back of an armchair. "I don't need any help."

Alice gave him a warm smile. "You do, Brad, and you know I can tell when you're not telling the truth."

Brad looked at her and squinted. "Yeah," he said. "How do you even know that?"

"That's not important right now," Grayson said, moving into the small studio. "What's important is that you need to pack your bags. We're taking you to a safe place."

Brad's eyes went wide. "A safe place?" He looked defiant, but then the look evaporated. "What place is safe?"

"We can't tell you that yet," Kaya said. She walked toward the closet near the bed. "Do you have a suitcase, or a gym bag in here?"

Brad stood still. "I don't understand what's happening here."

Alice moved him over to the bed and made him sit down before taking the spot next to him. "We know you're scared, Brad," she said. "We know you want to get away. We want to get you away, but we don't want to lose you. We just want to help. We have a place you can go, and the only people who will know where you are will be the people in this room. Mrs. Katz won't even know. After we get back, we'll make sure she knows you're in a safe place."

"You'll have to leave your cell phone and laptop here," Grayson said, palming Brad's phone. "They're traceable."

"Do you think I'm in some sort of danger?" Brad asked.

"We think you could be," Alice said. "And *you* think you could be."

Brad shook his head. "There's no way that you could know what I think," he said.

Kaya came back with two gym bags. "Put in enough for a couple of weeks," she said. "Underwear, jeans, shorts, shirts, socks, something to sleep in. Get any toiletries you need, any medication. If you forget anything, you can just buy it there."

"Where?" Brad tried one more time as he stood and walked to his dresser.

"With a friend," Grayson said. "Someone we can trust. You'll have to trust us."

"The other day in the park," Brad said, placing a pile of boxer shorts into the bag. "Was that legit? Were you like, undercover or something? But I didn't tell you anything."

"You told us enough," Kaya said. She touched Brad's arm. "You didn't have to say much."

They continued to pack Brad's belongings. "It will take about three hours to get there," Grayson said. "You can sit up front with me.

You can control the radio if you want. If you have any snacks, you can bring them."

"We're driving?" Brad asked, opening his refrigerator and taking out an apple. He reached back in and grabbed another one. Then he took some Clif bars out of the cabinet. "Three hours away. Is that far enough?"

"If we succeed in not letting anyone know where you are," Alice said. "Do you want to bring your hand-held games?"

"I can't bring my game system?" Brad asked.

"We have to keep it lowkey," Kaya said. "If you need to, you can find an arcade where we're going."

"They have arcades?" Brad asked. "I guess it can't be all bad."

A half hour had passed since the group of adults had awoken the teenager. It was seven thirty. Time to go. They left the apartment, and Brad locked the door.

At Grayson's car, Brad asked, "A Prius?" He shrugged. "I guess that's okay, but you should check out the electric cars that are coming out. Have you seen the Teslas?"

Grayson smirked as he loaded Brad's bags in the hatchback. "Do I look like I can afford a Tesla? I wouldn't mind having an electric car someday, but I have to wait for the prices to come down. I got this car used. It's two years old and it already has fifty thousand miles on it. A new car is not in my near future. Plus, this is safe for a baby."

"Who's having a baby?" Brad asked. He looked at Alice. "Not you?"

Alice laughed. "Grayson is married to Kaya," she reminded him. "Kaya's having a baby next year. But she's not showing yet. That takes a while to happen. Get in. We need to hit the road."

"Which road?" Brad asked innocently.

Grayson laughed. "You'll see when we get on it."

They had been riding for about forty-five minutes, superficial conversation passing the time. Grayson and Brad talked about local sports teams. "I played JV basketball freshman and sophomore years," Brad said. "But then a lot of the guys got really tall, and I stayed under six feet. I tried out for varsity last year, but I was cut, and I didn't want to be the oldest guy in JV, so I quit."

"I didn't play anything at Wisteria," Grayson said. "But Kaya was a varsity cheerleader all four years. She was pretty well-known."

"Did you know the Wisteria girl that fell off the pyramid ten years ago?" Brad asked Kaya. "That happened at my school."

Kaya rolled her eyes. "I might have been a bit familiar with her," was her vague answer.

Alice nudged Kaya. She took her hand and sent her a thought. Kaya nodded.

"Brad," Kaya said, putting her hand on his shoulder in the front seat. "Listen, we're not telling anyone where we're bringing you for your safety, and I know you said that you don't know where your mom went, but what do you want us to tell her if for some reason she does show up and is looking for you? I would hate for her to worry."

Brad continued to look forward, out the windshield. "I don't think she'll come looking for me," he said softly. "I-I mean, I don't think she'll come back. I think she left for good. I don't think I'll see her again."

Kaya squeezed his shoulder. "Okay, Brad," she said quietly. "I'm sorry. I didn't mean to say anything to make you upset."

Brad turned to look at her. "No, you didn't say anything bad," he said. "It's just . . . it's just that I miss her, you know? I wish I could see her again, but . . ." His voice trailed off. Kaya could hear the voice in his head telling him not to cry. Just don't cry. Don't blink. She removed her hand from his shoulder. She had heard enough.

Alice reached for her hand. *I don't think he knows if she's alive,* Kaya told her through her thoughts, *but he's pretty sure he'll never see her again. He suspects very strongly that she's dead. He doesn't think she would ever leave him with his father without her there to protect him. Either she's being held against her will or she's dead.*

Alice sighed out loud. *I'm sorry to make you do that,* she thought. *I know that was hard. But we have to help him. We have to know the truth for him to be able to move on. I still can't believe that Shari could be dead.*

Kaya squeezed Alice's hand and then pulled her own away. She herself could not believe that she was involved in something that could involve murder. She was glad Grayson was with them on this trip. She felt safer with him there. Despite her desire to be a law enforcement officer, Kaya didn't think she had the skills yet to keep herself and Alice safe in a dangerous situation. She would someday, but now, she wasn't just thinking about herself. She had a baby to think about, too.

"Alice," she said. "I want to try something, if it's okay."

"What is it?" Alice asked, wondering if it was another mind game.

Kaya looked at the front seat. Grayson and Brad were talking animatedly again as Brad adjusted the radio controls. "I want to try to read and project thoughts without touching," she said quietly. "I know I'm gonna need to have those skills before I ever have a chance to be alone with . . ." She gestured toward Brad. "Well, you know."

Alice nodded. "Okay," she said. "What can I do to help?"

Kaya smiled. "Thanks," she said. "You might be more receptive than other people since you have skills, too, but it's a good place to start. Here's what I want you to do. We'll start by taking a few deep breaths together, to center ourselves. Then . . ." She grinned. "Then I want you to think about something meaningful to you. For example, you can think about the reason that Tony's car was parked in front of your house at seven this morning when we came to pick you up!"

Alice's hand shot to her mouth. "Kaya!" she exclaimed. "How on Earth would you know that it's Tony's car? People park in front of my house all the time. It's public. What, have you been stalking us? That's just creepy."

Kaya laughed. "Oh, Alice," she said, shaking her head. "You just fell for the oldest trick in the book. You know how I knew that was Tony's car? Because you just told me, you idiot! You have to be more careful than that if you want to keep secrets!" She gave Alice a warm smile. "You don't have to tell me anything you don't want to, but maybe, just maybe, you can tell me how you're feeling this morning. That's all. Just how you are. I don't have to know the details."

Alice nodded. "Okay," she agreed. "I can do that."

Kaya nodded back. "Okay," she said. She sat back against the seat, concentrated on her posture, and closed her eyes. Then she opened one of them. "But a few details *would* be welcome." She closed her eye again and then led Alice through a breathing exercise.

The two women breathed together for some time. Then Alice heard a voice in her mind. *Can you hear me?* Her eyes snapped open. She looked at Kaya, who was looking back at her. She nodded. *Great! It's working! Now you try to send a message back to me.*

What do you want me to say?

Kaya shrugged. *Anything. Why don't you tell me about how you and Tony first met, to start.*

Alice nodded. *I was five. I started kindergarten. I was in a class with Emilie, who turned out to be my best friend. I didn't know she had a brother at first, let alone a twin. I was going to play at her house after school one day, and when we got to her mother's car, Tony jumped into the back seat with us. I had never noticed him before, and I thought he was in the wrong car. Oh my God! I can actually hear you laughing! That's so cool.*

Kaya smiled. *So he was your best friend's brother. When did he become something else to you?*

Alice didn't even have to think about her answer. *We were watching* Field of Dreams *on video. It was my favorite movie. It still is. It was one of the parts of the film where something happened that gave me the chills. I looked up to make eye contact with Emilie, but she was looking at the screen. That's when I noticed that Tony was watching me. Not in a scary way. Just observing me, watching my reactions. It really threw me for a loop.*

How old were you? Kaya wondered.

Alice felt like she was being interviewed. But it was good practice, and she was feeling kind of warm and cozy about Tony at the moment. *We were fourteen. I had never thought of him as anything but a minor annoyance. He was always around, him and his best friend Josh. But suddenly, he wasn't just Em's brother anymore. He was a guy, with more dimensions than I had ever realized. He saw me looking back at him and he turned away. That was when I knew he liked me.*

Kaya sighed audibly. *Puppy love. That's the sweetest. How long was it before you went out with him?*

It was more than two years, Alice admitted. *Two years of watching, and tiptoeing around each other. I wasn't sure how I felt about him. But the more I watched, the more I realized what a nice and gentle guy he was. He doted on Emilie, and he would help her with anything she needed. But he wasn't a sap. He didn't let anyone walk all over him. He had good instincts. I started to notice that he was like that in school with his friends, too. He would help them, or include them. He was kind. It made me feel warm to watch him. I wondered what it was about me that he liked. I didn't think there was anything special about me. Remember, my skills didn't emerge until I was seventeen. But he seemed to like me. I found myself wanting to spend more time with him. I would try to include him when I was at the house with Em. I only wanted to go to her house, and not to mine, since Tony was at her house. Em started to notice, and one day she confronted me. I confessed that I had a crush on her twin, and she was shocked.*

Laughter erupted inside Alice's head. *One of my friends had a crush on Graham freshman year,* Kaya said, *but she never told me. I ended up hearing it in her thoughts. But Graham would never have acted on it.*

Too much of an age difference, and he was already into Gina by then anyway. What did Emilie say?

She didn't say much at first. She kind of ignored it. But then, I guess, she came to terms with it, and the idea grew on her. She told me she watched us when we were together, and we looked good together. She ended up telling Tony that I liked him, and that he should ask me out. I was horrified, but then he did it.

And history was written? Kaya asked.

Alice shrugged. *I guess so. Over time, as we got to know each other better, we learned more and more about each other that we liked. We both liked a lot of the same bands, and the same movies. We both didn't care so much about school sports and spirit. He has this great sense of humor. Like, he doesn't even have to think about it. It's just there. And he thinks I'm funny. I finally asked him what it was about me that he liked, and he told me. He said that first, it was that Emilie always talked about me, and she said wonderful things. She loved me. And then he said he thought I was pretty. He loved my brown hair and brown eyes, even though that's what most people have. He liked the dimple on my right cheek. He liked all the things about me that I thought were average. I mean, that was pretty amazing, right? But then he, Tony, said that he liked my kindness. That's what blew me away the most. He was the kindest person I'd ever met, and he admired my kindness. I was blown away.*

Kaya's head tilted. *The way you talk about him . . . you still sound blown away.*

Alice's cheeks got hot. *I tried to convince myself that I didn't love him anymore when I came back from college. It was easy when I was at school. I never saw him. But then, there he was at Em's house again, being her twin, and being in my face. But things were different. My parents were gone, my sight was going. I had to find a way to support myself, to figure out my next steps. I knew right away that Tony still loved me. I could see the sadness in his eyes when he saw me. But the most amazing thing about that man was that when I told him I wanted to be friends, he took that to heart. He didn't take it to mean that I wanted us to just be civil with each other. He really wanted to be my friend, to be there for me, for whatever I needed. He never pressured me. Em did. She still does. But not Tony. Tony took his cues from me. He stayed close, but not too close. He told me that he would still be there for me if I started to see someone else, but I knew that wouldn't happen. I didn't want to be with someone else. It was either Tony or be alone. And for a long time, I chose to be alone.*

Kaya reached out as if to touch her hand, but then she remembered not to. *So then what changed last night?*

Alice closed her eyes. *You and I talked the other day. You helped me think about things, and how I could let Tony know what I wanted and not be scared that his love would swallow me up once my vision was gone. It made a lot of sense. I never stopped loving Tony, Kaya. I might have said I did, but I didn't. You're the first objective person I've been able to share my thoughts with, both literally and figuratively, since I've been back in Florence. I can't talk to Em, or Carla at work, and my parents are gone. I know a lot of people, and some of them I would call friends, but not the kind of friend that I can trust. You know, everyone knows everyone around here. But you're like a breath of fresh air, Kaya.*

Kaya smiled. *I'm glad I could help. Your story is so much better to tell than mine and Grayson's. Ours is just about chocolate pudding. And then we were married and pregnant.*

Alice laughed out loud and then covered her mouth quickly.

"You ladies doing okay back there?" Grayson called out. "You've been as quiet as mice. I thought maybe you'd both fallen asleep." Kaya laughed and then reached across the middle of the seat and touched Grayson's shoulder. Grayson smiled. "I love you, too," he said.

Brad shook his head. "You guys have a really weird way of communicating with each other," he said. "It's freaking me out."

Kaya turned back to Alice. *And what about last night?*

Alice tried not to smile. *We went to dinner, to a place that meant a lot to us. We talked, and after, we kissed in the car. Then he walked me to the door, and we kissed again. And then he and I walked my dog Pony, and when we got back, I asked him to stay. And he did. And it was wonderful. We had only been, you know, together, a handful of times after prom senior year, and then we broke up. I went on to date other men, but Tony didn't have any romantic relationships. I did find out last night that no dating didn't mean no, um, encounters, though. And to be honest, I'm glad. I thought I'd have to teach him a few things, but I really didn't. He was loving, and gentle but not too gentle if you know what I mean. And he was honest with me. He told me about the time while I was gone, and I told him my truth, too. I told him about my fears, about my vision, and everything I had told you, and he told me about his fears, also about my vision, and what it would look like for us going forward. We meant to go to sleep early because I told him I had to get up early, but we were up most of the night talking, and, well . . .*

No wonder you look so tired today. Kaya broke the connection and took Alice's hand. "I'm really happy for you, Alice," she said. "It sounds like you two are heading in the right direction. It sounds like the chemistry you had at age fourteen is still there."

Brad sighed from the front seat. "It's hard to follow your conversation when you talk in fragments," he said. "It's like all of you read each other's minds or something."

Alice, Kaya, and Grayson all laughed.

"I can't read minds, Brad," Grayson said. "And I can promise you," he glanced at Alice quickly, "that I'm not lying."

12

"BRAD, I'D LIKE YOU TO meet my very good friend, Dr. Blake," Kaya said. She was almost bouncing on her feet from excitement. She had just pulled out of an embrace with the professor, and she was smiling from ear to ear. "He gave me away at my wedding. He's like my second dad, and he'll be hosting you for a while, until we can work out another plan."

Dr. Blake smiled and shook Brad's hand. "It's very nice to meet you, young man," he said. "Kaya's been telling me all about you. You've certainly impressed her in some way. She only has good things to say." He turned to Alice. "And you must be Miss Telman." He shook her hand, too. "Kaya always refers to me as Dr. Blake, but I'm retired from the university now, and I'm just emeritus. You can call me Rigo. That's what my friends call me." He turned to Kaya. "That includes both of you, Mr. and Mrs. Grayson."

Kaya beamed. "Grayson is my husband's first name, Dr. uh, Rigo. God. That sounds so weird to say out loud. But our last name is Pike. You know, like Christopher Pike, the first captain of the U.S.S. *Enterprise*."

Dr. Blake laughed. "You finally found a reference I can understand," he said. "Kids these days tend to refer to *Star Wars*. I saw the first movie. Or is it the fourth movie now? It was the first movie when it came out. Now that I have more time on my hands, I should get the video tapes and watch them all."

"We have the boxed DVD set," Grayson told him. "We could loan it to you."

"Well, that would only work if I had a confounded DVD player," Dr. Blake said.

Alice looked at Dr. Blake. "What kind of a name is Rigo?" she asked. "Is it short for Rodrigo? You don't appear to be Latino to me."

Dr. Blake shook his head. "No, not Rodrigo," he said. "But it is a nickname. It's short for Dirigo."

Alice burst out in a laugh. "Oh, I'm so sorry," she said. "I meant no disrespect by laughing. It's just that I went to the University of Maine. I spent four years in Maine. I took a class in the history of Maine." She smiled at Dr. Blake, and he laughed.

Kaya looked back and forth between the two of them. "I don't get it," she said. "Let the rest of us dummies in on your private joke already!"

Alice turned to Kaya. "Dirigo is the motto of the state of Maine," she said. "And it just makes sense that it's Dr. Blake's name. Didn't you say he was your brother Graham's mentor? *Dirigo* means 'I guide' in Latin."

Kaya's mouth fell open. "Get out!" she shouted. "No way! Are you kidding me?" She looked at Grayson. "Can you believe this shit? First, we have Alice, the truth giver. Now we have Dirigo, the guide!"

Grayson put his arms around her waist. "Archetypes," he said. "And don't forget, Kaya, my doobage!"

Brad's ears perked up. "Doobage?" he asked. "Where?" Grayson laughed.

"Wait," Kaya said. "I think I'm missing something. What's an archetype again?"

"You know, like in books and stuff," Alice said.

Kaya shook her head. "What exactly is an archetype?"

"I'll explain it to you later."

"Let me show you to your room," Dr. Blake said. He lifted one of Brad's bags. Then he put it down. "We'll have Pike bring this bag up later. Follow me up the stairs."

Alice, Kaya, and Grayson were left on their own downstairs. "We should sit down," Kaya said. "I've been here enough to be allowed to make that decision. I'll take the La-Z-Boy. I'm the only pregnant one here, and I need to be pampered." She eased herself into her seat and used the lever on the side to recline it all the way back. "Ahhh," she said.

Alice walked around the room and squinted at the bookcases. "He's got a lot of really cool texts here," she said. "He's a psychologist?" She looked closer. "Oh. He wrote some of these books. That's cool. I took Intro to Psych freshman year. I'll have to check my books when I get back home to see if we used one of his books. Is he divorced?"

Kaya shook her head. "He was married a long time ago," she said. "His wife had MS, and she died when she was forty-two. They never had kids. That's why he likes working with students so much. I guess if he did have kids, they'd be about our age now, or maybe a bit older. I do feel really close to him. He helped me so much when I was in the psychiatric hospital." She went quiet and closed her eyes.

Grayson kneeled by the chair and took Kaya's hand. "You had a lot of help back then," he said. "We were all there for you. Me, Graham, your mom, Sergeant Morris, and Dr. Blake. You were never alone. Don't ever forget it."

Alice watched this scene. She had heard the story of Kaya being held at a psychiatric hospital after being misdiagnosed with psychosis, and then being kept against her will after accusing the administrator of wrongdoing. She didn't know that Kaya still had such strong feelings about that time. Trauma was hard to get past. Alice had lost her mother. That traumatic event went on for three years. Then she had to watch as her father drowned his sorrows in gin and vodka. Luckily, she was away at college most of the time during that, so she only had to see the damage when she was home on vacation. It was one of the reasons she didn't come home very often the last two years of school. It was one of the reasons she went without seeing Tony. Now both of her parents were gone. She missed them. But when she thought of them, it was hard to see past their final years and all of the pain. It was easier sometimes to just not think about them at all. Living at their house didn't help. Losing her vision did help in some ways. She didn't have to look closely at the old wallpaper that was put up in the 1970s, or the ugly linoleum pattern on the kitchen floor. But the smells were still there, and the sounds of the house creaking at night. Those two senses were vivid for Alice.

She thought of doing some deep cleaning, and getting a white-noise machine, but she never got around to it. She just learned to live with the distractions.

Dr. Blake padded back down the stairs in his slippers. "Brad found my Wii. He said it wasn't as good as his PlayStation 3, but he was willing to compromise for his safety." He sat on the couch. "So, Kaya, what's new with you? I haven't seen you since the wedding. How's Graham and Gina's baby coming along? Mason, a good, strong name."

Kaya smiled. "Mason is so cute," she said. "You know, for someone who can't hold his own head up yet. But he's been smiling regularly. Oh, I have some pictures." She took out her phone and found her picture file. "Here, just scroll to the left." She handed the phone to Grayson, who handed it to Dr. Blake.

Dr. Blake looked at the first photo. "Wonderful!" he said. "Oh, wait a second. I must have touched something I shouldn't have touched. Oh, how do I get back to it? Do I hit this button? Wait, how did I get to a calculator?"

Grayson looked at Kaya and smiled. Then he sat down on the couch and took the phone from Dr. Blake's hand. "I'll get them back for you."

"Why don't you just hold the phone for me, son, and I'll tell you when to scroll. Ah, yes. Oh, and you have some pictures on here from your wedding, too. Look at you, Kaya. You were such a lovely bride. You've always been lovely. Are you ready to start the academy in September? They'll be lucky to have you."

Kaya looked at Grayson, and then back at Dr. Blake. "Dr. Blake—I mean, Rigo—Graham hasn't told you the news? I'm not going to the police academy this year."

Dr. Blake's eyes went wide. "You're not?" he asked. "What happened? Change of plans?"

Grayson chuckled. "I'll say," he mumbled.

Kaya grabbed the lever on her chair and sat up. "Dr. . . . Rigo, I mean, Rigo, I would have told you earlier. But, like I said, I guess Graham left it to me to tell you. It turns out that Grayson and I are expecting a baby! So no police academy for me just yet."

"Oh!" Dr. Blake said, his hands clapping together. "Kaya, Pike, congratulations! Oh, my! This is *wonderful* news! Your child and Mason will be close in age—kissing cousins." He sniffed. "I feel like I'm starting to have grandchildren. I never thought . . ." He sniffed again and then pulled his handkerchief from his pocket and dabbed at his eyes. "I'm so happy for you all. When is the baby due?"

"Strangely enough," Kaya said, "February fourteenth. Valentine's Day. I doubt the baby will come that day, but it would be nice. It would be a fun birthday for a kid to have."

Dr. Blake nodded. "I wonder . . ." He stopped himself.

Kaya smiled at him. "You wonder if the babies will have the knob."

Alice looked at her baffled. "The knob?" she asked.

Kaya laughed. "Yes, that's what we always called the anomaly in my brain. The one that my father and Graham have, too. And maybe you, as well."

Dr. Blake turned toward Alice. "You know that the invitation is always open for me to check you for knobs, my dear."

Alice laughed. "I'll keep that in mind."

"Maybe Tony would be interested to know if you have a knob," Kaya said under her breath. Alice cracked up.

There were footsteps on the steps. "Hey, you guys," Brad said. "Are you all sticking around for a while, or are you heading right back?"

Alice walked up to face him as he reached the last step. "We're sticking around for a couple of days," she said. "We want to make sure things go well and you settle in okay. But we'll be staying at a hotel."

Dr. Blake shook his head. "You know you're all welcome to stay here with me. I have plenty of room."

"No," Kaya objected. "It would be too much. You and Brad need to get acquainted. We'd just be in the way. We'll stop by for a few hours each day. I want to go visit Sergeant Morris, and we'd like to show Alice the sights on campus."

Brad nodded. "Then I think we should all sit down and have a talk before you leave here today. Like now."

Alice nodded. "I think that's only fair," she said. She took Brad's hand and led him to the couch. She sat down, and he sat next to her. Grayson sat on the floor next to Kaya's chair, and Dr. Blake took the other chair. "We'll let you start, Brad."

"Okay," Brad said. "First of all, what the hell is going on here? Why did the three of you kidnap me and bring me here?"

Dr. Blake smiled. "Brad, you're free to go at any time, I promise," he said. "You're not a prisoner here. But I'm hoping after we all talk this out, you'll choose to stay, for your own safety."

"My safety," Brad said. "You keep talking about my safety. And you made me leave my cell at home. I'm pretty much incommunicado. You didn't even tell Mrs. Katz I was going, or where you were taking me. Fuck, you didn't even tell *me* where we were going." He turned to Dr. Blake. "Sorry about the language, dude."

Kaya sighed. "Brad, you don't really know me or Grayson," she said. "You think we're weird. We *are* weird. And you have no reason to trust us. And after we tell you more, you'll have even less reason to trust us. But I'm gonna try." She took a deep breath. "Alice and I know, and I can't tell you how except that no one told us anything, that you're afraid. We don't know exactly what happened to scare you, but we know it's because of your father, and we know that you've been asking for money from all of the people in town so you can get away. We know that you want to go to New York City."

Brad shook his head. "No. Uh uh. There's no way. I've barely even thought about the city, let alone said it out loud. I know I never wrote it down anywhere. What, are you guys psychic or something?" Realization came to his face. "Is that why you guys are always laughing at nothing, or you give answers to questions that aren't asked? I mean, can you read each other's minds? That would be harsh, man!"

Kaya looked at Alice and then back at Brad. "It would be cool to be able to do that stuff, wouldn't it?" she asked. "But no one can read minds, Brad. That's something you see in the movies. I'll admit, I'm really good at telling how people feel, and then figuring out what's going on with them, but it's probably because I majored in criminal justice in college. I'm pretty good at investigating stuff. It's my passion. But whatever reason we know about you, we do know, and we care about you. Well, Alice cares a great deal about you, and we're just getting to know you, but we care about Alice, so there you go."

Alice stood up and stepped in front of Brad. She crouched down and put her hand on his knee. "Brad, I work for the D.A.'s office," she said softly. "You know that. I know all the details about the case with your dad. I did a lot of work on it. I know he did a lot of bad things. And I know that your mom is gone." She felt resistance in Brad's body. She kept her hand still. "I know that you think that she's either in trouble, or . . ."

There was a silence. Then Grayson spoke. "Brad, my mom died when I was twelve," he said. "She was killed during a mugging while we were in the city shopping during the Christmas season. She was cooperating, trying to get her wallet out of her coat, but the guy got nervous and panicky, and he hit her. He knocked her to the ground, and she hit her head on the sidewalk. The guy took off. I was with her, man. I was powerless. I watched it happen. I just stood there, and stared at her, until the police got there, and they had to physically move me away from her body. I can assure you, I was never the same after that. I blamed myself for a long time. I thought if I had just stood up to the guy, I could have stopped him. But you know what? He had a knife. He probably would have stabbed me to death, in front of my mother, and then she would have had to live with my death for the rest of her life. It's not a lot of comfort, but I decided a long time ago that everything I did was going to mean something. That's why I'm here today with Kaya and Alice and you. It's because I feel like I can help. I can't stand on the sidelines and watch people get hurt. So now you know why the three of us are here with you today. And now what we need to know from you is: what has scared you? And what happened to your mother?"

Brad squirmed in his seat. Alice still had her hand on his knee. She could feel that he was wrestling about what to tell them, if it should be the truth. The truth seemed to win out.

"He-he threatened me all the time," he finally said. "It was no picnic, living with Chet. He's an asshole. I'm glad he's in prison. But he could get out, and it could be because of me. It could be because of my testimony. I was sixteen, and I didn't have a guardian with me when they talked to me. They could say that it wasn't valid. At least that's what his lawyer told me."

Alice shook her head. "We don't think that's gonna happen. At least we're gonna do our best to keep it from happening. They're desperate. They're not even saying that Chet didn't commit fraud with that scam. They're just trying to get out of the manslaughter charge. That would take years off of his sentence. We don't want to allow that."

Brad nodded. "Please don't let him get out," he begged. "He's dangerous. He knew about Mrs. Corrigan and her insulin. He knew, and he still pushed to get more of her money. He told her that he needed the front money to feed us, his own family. That was a lie. But she was such a good-hearted woman, and she believed him. She babysat for me when I was a little. She was my grandmother's friend. My grandmother died during this whole thing, too. I think it was from shame from what my dad did. But my dad has no conscience. He's called me before, from prison."

Kaya's face went white. "He has? Don't they monitor their calls in prison?"

"They're supposed to," Alice said. "Maybe the guards aren't aware of the circumstances?"

Brad shook his head. "They know. I'm guessing there are some bribes going on." He paused. "I think he has someone on the outside, helping him. Someone who can get stuff for the guards, and for him. He's said things to me that make me think that they could be watching me. I've felt like I was being watched sometimes. I keep my shades and curtains closed all the time. I don't go out alone at night."

"Oh my God," Alice said, her head shaking. "Brad, I'm so sorry. You must get so terrified."

"I told the officers at the police department about how Chet was involved with Mrs. Corrigan," Brad said. "I had to. I couldn't let them think that she was just a senile old lady who couldn't take care of herself and didn't take her medicine. It wasn't true, and her relatives needed to know. They lived out of town. They had no idea this was all going on. She never told anyone. My mom, she was gonna tell. She told me. She was planning on going to the police to tell them what she knew, what she heard Chet say around her."

"But she didn't?" Grayson asked.

Brad shook his head. "No," he said. "She told me that, and then, the next day, she was gone. I-I've always assumed that something happened to her, but everyone always insisted that she took off. Some of her stuff was gone, and her car was gone. Her purse, and her credit cards, and everything were gone. It really looked like she left. And Chet kept cursing her for leaving. He told me that she left, and he was mad. He said he was mad enough to go after her, to find her, but that he wouldn't. I always found that strange. Chet wasn't the kind of guy to let his woman just take off. She was *his* woman. He was the one in control. But he was so angry. I wanted to believe him. I wanted to believe that she had taken off, and that at some point, she was gonna come back for me, and then maybe he'd just let us go. But two weeks went by, and there was no word from her. Nothing. Chet had declared her missing, and the police thought they had enough information to show that she had just left us. I mean, who could blame her, right? There was no sign of any kind of crime.

"But then, after those two weeks, I did it. I went to the police, and I told them everything I knew. Everything my mother was going to tell them. I was there for hours, talking. They recorded me. They asked me if I wanted to call anyone, someone to support me, but I didn't have anyone. They offered me a lawyer, but I said no. I just kept on talking. They kept giving me soda to drink and escorting me to the bathroom. They went out and got me lo mein from the Chinese restaurant. When I was done talking, they had me sleep on a cot in a room at the police station. They watched me all night. When the next day came, they had to decide what to do with me. They couldn't send me back home to Chet. They knew it wasn't safe. So they made some calls. They ended up talking to the father of one of my school friends, Jeffrey, and he agreed to take me. Jeffrey's father was an ex-cop, and he still worked in security. They figured he could keep me safe. They arrested Chet a few days later, and then the judge remanded him to custody. They knew he would take off if they let him go. I didn't see him again until the trial."

"Wow," Dr Blake said. "That must have been a horrible experience for you, having to testify in front of your own father. To have to see him there in the courtroom, watching you."

Brad nodded. "It was. He stared at me. I tried to not look at him, but sometimes I couldn't help it. He had such hatred toward me in his eyes. When I saw that, I just knew. I knew that he had killed my mother. I told the cops what I suspected, but they never found any evidence of anything. They still insisted they would have found some evidence, somewhere. No body, no crime. But she never would have left me. She told me the day before she disappeared. She said that she would take care of him, make sure he went to prison, and we would get away from him. She said that no matter what happened, she would never leave me behind. It was me and her, against the world. That's what she always said, especially when it got really bad over the years. So then why would she go the next day and just abandon me? It makes no sense at all."

"No," Alice agreed. "It doesn't make any sense. Shari loved you so much. I knew Shari. Not well, but I knew her. She wouldn't leave you,

Brad. I'm so sorry. You've been through so much, much more than what most adults have had to go through in their entire lives. Your mother wanted to protect you, but she didn't have any support to help her. She was going to do what she thought she had to do, but she was never able to do it. But you were able to do it for her. You have a lot to be proud of, Brad. You stopped him. You got him off the streets, just like your mother wanted."

"Yeah," Brad said. "I know. I did what I had to do. But now, I think I might have signed my own death warrant. I'm the one who went to the police. Alice, if my father gets out of prison, I'm totally a dead man."

13

ALICE'S RINGTONE WENT OFF. IT was "Isn't She Lovely" by Stevie Wonder. She grabbed her phone. Everyone was looking at her. "What?" she asked. She answered the call. "Hey, Tony. Can you hold on a minute?" She covered the mouthpiece. "So I like Stevie Wonder. Sue me. I'm gonna take this upstairs."

She ran up the stairs and went into one of the bedrooms that didn't have any personal belongings in it. She closed the door and sat on the bed. "Hey," she said affectionately.

"Hey, sexy," Tony said.

If any other guy had ever greeted her like that, she would have hung up on them, but this was Tony, so she chuckled. "'Hey, sexy' back to you. How are you doing?"

"I was a mess at work today. I couldn't stop thinking about last night. I think I might have dozed off during lunch, but then I dreamed about you."

Alice felt warm. "What was the dream?"

"I think you had turned into a giant turkey sandwich."

Alice laughed. "So it was a good dream. But you made it through the day."

"And you made it to your destination safely," Tony said with relief in his voice. "I've been worried about you."

"Why?" Alice asked, letting herself fall back on the bed, closing her eyes.

"Well, you went off with your friends and you couldn't tell me where you were going," Tony said. From the sound of his voice, Alice imagined he was lying on his back on his bed, too. "I know that you can't tell me anything about what you're up to because of your work, but it makes me a little nervous for you. Do I need to worry?"

Alice smiled. It felt good to have someone worry about her, even if it was unfounded. "No," she reassured him. "You don't need to worry. I'm sitting in a nice bedroom on the second floor of Kaya and Grayson's friend's house, lying on the bed. It's air-conditioned, and it's a sweet place. Everything's going as planned so far. I'll be home in two days, and maybe we can plan to get together that night."

"Hmm." Tony purred softly. "I think I'm free that night. Alice, last night was so amazing for me. I hope it was amazing for you, too."

"Hmm," Alice said back. "It was. It was a wonderful night. Not just making love, Tony. Just, staying up and talking all night, and holding each other. . . . It was perfect."

"I think so, too," Tony said. He paused. "I guess after all that, I just need to talk some more about what comes next, you know? I mean, it's not like you're someone new I met, and I need to figure out what it's all about. We have a history. A long history. A wonderful history. And now I want to make new history with you."

Alice's heart was pounding. "I want that, too, Tony," she said. "I think we made a good start last night. We talked, and we told each other a lot. We'll see each other again when I get back. I think we'll be seeing a lot of each other. A lot."

"I know," Tony said. Alice was sensing something strange coming from him. She couldn't place it. It wasn't the truth or a lie. It was something in the middle. Something true and false at the same time. He wanted something from her, and he wasn't sure how to convince her. But he was going to try. And he was going to try right then. "Alice, I don't see any reason for us to wait, to go through a whole courting ritual. I already know I love you. I know I want to be with you. It's even more now than it was when we went our separate ways before college, because now we're friends. We have all the components we need to make this work, for a long, long time. I think that we should consider the offer I made to you a couple of weeks ago, about me moving in with you, in your house. Or you moving in with me in my apartment. Or even, we could sell your house and find another one that belongs to just you and me. Think about it, Al. It would be so great. We wouldn't have to wonder about when we'd see each other. We wouldn't have to plan anything. We would come home to each other every night and wake up together each morning. I can almost sense it now. It would be so great."

Alice could feel it too. It would be so nice to have Tony there any time she wanted him and to be able to hold him whenever she wanted to. But something was holding her back from just saying yes at that moment.

"Tony, why the rush?" she asked. "I mean, yes, I do see us being together. When I think about our future, it's me and you. I have no question about that. But maybe it would be fun to have the courting rituals. I mean, think about it. It would be fun. You know, to sort of do things in order again. In a sequence. I think it would make good memories for us. Something we could tell our grandkids."

There was a pause. "Alice, I hear what you're saying," Tony said. "I do. I mean, it does sound nice, but we're in our twenties now. We have other things to think about, like money, and work, and all that stuff. The sooner we move forward, the sooner we can start planning about all that stuff. We can start saving for our retirement, and all that. We can consolidate. It's better for the environment, you know, to down-size and everything. It just makes sense."

That's when it hit Alice. Tony was lying. He was totally lying to her. He didn't care about all of that stuff. Well, it wasn't that he didn't care; it was that the things he was saying were not his motivation to move in with her. It was something else that he wasn't saying. He was not being truthful with her, and that hurt. She wanted him to always be truthful, no matter what. "What is it you aren't telling me?" she asked him. "Is there something more?"

"What?" Tony asked. "No. There's no other reason. I just want to be with you. It's that simple."

Only it wasn't that simple. If it was, Tony would be telling her the truth. She felt like her throat was constricting. How could she start back up in a relationship with a man that was clearly lying to her about something so important? And she had no idea why. If they were in Florence, she would have Kaya touch Tony's arm and read his thoughts. Then she would know. But she didn't have that luxury. She was over two hundred miles away, and she couldn't look into his eyes to ask him what this was all about.

"Tony," she said softly. "Listen. I have to go. I left everyone downstairs, and we have some important things to talk about before it gets too late. You know, about my work project. Why don't we talk about this again later? Like tomorrow? I can call you tomorrow night. And we'll talk."

"Oh. Okay." Tony paused. "Yeah, it can wait. We don't have to make this decision tonight. We have time. Al, I love you. I love you so much."

Alice closed her eyes. She almost couldn't speak. "I love you, too," she managed. She did love him. But she didn't know if she could trust him. "Goodbye." She hit the end button and dropped the phone next to her head. She stared at the ceiling. There was a light fixture above her. It was round with what looked like gold paint finishing. It was blurry. She tried to count how many gold lines were painted on the glass, but they all ran together. She closed her eyes tightly. She pictured Tony's face. She stared into it in her mind. She looked at his eyes, his honest eyes. She didn't know if Tony had ever lied to her before. Why was he lying now?

She picked her phone up again and called another number. "Em?" she said when her best friend's voicemail answered. "Em, I have a problem, and I need to talk to you. Call me back when you get this."

It was ten minutes later when her ringtone, "You're My Best Friend" by Queen, started up. Alice had been dozing off on the bed. She startled. "Em!" she said into the phone. "That's for calling back."

"What's wrong?" Emilie asked. "You sounded like you were panicking in your message."

"I might be," Alice admitted.

"What happened?" Emilie asked. "From what I heard from Tony, the two of you had a great night last night. I was actually surprised not to hear it from you."

"I had a thing," Alice said. "I'm out of town with Kaya, and a couple of other people. I'll be back in Florence in two days. But I just got off the phone with Tony, and I'm just baffled. He said some stuff, and I just don't know why." She tried to keep her voice controlled. Tony might be the love of her life, but he had shared a womb with Emilie for nine months at the beginning of their lives. "I thought maybe, you know, I could run it all by you."

"I-I guess that would be okay," Emilie said.

The restraint in Emilie's voice threw Alice slightly. "Okay," she said. "It's just . . . well, he keeps talking about us moving in together. He talked about it a couple of weeks ago, too, but I brushed it off. I thought he just wanted it so he could take care of me. But just now, when we were speaking on the phone, he brought it up again, and he was lying to me, Em."

"What?" Emilie asked, obviously confused by this concept. "Why would he lie to you?"

"I have no idea," she said. "He was going on and on about all the reasons that he wanted to skip a few steps and just go right to living together. I mean, it sounds nice on the surface, but, you know, I want to be wooed! It's gonna be the last time in my life I'll have the chance, right? I mean, this is it. Me and Tony."

"Oh, Al!" Emilie exclaimed. "I had no idea! I mean, Tony was over-the-roof happy this morning, but I didn't know that you felt that way, too. I mean, I knew it in my heart, but I hadn't heard it from you yet. You have no idea how happy this makes me!"

Alice closed her eyes. "But Em, what about the fact that he lied to me?"

"How did he lie?" Emilie asked. "I mean, he said he wanted to live with you, to have a life with you. Why does it even matter why? Is it what you want? If it is, don't think into it that hard. Just go with it."

Alice focused her thoughts. Something still seemed off. "Emilie, did Tony talk to you about wanting to move in with me, when you talked to him this morning?"

"Well, yeah," Emilie said. The pitch of her voice was getting higher, but Alice could sense no lie. At least not yet.

"Why did he tell you that he wanted us to move in together?"

"Well," Emilie said, dragging out the word, "he has a lot of reasons. He loves you." Still the truth. "He wants to be with you." Also the truth. "You know he wants to help you, as much as you're willing." Alice had heard that truth from Tony himself. "And I guess that's it. Isn't that enough?"

Alice's heart dropped. Emilie was lying to her. A clear, bald-faced lie. "Emilie," she said softly. "Why are you lying? What is it? What did he tell you?"

"Alice, just drop it, would you? He loves you. Isn't that enough? He'd never hurt you. So maybe he has other thoughts that he doesn't want to share with you. That should be okay. Most people don't have the talent that you have, to tell if someone is lying or not. Actually, Al, why could you even tell if he's lying? Weren't you talking to him on the phone? You've never been able to get a feel if someone was lying to you over the phone."

Alice froze. She had been so wrapped up in trying to figure out why Tony was lying that it hadn't even occurred to her that she was sensing a lie through the cellular service. "I . . . I don't know," she said. "I have no idea. I've only ever been able to tell in person, if I'm right in front of someone." She thought for a moment. "It seems like since I met Kaya, my abilities have gotten stronger. She's been in my mind, sharing her thoughts, and I can share mine with her. And she's getting stronger too. She used to have to touch people to read their thoughts, but now she can do it from a distance. I guess the two of us together make each other stronger."

"That's so amazing!" Emilie said. "Al, this means there might be no end to what you can do! You might be able to hear other people's thoughts, too. That would help you so much in your job. You could do so much good in the world. Just think about it!"

Alice wanted to think about it. She wanted to talk about the possibilities, all the things she could do, and how she could help people. But at that moment, she couldn't focus on her abilities. She needed to focus on the here and now. "I-I want to talk to you more about this, Em, but right now, I just need to know the truth. I . . . I want to be with Tony, like I said, but not unless he's totally honest with me. I can't let things go forward without the truth. You remember what it was like with Jackson in college. All the lies! I couldn't catch him in any, but I knew they were there. I ended up breaking up with him and never knowing the truth. I don't want to live with unresolved lies with Tony. It would eat me up inside, and eventually, I would break. I don't want that, Em. Please! Be honest with me! What's he hiding?"

"Alice, you have to trust me," Emilie said. Alice could hear that her best friend was crying, but she couldn't imagine why. "And you have to trust Tony. He's not really lying to you. He's just leaving something out. He's not ready . . . he doesn't want to say it. Please don't make him." Emilie started to sob.

"Em!" Emilie was telling the truth. Alice was horrified. "I-I'm sorry. I didn't mean to upset you like this. I really didn't. I-I want to back off, and just let it go, but now I know I can't. Whatever it is, maybe

I can make it okay! Maybe I can help. I don't want Tony upset, but I don't want you to be upset either. Please, Emilie, just tell me. What is it that Tony's not saying?"

"It's his eyes," Emilie said, trying to control her voice. "It's because you love his eyes."

Alice's forehead wrinkled in confusion. "Of course I love his eyes," she said. "He has beautiful eyes. But what does that have to do with moving in together?"

"It's not about moving in together," Emilie insisted. "It's about what it represents. Alice, he wants to be with you, for things to get to the next step. It's because of what you said about his eyes. You told him you remembered his eyes, that you could even see him when you closed your own eyes. You told him that even when you lost your sight, you would always remember his eyes."

"I remember thinking that," Alice said, "but I don't remember saying it outloud. Did I say it in my sleep? Or did he read my mind?"

"Alice," Emilie said. "No. He can't read your mind. I would say no one can do that, but I know that's not true. But Emilie, what you said, it got to Tony. He thought about his future with you."

"He wants to move in together before I lose my sight," Alice whispered.

"No," Emilie said. "That's not it. It's not it exactly. Yes, he wants to be able to have experiences with you while you can still see, yes. He wants you to be able to remember the sights you see together, the colors, the textures, everything. But there's something else he wants for you, and it's the most important thing that he's ever wanted in his life." She paused, and Alice could hear her crying again. "Alice, Tony wants you to see the eyes of your children. He wants you to be able to look into them, and see them. He wants you to remember them, even when you close your eyes, and even when your vision is gone. And he knows that you're running out of time. He doesn't want you to run out of time."

Tears were running down Alice's face before she even realized she was crying. She felt numb, from the top of her head to the tips of her toes. She couldn't speak. There was silence between the two friends as they cried together over the miles.

Finally, Alice pulled herself together. "He wants me to look into my baby's eyes," she whispered.

"He does," Emilie said.

Alice sniffed. "He really loves me."

Emilie laughed. "You're just discovering this now? Yes, Alice Telman. My brother loves you that much. I wish I could meet someone who loves me as much as he loves you. But I have to ask you . . . do you love him just as much?"

Alice nodded her head so hard that her tears shook off of her cheeks. "I do," she said. "And we can have it all, Em. We can move forward, and he can woo me while we do it. Neither one of us has to give up anything."

"You don't," Emilie said. "You *can* have it all, and when you do lose your vision, we'll all be there to help you. I'll come back to Florence next year, and I'll be there for you, to help you with my little nieces and nephews. I'll describe everything to you, and then you can picture it in your mind. I'll use the most precise language I can come up with. It will be like you're looking at everything yourself. You'll have the perfect life, Alice."

"It will be the perfect life," Alice whispered, trying to believe that herself.

There was a knock on the door, and Kaya poked her head in the door. "Alice?" she asked. "Are you in here? Oh, there you are. Are you okay? Are you crying! What happened?"

Alice raised one finger. "Emilie," she said into the phone. "I have to go. I'm sorry. I wish we could talk more. We'll talk again when I get home, okay? But I'll talk to Tony again. I-I'll listen to what he has to say, and I'll keep an open mind."

"That's all I ask," Emilie said. "I love you so much, Alice. Take care of yourself. I'll talk to you soon."

"Bye," Alice said. She hung up. She looked up at Kaya. "Something's happened," she said.

Kaya sat down next to her. "Something with Tony?" she asked carefully.

"Yes," Alice said. "Something happened with Tony, too, but that's not what I'm talking about. Kaya, I was able to tell if people were telling the truth or lying over the phone. I've never done that before. I didn't know I could. Do you know what this means?"

Kaya nodded. Then she smiled. "I do," she said. "At least I think I do. I've noticed changes in me, too, ever since my father came back in my life, and since I met you. It's like all of the thoughts are coming more easily to me now. I can focus on specific things and not have to listen to the background noise. I can encapsulate thoughts like my dad does, and I can read and send thoughts from a distance. Before all of this, I couldn't send thoughts, just read them. That makes me able to have whole conversations with people who don't have our skills *inside of our heads!* My husband and I can communicate from across a room. Just think about what we'll be able to do with this parlor trick! But you, too! Your skills are getting stronger. It makes me wonder if maybe you and I can even learn to home in on each other's skills. Maybe I can sense the truth, and maybe you can read thoughts. We both just started out with the ones we know that came naturally to us. We might have to learn the other things over time."

Alice nodded. "You could be on to something. I haven't read any thoughts on my own yet, but I feel like I could. I've had your thoughts in my head, and my mind feels like it's expanding. It's just a matter of time and practice. What else do you think we could do? Do you think there are other things? What are these brains of ours capable of?"

Kaya laid back on the bed. "I don't know," she said. "I almost don't even want to speculate. Could you imagine? What if we can move things with our minds? Have you ever heard about people who could bend spoons? I want to bend spoons! The only time I've ever bent a spoon is when the ice cream was too hard, and I couldn't scoop it out. My mom got really mad."

Alice lay down next to Kaya. "I don't know about bending spoons. I'd like to be able to fly or breathe underwater. Superman or Aquaman. But women instead of men. We could swim deep below the sea and search for mermaids."

"And then fly home in time for dinner."

Alice laughed. "Where is your baby during all of this?"

Kaya smiled. "She's with me all day, but when I go out at night to fight crime or search for mermaids, she's at home with her daddy."

"She?" Alice asked. "Did you find out it's a girl?"

"No," Kaya said. "It's just how I imagine the baby. But I'll still be happy if it's a boy. But it sounds better to say *she* than *it*."

"Yeah," Alice said. She folded her hands over her belly. "What color eyes do you think she'll have?"

Kaya thought about it. "Well, I have blue eyes, and Grayson has brown eyes, so I would guess either brown or maybe hazel. I don't know what color his mother's eyes were. I never met her, and I haven't really looked close at his pictures. He didn't move to Wisteria until junior year, when his father decided they needed a new start. Thank goodness he did. But if his mother's eyes were blue, there's a chance the baby could have blue eyes. I don't really care though. As long as she . . ." She stopped herself.

Alice turned to look at her and smiled. "You don't have to monitor what you say for me, Kaya," she said. "You were going to say as long as she has eyes that work. I want that for your baby, too." She paused. "I want to tell you what happened with Tony tonight, but I don't want to talk about it. Can you just encapsulate it and take it from me? That would make it easier."

Kaya looked at her and then nodded. "Okay. I think I can do that, no problem. But I'll hold your hand. I think it would make it easier for me, since I've never done this with you before."

Kaya was lying; she didn't need to hold her hand. Alice smiled at her. She gave her friend her hand. She felt the warmth. It made her feel safe. "What do I need to do?"

"Just think about what happened," Kaya said. "Just imagine it in images if you want, instead of words. Just relax. Let the bed hold your head and support it. Let your whole body sink into the mattress. It's a nice, soft mattress. Maybe the pregnant girl and her husband should sleep in here tonight. . . . Just relax. Breathe. . . . Okay." There was quiet for a minute, and then another minute. Alice didn't feel anything happening inside her head. She thought maybe it wasn't working. But then Kaya's eyes opened. And then they teared up. "Oh, Alice," she said. She wiped her cheek. "I'm so sorry. Pregnancy emotions. I just can't believe Tony! He's . . . he's amazing! What are you gonna do?"

Alice moved her head back and forth on the bed. "I don't know," she said. "I haven't had time to process it at all. But it all makes sense. What he wants. I never thought about the eyes of my children. It's like, now that the thought has entered my mind, it's as if I have to see them. I have to memorize them. I have to remember them forever. How could I not? I want to do it for Tony, because he wants it for me. But then, I also want to do it for myself. But here's the problem: Tony and I have only been on one date! How can we be sure this is going to work? I haven't spent any time as his girlfriend for over six years! I've been his sister's best friend, and his friend, and I've been a completely separate person from him for over four whole years. I've had other relationships. I want to have experiences with him. With him as my boyfriend, and us deciding together when it's time to move in together, and when it's time to get engaged, and married. But do I really have that luxury? Will I be able to live with it if I don't see those tiny baby eyes?"

Kaya sat with that for a while. "I don't know," she said. "What about a compromise? What if you both get what you want?"

"I was thinking that too," Alice said. "But before I could work out the details with Emilie, you came into the room. How do I do it?"

Kaya shrugged, which was a difficult thing to do while lying down and holding her friend's hand. "You talk to Tony and you figure it out together," she said. "He doesn't decide your future and you don't decide your future. You become a team, and you come up with a game-plan, one you can both accept."

"A team," Alice said. She thought about it. "I like that. I like the idea of me and Tony being a team. We were a team in high school, and we can be a team again. And you and Grayson, and Emilie, you can all be on our team."

"And Rigo," Kaya said. "He can be our guide on this journey!"

Alice laughed. "Do you think it's a coincidence that we all have names that match our skills?" she asked. "I mean, Rigo has been a mentor to Graham, but he's also been a guide to you on your journey. He even walked you down the aisle, which is another way of guiding you. And then there's me and the truth. This is what I meant earlier by archetypes."

"I've heard the word *archetype* before," Kaya said, "but I just pretended to know what they are. You said you'd explain it to me."

"Uh," Alice said. "Let me try to channel my college lit professor. Okay. Here it is. In ancient literature, every story had a hero, a villain, a damsel in distress . . . and lots of other characters that made up a tale. Those were the archetypes. I want to say there are twelve types, but I can't remember them all. Oh, there was the lover. I always liked the lover. Then, as time went on, other books were loosely based on those archetypes. There are others, too, besides the twelve, more modern ones, but you can still kind of fit them into the originals. Like the whole justice and truth thing that Graham said about me. When you think about justice, you probably think of a statue of a woman with a blindfold, holding scales. So that's like an archetype. It might be sort of a hero, or maybe a wise person. If someone was to write a story about someone that represents justice, they would probably look on the internet for a name that means justice, or in my case, truth, like

Alice, to give the reader a clue of which archetype they were going for. And then they would make them go blind. It's symbolism, but it also follows an ancient formula. The hero is triumphant in the end, and the villain fails."

"So in our story," Kaya asked, "what would I be?"

Alice considered this. "I don't know," she said. "I would guess the hero, but then I don't know what that makes me. I'm the hero in my own story."

"Or maybe you're the lover," Kaya teased.

"Or maybe I'm the hero, and Tony's the lover."

"Oh yeah." Kaya said. She rolled over to face Alice. "I guess I get it now. So then Rigo is kind of a wise man in our lives. Having a name that means 'guide,' or even 'mentor,' is kind of ironic, right?"

Alice shook her head. "*Ironic* is the opposite of what you'd expect, like a really tall guy being called Tiny, or a really quick person being called Slowpoke. That's what makes it funny. This would be more the opposite of irony. Maybe congruence."

"So irony is saying the opposite, and then congruence is opposite of irony, so it's kind of ironic to irony."

"I'm getting dizzy thinking about it," Alice said. "That must mean you have it right."

14

"HOW WAS YOUR TRIP?" CARLA asked. "Where was it you went again?"

Alice gave her boss a half grin. "I told you it was a secret. Carla, this is the friend that I told you about, Kaya Pike. Kaya, this is Carla, the assistant district attorney."

Carla smiled and held out her hand. "It's nice to meet you, Kaya."

Kaya appeared starstruck. "It's-it's nice to meet you, too." She shook Carla's hand and then looked at her own open hand. "I'm so excited to be here!" she said. "I majored in criminal justice at State, and I just graduated in May. I hope that someday I can work with the D.A.'s office on big cases. I'm not sure how yet. I'll probably start with the police academy, but not yet because I'm pregnant, but when I decide—"

Carla gasped. "Oh, wow, congratulations!" she exclaimed. "That's so exciting! How far along are you? When are you due?"

Kaya's eyes were like dishes. "I, well, I'm due in February, about nine weeks now."

Carla looked excited. "I'm so happy for you! My wife and I have a daughter, Tasha. She's nine months old. Kaylie carried her, and I'm going to carry the next baby, if everything goes the way it's supposed to. How are you feeling? Have you been sick at all?"

"I-I was a bit sick at first," Kaya said. "I get nauseated from time to time, but I'm lucky. I haven't had bad morning sickness. I have more of a bad morning eating problem. I'm always starving."

"Kaylie got sick a lot," Carla said. "I'd rather be hungry. Alice, are you expecting someone?"

Alice turned to the lobby. Peter Reed had just walked in and was looking around. "Kaya, it's your dad."

Kaya waved to her father. "He wanted to come with us today to meet with you, Carla," she explained. "He's sort of like my bodyguard or something! I hope that's okay."

Carla nodded. "Hello," she said to Peter.

Peter smiled at the women. "Hi, I'm Peter Reed," he said, holding out his hand to Carla.

Carla smiled. "I'm Carla Poppet, Assistant D.A. Nice to meet you, Mr. Reed."

"It's Peter, please," Peter told her. He turned to the other two women. "Hey, Kaya." He kissed her cheek. "Hello, Alice, right? We met briefly last week."

Alice nodded. "It's nice to meet you officially, Peter."

Carla cleared her throat. "I'm gonna go get Melody to sit in on the meeting with us. She's been working on the McHale case since the beginning. I think she's upstairs. I'll be right back." She turned to walk down the hall.

"Dang," Kaya said. "I have to go to the bathroom. I have to go at the most inconvenient times. I had a super big smoothie for breakfast. Alice, where's the ladies room? Are you okay waiting here with my dad?"

Alice nodded. "It's right over there. We'll wait for you when Melody gets here."

Kaya walked away, and Peter turned to Alice. "So everything went okay, on your trip?"

"It did," Alice said. "Better than we even thought. Everyone's being cooperative and getting along really well."

Peter nodded. "That's great," he said. "Now, if we can get your office to agree with our plan, we can try to wrap this all up before Brad has to start school in the fall."

"That's the plan," Alice said

Carla came back with Melody in tow. "Peter, I'd like you to meet one of our up-and-coming attorneys, Melody. Melody, this is Peter. He's the father of Alice's friend. Where did she go off to?"

"The bathroom," Peter said. He looked closely at Melody. "Have we met before?"

Melody looked at his face. "I don't think so," she said. "I'm from Wisteria, not Florence. Although, to be honest, that's not saying much."

Peter laughed. "No, I'm from Wisteria, too. I didn't grow up there, but I moved there in my early twenties."

"Oh," Melody said. "That's cool. You have a daughter. Did she go to Wisteria High?"

"A daughter and a son, and yes, they both went there, but I think they'd be pretty far behind you."

Melody smiled. "I was a teacher there," she said. "I taught civics after college and before law school. Maybe I had one of your kids in my class."

"I . . . I wasn't around during that time," Peter said, "so I never met their teachers." He turned to look toward the hall. "Oh, here comes my daughter now."

Kaya walked back in the room. Alice walked up beside her. "Kaya," she said, "I think I've told you about my friend Melody? Melody, this is my friend, Kaya."

Kaya and Melody faced each other, and both sets of eyes went wide. "Miss Green?" Kaya asked.

"Kaya Reed?" Both women made excited screeches and then ran into each other's arms. "Kaya, it's so good to see you! You look great! Are you back in Wisteria now? You finished college?"

Kaya nodded. "I got married!" she said, and she showed off her ring.

"To Grayson Pike, I'm guessing?"

Kaya laughed. Carla looked back and forth between them. "Kaya was just telling us that she's expecting a baby in February!"

Melody's mouth dropped open. "Oh my God, Kaya! Congratulations!" She hugged her again. "I can't believe it! I think you're my first former student to be having a kid! Man, I feel so old!"

Peter stepped closer to the two women. "So Melody, you were Kaya's teacher?" he asked. "That's really cool."

Kaya turned to look at her father, still grinning. "Miss Green was my cheerleading coach, Dad," she told him. "She was an amazing coach! I looked up to her so much! She made cheering so much fun and she really encouraged me. I was kind of in a bad place starting freshman year, and she . . ." She stopped. "Sorry, Dad. I didn't really mean to say that."

Peter shook his head. "No, it's fair of you to say that." He looked at Melody. "I . . . left my family that year. I went off to try to figure some stuff out. I was gone for a long time, but I'm back now. Thank you for being an important person in my daughter's life back then. It makes me feel better to know that there were people looking out for her."

Melody bent her head down. "I was there when she fell," she told Peter. "I became much more careful after that incident. Thank goodness Kaya was okay, and she came back to cheerleading when she recovered."

Kaya looked back and forth between her father and her former coach. "I . . . maybe we can all go get a coffee, or an herbal tea when we're done here." She motioned toward Alice and Carla. "We came here to have a conversation with Ms. Poppet—"

"Carla."

"—Carla, and I don't want to waste her whole afternoon."

Carla laughed. "Really, it's okay," she said. "Things are kind of slow here this summer. We could use some good distractions. But why don't we all head to the conference room so we can talk. I'm intrigued by what you and Alice have to say to us, Kaya."

The group made their way to the conference room. Carla sat on one end of the table, Melody on one side of her, Alice on the other, Kaya next to Alice, and Peter across from her, next to Melody. Kaya tried to stop herself. She made her biggest effort. But she had felt it already. There was something between her father and Melody, some kind of attraction, an instant attraction. The thought excited her. Her father, and her old coach, eyeing each other like high school students. She lazily let her mind wander into her father's mind . . . and then pulled it out quickly. Yes. He was thinking about Miss Green. He was thinking some very strong thoughts about Miss Green. She then took a quick trip into the lawyer's head, and she found her father roaming around in there. She let the images and words go with a smile and focused her attention on the district attorney.

"So, Kaya and I wanted to talk to you both about the McHale case," Alice said, suddenly all professional. "We have some information, and we think we have a way to get some more."

Carla perked up. "You found a way to block the appeal?"

"No," Alice said. "Not exactly. But I don't think the appeal has a leg to stand on. But what we want to focus on is the disappearance of Shari Coombs."

"Shari Coombs?" Melody asked, looking confused. "She took off before all of this even happened. What about her?"

Alice looked at Kaya. Kaya shot her a thought. *You've got this. I've got your back.* Alice nodded and looked at her boss. "That's just it," she said. "We have reason to believe that maybe Shari didn't take off after all. Carla, we think that Shari might be, well, dead."

"Dead!" Carla exclaimed. "Why do you think she's dead? She packed her bags, got in her car, and took off into the night never to be seen again. We found no evidence that she was murdered. No blood, no body. No concerning tire tracks. No eyewitnesses. As far as the Florence Police are concerned, Shari Coombs was there one minute, gone the next. To be honest, no one blamed her. She wanted to get away from Chet McHale. It was probably the smartest thing that she ever did. No one could blame her!"

Alice took a deep breath. She held it for a few seconds, then exhaled. "Except for Brad McHale."

"Brad!" Melody said. "Did he tell you something? Did he witness something? I talked to him back then, and he said he didn't see anything. He barely said anything. I think he was in shock during the whole thing, from the moment he went to the police station to turn in his father until . . . until Chet was locked up awaiting his trial."

"He's still in shock," Kaya said. "He's still struggling. Carla, Miss Green, Brad and his mother were very close. Just the day before she disappeared, she swore to him that she would never leave him. She was going to turn Chet in."

"What?" Carla asked. "He never told us that."

"She told him," Alice went on. "She had it all worked out. She was going the next day to talk to the police, to tell them what she knew about Mrs. Corrigan's death. Brad thinks that his father found out. Maybe Shari let something slip, and he got mad, and then, well, I have no idea what he did. But Brad is convinced that his mother is dead. And that his father will come after him next."

Carla and Melody looked at each other. "Mel, we need to get Bob to send a patrol car over to keep an eye on Brad's place."

"That's not necessary," Kaya chimed in. "Brad is gone. He's in a safe place."

"What?" Carla asked sternly. "You've taken it upon yourselves to take Brad away? What place is safe enough for him?"

Alice squirmed uncomfortably. "I can't tell you that, Carla," she said. "It's really safe. I'm sorry that I didn't come to you first, but it seemed so desperate. Brad was planning on taking off, to get away somewhere that Chet would never find him, and I was worried that if that happened, we'd never be able to find him either, or protect him. Kaya and her husband and I brought him somewhere safe this weekend. He's in very good hands, and no one knows except for the three of us and the person Brad's staying with. We didn't let him take any electronics that could be used to trace him. There's a police officer there that knows to keep an eye on the house, but he doesn't know the reason why. Brad is truly safe."

Carla sat silently, taking in all of this information. "Alice, I can't say that I condone your behavior on this," she said. "You should have come to me. And you didn't. But it sounds like Brad is indeed safe. If what you say about Shari is true, we'll need access to Brad. You'll be in charge of making sure that we can have that. What is the plan that the two of you came up with?"

"It's a bit complicated," Kaya said. "That's another reason I asked my father to come along. He can vouch for us, that everything we say is true."

"You'll need vouching?" Melody asked. "This is intriguing indeed."

Alice chewed her lip. Kaya nodded at her. "Carla," she said. "You know something about me that a lot of people in Florence don't know. You know that I can tell when people are being honest. Do you know why that is?"

Carla shrugged. "I just always assumed that you had good instincts. You're good at reading body language, and the slight changes in voice tones when someone is lying. I've heard of people who are really sensitive to things like that."

Alice nodded. "Okay," she said. "That's as good a reason as any. But what if it was something else?"

Carla looked skeptical. "What something else?" she asked. "What, like you can read minds?"

Alice laughed. "Another, just as good a reason as anything else. The simple fact is, there's no solid explanation, but you've accepted it as a fact that I can do it, right?"

"Well, of course," Carla said. "I've seen it with my own eyes. There's evidence. I'm a strong believer in evidence. That's what's gotten me as far as I've gotten in my career. I believe what I see with my eyes and hear with my ears. I keep an open mind. Evidence is key."

Alice nodded. "Then I'll proceed," she said. "What if I told you that Kaya and I—"

"—and my father," Kaya interrupted.

"And Peter," Alice added, "are able to know things that other people think? Would you believe that?"

"I . . ." Carla started, looking at Melody for support. "I don't know. I mean, like I said, I'd need to have evidence."

"We're prepared to give you evidence," Kaya said. "We're not going to tell you how we do what we can do, but we will show you what it is that we can do."

"Why?" Melody asked. "What do you have to gain from putting on a dog and pony show for us?"

Kaya gave Melody a warm smile. "We have a lot to gain," she said. "There's a young man out there who's scared to death for his life, and we can help keep him safe. I swore to never, ever share what I'm going to do in this room with anyone outside a very specific circle of people. But I think it's important enough to give you a little peek. Can you understand that, Miss Green? You know me. I'm the same girl I was five years ago when I was your head cheerleader. You believed in me then. Please, try to believe in me again."

Melody sat back in her chair. "Okay," she said. "What do you want me to do?"

Kaya grinned. "Great! Um, does anyone have a deck of cards?

Carla excused herself and returned with a deck of cards from her desk drawer. "I got these as a white elephant gift last holiday season. What do you want me to do with them?"

Peter finally spoke. "Take them out and shuffle them," he said. "Then, when you feel they're mixed enough, cut the deck."

Carla complied. When she finished shuffling, she held the deck below the table. "Okay," she said. "What now?"

"Look at the card," Kaya instructed. "Don't say it out loud. But say it inside your head."

Carla nodded. "Okay."

"It's the queen of diamonds," Peter said.

Carla shook her head. "No," she said. "It's the three of hearts. But that wasn't what I said in my head."

"What did you say?" Peter asked.

Carla's face flushed. She slammed the card on the table. "I said queen of diamonds," she admitted. "I wanted to make sure that you weren't somehow able to see the card."

"How did you do that?" Melody asked, spinning to look at Peter. "Is it some kind of trick?"

"No," Peter said. "It's not a trick. You try it. Actually, why don't you leave the room, go back to Carla's desk, look at a card there, and then put the deck back in the drawer. Then come back here and I'll tell you your card."

Melody looked at Peter suspiciously but did as he said. One minute later, she came back into the room. "I looked at two cards," she said. "You know, just in case."

"Now think of those cards," Peter said. He concentrated. "Eight of clubs, and, oh, seven of clubs. Maybe Carla didn't shuffle them well enough. And by the way, six-foot-one."

"What?" Melody asked.

Pete smiled. "You were wondering how tall I was. I'm six-one. Did I get your cards right?"

Melody blushed bright red. "Yes," she said. Then she pressed her lips together and looked down at the table.

"What does this mean?" Carla asked. "How are you doing this?"

"It doesn't matter," Kaya said. "My father and I, well, we can tell what people are thinking. And we think that we might be able to tell what Chet McHale is thinking, if you'll let us."

"What?" Carla said. "I don't know what planet you're all from, but on this one, we don't let civilians interrogate convicted criminals."

"We're not talking about interrogating Chet McHale," Alice said. "We were thinking that the sheriff's office could do that part. And that you and I could be there to observe. Kaya could be off to the side somewhere, but not too far away. She doesn't have to be right there to be able to get a read."

"But how do we know that Kaya can do what Peter can do?" Melody asked.

"Because," Kaya said with a mischievous grin, "I can tell you that right now you're wondering what it would be like to go out to dinner with my father, and my father is thinking about the most casual way that he can ask you out, despite the awkward circumstances. You're a bit worried because you remember how hard it was for me when he left, but then you can see how tight we are now, so you're thinking it might be okay. And then you have a thought about my mother, and if it would be a betrayal to her if you go out with my father, since you liked her so much, and her life was so hard back then. I can tell you right now, Miss Green, it would be okay with her. She's very happily engaged to my childhood dentist. So you're okay."

Melody started to slump in her chair, as if she wanted to disappear under the table. "Okay," she mumbled. "I believe you. Just no more reading my thoughts, okay?"

Alice smiled. Then she looked at Carla. "We need to do this," she told her. "We need to put this scumbag away for the rest of his life. If he did kill Shari, he needs to be punished, for her sake and for Brad's. Brad deserves to be able to feel safe in his own home."

Carla closed her eyes and sighed. "You're right," she said softly. "You're absolutely right. I mean, you're always right, Alice. That's why I've come to rely on you so much. We have to pursue this. We need a plan."

Kaya smiled. "We have a plan," she said. "We can tell you what we think would work."

"Is it dangerous?" Carla asked. "Because if it's dangerous, it's a hard no."

Alice shook her head. "If we do this right, Carla," she said, "Chet McHale will have no idea that we even had anything to do with all of this."

15

"DAD HAS A CRUSH ON my cheerleading coach!" Kaya said as she burst through Graham and Gina's door, Grayson in tow. "I need you to know before he gets here, because I'm gonna roast him *hard*!"

"Hello to you, too, dear sister," Graham said. He smiled at Grayson. "How do you keep up with her, man? Sometimes, I just get lost in the enthusiasm."

Grayson chuckled. "Cheerleader," he said as an explanation. "I'm not gonna discourage it. It has its benefits for me."

Graham held up a hand. "No," he said. "Dude, we've become friends, but we're not *that* friendly." He followed Kaya into the living room, where she sat down right beside Gina and put out her arms for the baby. "So Kaya, since your cheerleading coach at State was like eighty years old and gay, I'm assuming you're talking about Miss Green?"

Kaya made smiley faces at baby Mason. "Yes," she said in baby talk voice. "Yes, Grandpa Peter likes Miss Green! Mason, you might get a new grandma out of this!"

Gina laughed. "I remember Miss Green. She was a hottie back in high school. Is she still teaching over there? How did your dad meet her?"

"She's a lawyer now," Grayson said. "She works with Kaya's friend Alice. Peter went with them to their meeting over there, and it was lust at first sight between those two. And then Kaya started invading their brains . . ."

Kaya looked up. "It was for a good cause," she said. "I had to show the lawyers that I could help with the case. Reading their thoughts was the obvious way to convince them." She laughed. "And it was totally funny!"

"So it went well?" Graham asked. "Did they agree to go along with the plan?"

"They did," Kaya said. "At first, I thought that the A.D.A. was gonna have a stroke, but then she was all in. She's gonna set up a meeting at the state prison next week. I'll go with Alice and the A.D.A., and we'll have a detective and an officer from the sheriff's department with us."

Graham handed his wife a tall glass of ice water and then sat down next to her. "Are you sure there's no risk?" he asked. "I mean, we're talking about a guy that might have murdered his wife. Well, actually, his common-law wife, but murder is murder. And he was responsible for that other woman's death. He was convicted of it."

"Graham," Kaya said gently. "I won't even show my face. Apparently there's an interview room in there with a two-way mirror. I'll stay back there and observe. Alice will go in with Carla, that's her boss, but she won't have to say anything either. She can signal Carla if Chet's lying. And we all know what to do when we have enough information to implicate him. He'll never know it was us. And it will work. I know it will."

Graham nodded. "I trust you to do the right thing, Kaya," he said. The doorbell rang, and he stood up. "I just want you to be extra careful, since you're bringing Mason's little cousin with you everywhere you go." He opened the door. "Hey Dad," he said. "Did you forget your key again? We need to get you a keychain so you can put it with your car key. Come in. Kaya and Grayson just got here. They say you had an interesting day."

"Of course they did," Peter said as he walked into the living room. "Your sister has a mighty blabbermouth on her." He smiled at Kaya, holding her nephew. "Ky, I told you to show your skills, not humiliate your cheerleading coach. And me."

Kaya looked contrite. "Sorry, Dad."

"Oh, no," Peter said with a grin. "Don't apologize. You told me she liked me. I asked her out. We're going to dinner tomorrow night!"

"Hey!" Gina said with a smile. "That's fantastic! I can totally see the two of you together. I mean, I don't know if you have anything in common, but I can see you standing next to each other and stuff."

Peter groaned. "Not you, too, Gina," he said. "I thought you were the sane one."

Graham sat back down on the couch. "Where are you taking her?"

"I don't know," Peter said, sitting in a recliner. "I've been away for a while, as you're all aware. Where do all the cool kids go out to dinner these days?"

"First of all," Kaya said with a smirk, "all of the cool kids are like sixty now. But most of my friends like to go to Sammy's in Wisteria, or Couscous in Florence. Then there's Gaucho's, but I've never been there."

"Is that pizza place still on Cardinal Ave?"

"You can't take Miss Green to Aldo's Pies," Kaya protested. "You order at the counter, and they give you a number. Miss Green deserves a linen tablecloth and table service."

"She's right, Peter," Gina said. "She's high class. Cloth napkins and wine. Wine with a cork."

"A cork," Peter said. "Got it. Anything else I should know?"

"She's limber," Kaya teased. "Cheerleading, you know." She did the best she could to keep a straight face, but Gina couldn't help letting out a giggle.

Peter shook his head. "I'm not getting into this discussion with my children," he said. "But I will let you help me choose what to wear."

Kaya squealed. "Oh my God, I love it! I get to help dress my father for his first date with my teacher! It's kind of like the *Gilmore Girls* with a gender bender!"

The doorbell rang. Graham stood up. "It's like Grand Central Station in here."

Gina turned to Kaya. "He says that all the time. What does it mean?"

"I have no idea," Kaya said with a shrug.

Peter laughed. "It's something I used to say all the time," he said. "Grand Central Station is a busy train and bus station in New York City. Has Graham ever been to New York?"

"No," Gina said. "Ah. It's one of those parental phrases that get passed down from generation to generation. In my house it was 'who knows what evil lurks in the minds of man?'"

"'The Shadow knows,'" came a male voice from the hallway.

Peter looked up and saw him standing there with a smile. It was Steve Flagg. The dentist. His ex-wife's fiancé. "Hello, Peter," he said. "We weren't expecting to see you here. Are you still staying with Graham and Gina?"

Gina looked up at Steve. "We wanted him to stay," she said. "He's been helping us with Mason so much we didn't want him to move out."

Peter stood. "Nice to see you, Dr. Flagg," he said. He reached over to shake the other man's hand. "Is Janice here, too?"

"She's getting some things from the car," Steve said. "We just came from a dental convention in Wheeler. We picked up some goody bags for the kids from the vendor area. I'm sure we can wrangle one for you, too. Do you still have all of your original teeth, Pete?"

Peter smiled, showing straight, white teeth. "It's Peter," he said. "All original, Steve. Never had a cavity or a crown. No root canals or receding gums. Some people are just born with it."

"Hello!" Janice's voice came from the hallway. "Who needs a new toothbrush? I have floss!" She came into the room and quickly looked around. "Oh, Peter," she said. "I didn't know . . ."

"It's okay, Janice," he said. "I can go upstairs to my room and let you all visit if you'd like."

"Nonsense," Steve said, taking the bags of dental supplies from his fiancé's hands. "You're staying here. It's your home. We're all adults. We're gonna have to figure out how to deal with situations like this anyway. We share kids, and grandkids. Let's not let it be awkward every time we run into each other. Maybe we can all become friends in time. Right, Jan?"

Janice looked at the floor, and then looked up, a smile fixed on her face. "Yes, of course," she said. "Friends. All of us." She walked over to the couch, kissed her daughter and daughter-in-law on the cheek, and took the baby from Kaya's arms. "Hello, Mason. Grandma's here! Let me kiss those chubby little cheeks."

"He is a handsome kid, isn't he?" Peter stated. "Takes after his grandpa."

"Yes," Janice said, eyes still on the baby. "Gina's father is a very good-looking man."

Peter nodded. "Good one, Janice. Nice to see your sense of humor is still intact."

"Dad," Graham said. "Why don't you come in the kitchen with me and help me with the food?"

Peter nodded toward the group and followed his son out of the room. "Was I misbehaving?" he asked.

Graham stood facing him. "No," he said. "I just . . . well, you just have to help me keep things civil. Please don't give Mom and Steve a hard time, okay? Listen, Steve was there for Mom. It was six years after you left by the time they got together, and he still let her cry on his shoulder with her memories of you. None of this is Mom's fault." He turned aside and looked at the wall briefly. "It's not your fault either, but it also is."

"Fair enough," Peter said. He sighed. "It's not that I resent your mother or Steve. I'm happy for them. I'm glad that Janice found some-one to make her happy. It's just . . ." He sat down hard on a chair. "I'm not resentful. I'm jealous. I'm ridiculously jealous, Graham. I never stopped loving your mother. She was the one who stole my heart. I knew logically that she would move on, but emotionally, I was still hoping . . . It was a stupid thought. An immature thought. So I'm jealous. And I like Steve. I remember liking him back when I brought you and Kaya in for your cleanings. He made you laugh, and those gerbils—"

"Hamsters," Graham corrected. "He still has them. They're the de-scendants of the originals."

"Yes, well, hamsters, then. But the point is, I don't want to get in the way of their happiness. But it's hard to see them. I can see that they're perfect for each other. Maybe if your mother had been the one to bring you kids in every six months . . ."

"Mom loved you every bit as much as you loved her," Graham said. "For the first several years, she waited, hoping you would come back. She was ready to hear you out, to forgive you for why you left, no matter what it was. But then it got harder for her. When things happened with Kaya, and she had to face it all alone—"

"I know," Peter interrupted. "I get that. I wasn't there to go through it with her."

"Steve was there," Graham finished, sitting across from his father at the kitchen table. "If anything, he deserves your gratitude."

Peter looked at his hands on the table. "I know that, Graham. I know. I'll be good. I promise. But maybe you should have this talk with your mother, too. I've already explained to her why I left. She knows. I think she understands. But I don't know if she's ready to be my friend, like Steve seems to want. I don't blame her. I would love to have Janice in my life in some way or another, even if it's not as a partner. We were friends before. Maybe we can be again."

Graham put his hand on his father's hands. "Maybe instead of me explaining things to Mom, you yourself should tell her how you feel. Be honest with her. I think she deserves that. I think she's worried. She had memories of the good times with you, and I'm sure she's confused about her own feelings. Maybe you can help her."

Peter looked at his son and nodded. "You're gonna be a really great psychologist," he said. "You have a good grasp on the human brain."

Graham smiled. "I should hope so. I know the brain, but I don't have the skill of you and Kaya. And Alice too. But don't read Mom's mind, Dad. Let her use her words with you. Trust her words"

Peter nodded. "I will."

"Go back in there," Graham said, standing up. "I'll take care of the food."

Peter stood. He approached his son and embraced him. "Thanks, kid," he whispered.

He walked out to the living room. Janice was sitting on the couch between Kaya and Gina, and they were all fussing with the baby. Grayson and Steve were engaged in conversation in the den in front of the television, half-watching a baseball game. Peter grabbed a dining room chair from the table and pulled it in front of the couch.

Kaya looked up. "How is dinner coming?" she asked. "I'm hungry." Her stomach growled out loud. She put her hand over it. "And I'm nauseous. Excuse me." She stood and quickly left the room.

Gina reached for Mason. "I need to go change his diaper before I feed him," she said. "Again." She left the room with the baby.

Peter was left sitting in the chair, looking at Janice. She looked back. She gave him a forced smile. He smiled back at her gently. "You look great, Janice," he said. "You don't look like you've aged a day in ten years."

Janice's eyes brightened slightly. "Thanks," she said. "There were some years there when I think I aged decades in a matter of months. But then, I started to take care of myself again. I started exercising again, and eating healthier, and doing the things I enjoyed. I never would have gotten back to my old self without . . ."

Peter nodded. "It's okay to say it, Janice. Really. I understand."

Janice cocked her head. "Do you, though?" she asked. "I mean, I hear you saying that, but is it true? I'm not sure I get that feeling coming from you. I may not be able to read minds, but I can read faces. I'm under the impression that you don't approve of my relationship with Steve. That you find it, I don't know, maybe humorous. Like some type of joke. Peter, this is not a joke. This is my life."

Peter nodded again. "No, I know that," he said. "It's a life you pieced together on your own, all alone, and I respect that. Janice, it's not that I disapprove of you and Steve. No, he's a good guy, and you're obviously happy. I want you to be happy. It's just that . . . well . . . I had always just hoped that you would be happy again with me. I know that that can never happen. I think I knew that right after I left, but still, the thought of someday coming back to you, hopefully with answers as to why I was the way I was, that's what kept me going."

"You mean to tell me that all this time, all these years, you've been celibate, waiting to come back to me?"

Peter laughed and then rubbed his hand on the side of his neck. "Janice," he said. "I'm not gonna lie to you. It *was* nine years."

Janice nodded. "I thought so."

"But that was sex. I'm talking about love. I've never stopped loving you."

Janice closed her eyes. "We can't be having this conversation," she said. She looked over at Steve. "I mean, maybe we should go somewhere else and talk."

Peter nodded. "Let's go outside for a minute."

They both stood. "Steve, honey, I'm gonna step outside for a cigarette real quick," Janice said.

Steve nodded. "Okay, Jan."

"Peter's gonna keep me company."

Steve looked at Peter. Then he nodded. "Okay. Watch out for the mosquitos out there."

The two ex-spouses walked out the door, and Peter closed it tight. Janice sat down on the concrete steps, and Peter sat next to her. "When did you start smoking again?"

Janice lit her cigarette. "Right now," she said. Then she laughed. "I just keep them in my purse in case I need them. I smoke maybe once a month if I'm feeling stressed out. Then I feel sick, and I don't smoke again for a long time. I haven't had one for two months this time." She inhaled and then blew out the smoke. "This is horrible," she said, and she coughed.

Peter laughed. "You are a walking contradiction, Janice Reed. I'm assuming you kept the name. At least until your wedding. Late August?"

Janice nodded. "August 29. Labor Day weekend."

"I'm sure it will be a lovely ceremony. I'll offer to watch the baby for the kids."

"I'm sure we'll be inviting you," Janice said. She took one more draw on her half smoked cigarette and then stumped it out on the step.

Peter shook his head. "Don't invite me."

Janice looked confused. "You don't want to go? C'mon, Peter, we can do this!"

"No," Peter said softly. "No. This is your day. I want you and Steve to be the focus. I don't want Jim and Selma to have to explain to their friends why their daughter's ex-husband is there, and where he had been all these years. Just let it be about you two, and the kids, and your friends. I'll still be here after. We can still be friends. We can find our way back to being friends."

Janice looked at his face. "Are you sure? After what you said in there, about loving me?"

Peter shrugged. "I've lived with some pretty difficult challenges over the years, Janice. This will just be another one. I can manage to turn this love into something platonic. Even if you are still as hot as the afternoon sun."

Janice smiled. "I remember the first time you said that to me," she said. "It was the first time we met, down at the park. It was after you lost sight of your frisbee in the sun and it hit me in the chest. Then you stood and stared at my chest and asked me if it was okay. And when I said it was okay, you said, 'Baby, it's more than okay, it's smoking hot.'" She laughed. "All of my friends laughed so hard. I turned red. Kaya turns red when she's embarrassed, too."

"I was a lady killer back then," Peter said. "And I've still got it. Kaya hasn't had a chance to tell you yet, but I actually have a date tomorrow night."

Janice's brows rose. "Oh, really?" she said. "Another frisbee accident in the park?"

Peter laughed. "No," he said. "No. It's Melody Green. Miss Green."

Janice's mouth fell open. She stared at him. Then she laughed. "Oh my God," she said. "You and Kaya's old cheerleading coach? That's hysterical! How did you meet her? Were you watching cheerleading instructional DVDs or something?"

Peter shook his head. "She's a lawyer now, in Florence. Working for the D.A. with Kaya's friend. We met today. I asked her out. Kaya did some brain probing on her own and figured out we were attracted to each other. History is made."

Janice smiled. "I'm happy for you, Peter," she said. "I hope it works out well for the two of you. Let's go back inside, okay? I've got the horrible taste of cigarettes in my mouth. I should just throw away the pack. I don't think I'll need them anymore." She took the pack out of her purse and looked at it. "Then again, it's nice to know that they're there in case I need them." She shoved them back inside.

They went back through the door, and everyone was in the living room. Kaya was holding a wet washcloth to her forehead, and Gina was nursing the baby. Grayson and Steve were watching the game quietly in the den. Steve looked up at Janice and smiled. She went to his side and offered him her hand, which he took quickly. He kissed her palm and then squeezed her hand.

Graham came out of the kitchen. "The casserole is heated," he said. "It came from our neighbor Calvin, who's a chef at Couscous, so it'll be good. Mom, Steve, eat with us. There's a ton of food. Then we can try out all the new toothpastes you brought us. Dad, go in the kitchen and grab the bread. Kaya, do you need a ginger hard candy? We have some left over from Gina's morning sickness."

Peter went into the kitchen with a smile on his face. For the first time in the three weeks since he'd arrived back in Wisteria, he felt like he had come home to his family. And to a few extra members than he had anticipated.

16

TEN MILES AWAY, ALICE WAS waiting for Tony to pick her up for dinner. She was nervous. She was more nervous than she had been earlier in the day when facing the Assistant District Attorney of Charleston County. She was confident in what the team would be doing to get Chet McHale to confess his crimes. But her future with Tony wasn't as clear. They had spoken on the phone every night while Alice was away, but she had been too scared to bring up anything important over the distance. Now, they would be face to face, and he would expect them to discuss what the future would be bringing them. Alice had tried to prepare herself for the conversation, but nothing felt natural to her. She would have to wait to see how the words came out of her mouth. She hoped she wouldn't cry, but she stuffed her purse with tissues just in case.

Tony was fifteen minutes late. When he came to the door, he looked disheveled. "I'm so sorry I was late," he said, distress radiating from his words. "Things got a little out of hand at the lab this afternoon, and long story short, I spent a few hours in a safe suit scouring the floor with a bristly brush and stuffing paper towels into red hazmat bags. So yeah, there was a bit of paperwork to complete before we could all leave, and then I realized that my phone went into a red barrel with the disposable suit, and it had already been brought out to the incinerator. So, yeah, a bit stressful. At least it wasn't my fault."

Alice smiled at Tony. "I'm so sorry that your afternoon was so stressful," she said, putting her hand on his reddened cheek. "Fifteen minutes isn't that long to wait, and it was only a few years ago that we didn't all have cell phones so we had to sit and wonder. It was like old times."

"We might be late for our reservation, though," Tony said, looking at her cautiously.

"So then we go somewhere else," Alice assured him.

Tony let his solemn expression fall away from his face, and slowly it was replaced by a smile. He put his hands on either side of Alice's waist. "You are an amazing woman," he said softly. He reached over to kiss her. "I missed you while you were gone. I'm really glad you're back. I'll be happy when this whole Chet McHale thing is over." He pulled her into an embrace.

Alice closed her eyes and pressed her cheek into Tony's chest. "Me, too," she said. "Although some good things have come out of these last few weeks. I've made some new friends, impressed my boss, and I've found the best man in the world right back here in my life again, where he belongs."

Tony kissed the top of her head. "We'd better go," he said. "I actually preordered us some stuff at the restaurant, so I'd like to try to get there in time." He took Alice's hand and led her out the door. Alice locked the door and headed to the car.

When they got into the car, Tony pointed to the floor in front of Alice. "There are some CDs on the floor right there in the case. Can you hand the case to me?"

Alice reached down and grabbed the case. "It's heavy," she said. "Is this your entire collection?"

Tony nodded. "Yes," he said. "I keep them at work because I'm there most of the time. By the time I come home at night, I kind of want to veg out in front of the TV or read. But I wanted to bring them tonight because I wanted to put something on for you." He opened the case and fingered through the collection. "Ah. Here it is." He took the CD out of the case and pushed it into the player on the dashboard. "Prepare to boogie!"

The CD started and spoken word came over the speaker. Alice felt a smile crawl across her face. "Offspring?" she asked. "You've gotta be kidding me! I haven't listened to *Smash* for years! Oh, man! 'Nitro'! You still have this CD from high school?"

Tony smiled as he started the car. "No, I don't have my high school CDs anymore," he said. "I sold them at some point to get some quick cash. I found this last month at Music Exchange. I couldn't believe it! Remember when you and Em used to yell at me to turn it down? But then you both ended up loving it. You used to slam dance in her bedroom!"

"And then you requested they play 'Self Esteem' at the junior prom. And they did!"

Tony laughed. "We all got out there and danced so crazy, and everyone was looking at us like we were crazy!"

"Remember how Emilie's date, Chris, was looking away, pretending he didn't know us?" Alice chuckled. "But then Em dragged him out there, and he ended up dancing even more wild than the rest of us!"

"I think he took a few shots first," Tony said. He shook his head. "Remember after that prom? We ended up making out in the grange parking lot. All of our friends were going nuts looking for us, and when we came back in, I had lipstick all over my collar, and Emilie hit me in the arm!"

Alice's chest started to ache from laughing. "Okay, enough," she declared. "Oh my God. Those years were so fun, weren't they? I can't imagine us doing all that stuff now."

Tony turned toward her and grinned. "Really? Because I was thinking after dinner we could head over to the grange, and—"

Alice hit him in the arm. "Cut it out!" she said with a smile. "We have places to live now, with soft beds and pillows. That's what it means to be an adult."

They rode in silence for a few minutes. Alice noticed that all of her fear had run out of her. She felt totally at ease. This was Tony. She knew Tony. They had grown up together. He was no mystery. If Tony had lied to her, or omitted certain things from her, that only meant that he was waiting to tell her, or he was in the process of working something out. She didn't have to be afraid to talk to him. It would be the most natural thing in the world to do. Now she looked forward to the conversation.

"We're here," Tony said, pulling into a parking lot.

Alice looked outside the car. "We're eating at Sammy's tonight?" she asked, surprised. "I thought we would be going to Couscous. I didn't even realize we crossed over to Wisteria."

"I hope it's okay," Tony said as he unbuckled his seatbelt. "I thought we'd try something different. Something new for us. You know, new start, new restaurant."

Alice's eyes went wide. "Tony, this place is fancy," she said. "I don't know if I'm dressed right for Sammy's. I mean, I'm not wearing my diamond tiara!"

Tony laughed. "Maybe I brought one for you," he teased.

Oh no, Alice thought in a panic as she waited for Tony to come around and open her door. *I hope he's not talking about an engagement ring! No! Not yet!*

They walked into a dimly lit entry and approached the hostess stand. "We have a reservation for two for Baptiste," Tony said. "Antoine Baptiste?"

The hostess looked up from her book with a smile. "Yes, Mr. Baptiste," she said. "Right this way." She escorted the couple through the dining room to a small table in the middle of the floor. "Tabitha will be your server tonight," she said. "She'll be with you shortly. Would you like some wine to start?"

Tony smiled. "I ordered something ahead," he said to the hostess. He looked at Alice and winked.

"I'll be right back, sir," the hostess said. She turned and left.

"What have you done, Tony?" Alice asked.

Tony smiled slyly. "It's a special night. We're celebrating. We're together again, Alice, and it's worth a celebration, don't you think?"

Alice couldn't help but smile. "I-I do think." She reached her hands across the top of the table and took both of Tony's. "I really do love you, Tony," she said softly.

Tony grinned. "That means everything to me," he said. "I love you, too, Alice."

The hostess came back carrying two champagne flutes in one hand, and a bottle in the other. Alice squinted at the bottle. "Laurent-Perrier?" she asked. "I don't know that one. Tony, is it really expensive?"

"Maybe," Tony said. He watched the hostess pour the sparkling wine into the flutes. "Not Dom Perignon, but also not Mad Dog. Just enjoy. Remember, we're celebrating."

"What are you celebrating tonight?" the hostess asked as she poured Alice's drink.

Tony looked up at her. "I got the girl back."

The hostess grinned. "Well, congratulations to you and the girl." She looked at Alice and winked. Alice acted demure.

"Tony, this is too much," she said when they were alone again.

"Nothing is too much," Tony replied. "Don't worry. I'm not breaking the bank tonight. I hardly ever get to have a night like this, and I wanted to do it once. I won't wine and dine you every time we get together, so enjoy it while you can."

Alice nodded. "I will." She lifted her glass. "You make the toast."

Tony looked up in thought. "To new beginnings with old loves," he said. "To wonderful things to come and memories to share. To us."

"To us," Alice said. They clinked glasses, and Alice sipped her champagne. "This is so much better than the stuff we smuggled into senior prom. This doesn't burn my tongue!"

Tony laughed. "Yeah, we might as well have been drinking it out of a paper bag," he said. "I think that was Two-Buck Chuck, wasn't it?"

Alice almost spit out her mouthful. "Oh, Lord," she said. "Two-Buck Chuck! Yeah, we have come a lot farther than I thought!"

"Yeah," Tony said. He put his glass down. "Maybe we can talk more tonight about where we're going—"

"Hi!" the waitress said. "I'm Tabitha. Have you had a chance to take a look at your menus?"

"No, not yet," Tony said.

"I hope you're enjoying your champagne. Would you like anything else to drink tonight?"

Alice nodded. "Can we have two ice waters and a basket of bread?"

"I'll be right back with those," Tabitha said, and she departed.

"We'd better look at the menu," Alice said. She discreetly removed a small magnifying glass from her purse. "Let's see. The salad looks good. But I'm hungrier than that. I want something filling." She read the columns. "Linguine with clam sauce," she said. "That looks good."

"Do you want to get an appetizer?" Tony asked. "Maybe the mussels? I could go for some mussels."

"That sounds great," Alice said. "You're gonna get the roast beef, aren't you?"

Tony laughed. "Of course," he said. "It's a big slab of beef and comes with some form of potato. I love meat and potatoes." He put his menu down. "So again, when we talked the other night—"

"Have you decided?" Tabitha asked, stopping back at the table, putting down two glasses of water and the bread.

Tony looked up at her. He did not look pleased. "We'll have the mussels to start, and I'll have a caesar salad and the roast."

"How would you like it cooked?"

Tony started to tap his foot. "Medium rare," he announced.

"And your potatoes?"

Tony sighed. "Au gratin."

"And you, ma'am?"

Alice gave her order, and Tabitha walked away with their menus. Alice laughed. "Dude, calm down!" she said. "You look like you're gonna burst a vein in your forehead! She's gone now. Talk, before she comes back with the mussels!"

Tony gave her a lopsided grin. "Thank you," he said. "I don't know why I'm feeling so pressured. I just want to talk about this. I kind of feel like we left things hanging on the phone the other day, and I think we should continue our discussion."

"Tony?" Alice said.

"What?" Tony asked, looking into her eyes.

"I've been thinking about something, and I want to run it by you. Listen, I've been thinking of making some changes. I'm tired of living in a house that was decorated by my parents when Johnny Carson was still the host of The Tonight Show. I'm thinking of ripping out all the wallpaper and maybe getting an architect to come in and see if I can rip the wall down between the kitchen and the dining room and put up a breakfast bar. And don't get me started on the bedrooms. No one needs four bedrooms in a house that size. I'd like to make a master bedroom, with a bathroom. Maybe put in some hardwood floors. A deck out back. You know, bring it into the twenty-first century."

Tony stared at her. "Oh, okay," he said. "Yeah, I can see that. I mean, you're living in your childhood house. You want to make it your own. I don't blame you. There are so many memories in that place. I think that you'd make some really great choices in bringing it up to date. Maybe you could even sell it after, and make a profit."

"Or I could stay there," Alice said.

Tony nodded. He had a serious look on his face. "Sure," he said. "You could stay there. That would be good, too. I mean, you'll make it perfect for yourself, and then you'll want to stay there."

Alice nodded. "But here's the thing," she said. She waited a few beats. "I think that maybe it would be a good idea to have some help, you know, making decisions about what to do, to make it just right."

Tony nodded. "You could find a designer to help you with that. They could tell you about all the current styles, and bring you samples. It would be a really good idea to get some help with that."

Alice could see that Tony was feeling deflated. She had to reel him back in. "I was actually thinking that I might want someone I know to help me. Someone that knows me, and someone who I know and trust. Someone, you know, who might just end up benefiting from the alterations. Someone, you know, who will be living in the house with me when it's done."

Tony had been pulling his linen napkin between his two hands, but then he stopped. "Living in the house with you?" He burst into a grin. "You want to redo the house, and you want me to be part of it? Because you want me to move in with you?"

Alice smiled. "Yes!" she said. "But you won't be moving into my house. You'll be moving into *our* house."

"But Alice," Tony said. "That might take some time, don't you think? Like maybe a lot of time."

Alice nodded. "Yeah," she said. "And in the meantime, I'll have to find a place to stay. So I was thinking, while the work is being done to make the house our home, maybe Pony and I can stay with you?" She bowed her head and looked up at him hopefully.

Tony inhaled deeply. "I-I think we can make that work," he said. "I mean, we'll have to put a pet deposit down on Pony for possible damages, but that won't be a problem. It will be less than a bottle of Dom Pérignon!"

Alice laughed. She reached back for Tony's hands. "Tony," she said. She squeezed his hands. "I know what you were saying to me the other day. When we talked, I knew you were holding something back. At first, I thought you weren't being honest with me. I wasn't sure why. But I spoke to Emilie, and . . ."

"Oh," Tony said quietly. Now he looked down. "So, she told you why . . ."

Alice nodded. The tears started to develop in the corners of her eyes. "She did tell me, Tony. I-I don't even remember telling you my thoughts about your eyes. I have no idea how you knew. Did I tell you in my sleep?"

Tony shook his head. "No," he said. "You told me. You told me that you could see my eyes, that you could always see them, and you would always remember them. When you told me that . . . it hit me so hard, Alice. You were so open and honest. It made me think. I thought of everything we could be . . . but I also thought of everything you might miss. And I don't want you to miss anything. I know I'm moving quickly, Al, but I think it's okay for us. We've known each other for a very long time. There's not much else we need to learn about each other, although whatever there is, I want to know it. But, yes, I don't want to scare you away, but I also want you to have the best of everything."

Alice looked at her champagne and then back into Tony's eyes. "Please, Tony," she said. "Please tell me you're not going to propose to me tonight."

"What?" Tony asked. He looked at the champagne, and he laughed. "Oh, God, no," he said. "I just wanted to do something special for you. Something to show you how much you mean to me. There's no way I could afford a bottle of champagne, a dinner at Sammy's, *and* an engagement ring. No, you'll have to wait a bit more for that. And, when I do propose, I want it to be a surprise, but not the fact that I want to marry you. Just that I'm giving you the ring at that specific time."

Alice felt a wave of relief flow through her. "Oh, thank God," she said. "I don't think I want to be the woman who gets engaged after one date. I mean, one date plus two earlier years of dating. But yeah, let's hold off on that part now, okay?"

Tony nodded. He lifted his champagne flute and signaled for Alice to raise hers as well. "Here's to not getting engaged tonight," he said.

"Here's to that," Alice said, and they clinked glasses.

Tabitha came back with the mussels. "I hope I'm not interrupting anything," she said.

17

ALICE WAS NERVOUS DURING THE two-hour drive to the state prison. She sat in the back seat of Carla's county-issued sedan with Kaya, quietly holding hands and exchanging thoughts. Carla and Melody sat in the front having an animated conversation about work issues. After some time, the subject changed, and Melody started talking about her date with Peter. She had effectively forgotten that Kaya was in the car. Kaya started humming loudly inside her head to block it out, and Alice hummed along in solidarity. It appeared the date had gone well, and Peter and Melody would be seeing each other again. Alice knew that Kaya was happy about the situation, but she just didn't want to hear the details. Alice tried to distract her with a silent game of I Spy, and then they searched for out-of-state license plates. By the time they were done with those, Carla and Melody were talking about the McHale case.

"This is going to be tricky," Carla said. "We need to get him to say all of the right things. They have to be his words. It doesn't matter what the two of you sense from him. He has to confess. Otherwise, it's all conjecture."

"I'm pretty sure we can do it," Kaya said.

Melody smiled. "Kaya can do anything she sets her mind to," she said with affection.

Kaya blushed. "Miss Green has a bias," she said.

"Would you please call me Melody?" Melody insisted. "We're really not that far apart in age, and I'm your friend now, not your teacher. I'm not even a teacher anymore. And I'm kind of dating your father."

"You were a good teacher. Melody. Ugh, that just sounds weird after four years of Miss Green in high school."

"So, Alice," Carla said, bringing them back on track. "You'll give me the same signal as usual, right? You'll kick my foot if he's lying. But I remember last time you did that, you got really excited and stomped on my toe. Maybe just a firm but gentle nudge of my foot would be sufficient."

"Okay," Alice said. "I'll keep my excitement to myself. I'll keep a straight face. We don't want Chet to suspect that we know anything more than what we're saying."

"The detective will do most of the talking," Carla went on. "I've prepared him as to what to expect, short of telling him that we're working with real-life psychics. Kaya, if you catch anything from Chet that will help us, knock on the window. I'll come out and you tell me. Chet is never going to see your face or hear Alice's voice."

Kaya nodded. "We're gonna get some information," she said confidently. "There's no way he's not going to think about what happened that night. And when he does, we'll have him dead to rights."

"As long as he says it aloud," Carla warned. "Kaya, remember, he has to say the words. We have no evidence."

"We will," Kaya promised.

Alice sighed. "There's still a part of me that hopes that Shari's alive somewhere. I mean, for Brad's sake. And hers. It's so hard to think of her dead body being out there all alone and no one knows about it except the killer."

"I know," Carla said. "This isn't the first time I've been involved in an interrogation about a missing person. And most of them don't end up with the missing person alive and well. It's part of what we do, Alice. If you stay in the field, it's something to expect."

Alice nodded. She looked at Kaya, who was still trying to figure out how to break into law enforcement without first being a beat cop. Kaya smiled at her. She didn't have to be connected to Kaya's thoughts to know that Kaya would figure it all out. Kaya was good at that stuff.

They reached the prison, parked, and were greeted at the entrance by security. "Anyone wearing an underwire bra?" the female guard asked.

Kaya touched her breasts. "We all complied with the rules we were given," she said. "I'm wearing a sports bra that doesn't fit now that I'm pregnant. I feel like I have a uniboob."

Alice laughed. The guard nodded at the group. "Please put your bags on the moving belt. We'll hand-search them once they've been scanned. Please step through the X-ray one at a time. Please raise your arms. Thank you."

They were led through a set of locked doors, and then another. They were led to a room. The guard unlocked the door. "Please step through." They all went inside and found the detective and the sheriff's deputy already waiting. Everyone was introduced and shook hands.

"I'm curious to see how this goes," Detective Caron said. "I interviewed this loser back when he was first arrested last year, and I can't tell you how excited I was to see him go down for that old lady's death. He's a scum. I never really blamed that woman for taking off, but to be honest, it barely occurred to me that he might have killed her. He's a conman. You don't really expect that from a con. But you never know. Sometimes the preacher next door goes nuts and kills his entire family. So I'll take your lead, Carla. I'll start by asking him what happened to his wife."

"Girlfriend," Alice corrected. "They never married."

"I'll refer to her as Ms. Coombs. Mrs. Pike, you'll be watching from the other side of the mirror. Ms. Telman, you'll be observing quietly. Officer Beck will be here in case the scum acts up, and if we're lucky, to make an arrest for us. Are we all ready?" Everyone nodded. "Carla, Ms. Telman, let's go in, and a guard will bring Mr. McHale into the room from the back entrance. Melody, Mrs. Pike, you stay here with the guard."

Everyone took their places. Alice sat next to Carla, the detective across the table from them. The head of the table was reserved for Chet McHale. Minutes passed, and finally a buzzer sounded, and the door opened. A guard walked the shackled McHale into the room and sat him in the chair. The guard then went through the other door into the side room where Kaya and Melody were watching. Alice felt acid burning in her stomach. She wanted to reach out and throttle this man for what he had done to Brad, Mrs. Corrigan, and most likely Shari.

But she sat still. Kaya's voice came into her head. *Relax*, she said. *Don't let him see your fear.* She made a conscious effort to relax her face.

"Mr. McHale," Detective Caron said. "I can see that prison agrees with you. You look like shit."

Chet chuckled. "You came all the way here from Florence just to insult me. Good use of taxpayer money."

"No, Chet, we're here today to talk about the murder of Shari Coombs," Caron said.

Chet's face was impassive. "Someone murdered Shari?" he asked. "Where was she? In the city? I haven't seen her since she took off last year."

"Well, Chet, we have reason to believe that Ms. Coombs may have been dead since the day she disappeared. We think that she never made it out of the Florence area, and that she's still there, waiting to be found."

"What?" Chet said, attempting to cross his shackled hands in front of his chest, and somehow succeeding. "You think she offed herself or something?"

"No, Chet," Caron said. "Like I said, we think she was murdered. We would like to review your side of the events that occurred that night. Just to remind us, you know."

Chet nodded and thought for a moment. "Okay. Yeah. Sure. So I took the bus home that day because my friend was using the car. It was a busy day. It was late. Shari's car wasn't there. That was normal. Sometimes she stayed late at work. The kid wasn't there either. I thought he might have been with his grandma or something. I went inside and made myself a sandwich. Bologna, if you want to know the details. It was dry. We were out of mayo. After a while, I went back to the bedroom, and everything was a mess. I looked more carefully, and I noticed that some of Shar's things were gone. I checked the bathroom, and her makeup and shampoo and stuff was gone. I checked the closet and couldn't find her suitcases. That's when I figured she'd gone somewhere, and quickly. I called my mom's house and asked if they knew where she was. I talked to the kid. He had no idea. He thought she was home. So I waited. She didn't come home. I looked around for a note, but there wasn't any. I considered calling the police, but I had no reason to, really. It didn't look like anything illegal had happened. It looked like my woman had run off. I was pissed."

"What happened the next day, when Brad came back home?"

"He was worried about his mom," Chet said. "He said he was going to talk to her about something, and she wouldn't have just taken off like that. I told him to look around. All he needed to know was right there. The bitch had packed her shit and left us. No note. Nothing. She deserted her kid. But he wasn't convinced. He said he wanted to talk to the police. I told him to help himself. I knew the police wouldn't take a report. It was less than twenty-four hours, and like I said, she left on her own. She did leave. It was pretty clear. But it turns out the little piece of shit really went to the station to turn me in about the fucking diabetic bitch. And I was right. They never filed the missing person's report."

Detective Caron stared at him. "Okay," he said. "So that sounds a lot like what you told us last year. But in the meantime, Ms. Coombs had not come forward, even to contact her son. All of our witnesses have stated that she and her son were very close, and it was very unlikely that she would leave him without a word and still be out of contact one year later. What we're looking at, Mr. McHale, is a woman who can't come back because she's in fear for her life for some reason, or she can't come back, because she's dead."

"She has no reason to be scared," Chet said passively.

Alice kicked Carla's foot. Up until that time, much of what Chet said had been true. Sort of true. Shari's bags had indeed been packed. Her car was gone. Chet had been pissed. He did call his mother and speak to Brad. But there was more to the story. He was not sharing the whole truth. Only the truth he chose to remember.

"Did Shari take off often?" Carla asked.

Chet turned to look at her. He smiled. "No, Mrs. Assistant D.A.," he said. "Shar was happy with me."

Alice kicked Carla's foot, harder this time. "She was happy, was she?" Carla asked. "So happy to be with you, and your son. So happy, that out of nowhere, she packed her bags and left, with no word to either of you, taking you both totally by surprise."

"That's right," Chet said smugly. Alice kicked Carla's foot.

"Ouch," Carla said softly. "Okay, Chet," she said. "So you were caught totally by surprise by Shari leaving. Did you have any idea where she would go? I mean, everyone has some place they go when they're upset. A friend, a family member. Someone, or some place. A town, a city."

Chet shook his head. "I couldn't think of any place."

Carla nodded. "Okay," she said. "But if you could imagine any place that you think that Shari would or could go, where would it be? If you could picture where she is right now, where would it be?"

Chet shook his head again. "I have no earthly idea."

Alice kicked Carla's foot at the same moment that a knock came from the back of the mirror. Carla looked over at the detective. "Excuse me a minute," she said. She motioned for Caron to come with her.

Alice was left sitting in the room with Chet and the guard. She glanced at Chet. He looked at her with a sneer. "What's your name?" he asked. Alice turned away. "You're kind of cute," Chet went on. "Are you married? I'm not. You know, they allow us to get married. We can even have visits from our wives. I don't think Shar would mind at all." He laughed, and Alice felt she might vomit.

Carla and Caron came back to the room quietly. They both sat back down in their seats. Alice looked at one, and then the other. The two looked at each other with no expression and then looked back and Chet. Chet looked back and forth between both of them. "What was that all about?"

Carla exhaled. "Before we came to see you today," she said, "we put out a message to the media, telling them that we were looking for any witnesses that might have seen Shari the day of her disappearance. We have a hotline number, and people have been calling all day with tips. Most of them have been phony. But we just got a tip that we feel might be worth investigating."

"Someone said that they saw some activity at the lake that night," Detective Caron said. "It was a message on the voice mail, and they didn't specify which lake. They heard a skirmish but weren't able to see what was happening. It's enough information so that we can start a search of all the lakes in the area. We have the equipment to sweep all the lakes. We'll start with Cherry Lake in Florence, and then move on to Luna lake in Wisteria, and Blue Lake in Garrison. It's only a tip, but it's a place to start."

Alice tried to keep her expression steady. Both Carla and Caron were lying. Everything they said was a lie. Caron wasn't even telling the truth about being able to sweep the lakes. He was bluffing. But something was going on. Kaya had picked up on a thought. Something to do with a lake. Carla had asked Chet where he thought that Shari could be, and Chet had pictured a lake in his head. It was just that Kaya didn't know which lake. And Chet had to confess. *Confess*, she thought, looking at his repulsive face.

Chet finally spoke. "A skirmish at a lake?" He laughed. "That's not much to go on. But maybe Shar met someone at the lake after she left. That's possible. Maybe she had another guy. I wouldn't put it past that bitch."

Detective Caron nodded. "It could be," he said. "We'll consider all the possibilities. Maybe she did meet someone at the lake that night. Or maybe someone brought her to the lake."

A thought popped into Alice's mind. *Kick Carla's foot twice*, was what Kaya put into her head. Alice complied. Carla perked up slightly. "Yes," she said. "Someone brought Shari to the lake, in her own car. But that seems strange, doesn't it? I mean, she had her bags packed, all of her stuff. But then why would someone drive her to the lake in her own car? If she was leaving *with* someone, why make the stop at the lake? Why not just leave?"

Chet shrugged. "I have no idea," he said. "You'd have to ask Shar. Oh, that's right, you can't. She's missing."

Alice kicked Carla's foot once. He was lying. He did indeed have an idea why that would happen. *Just say it!* Alice thought. *You're getting yourself backed up against the wall. Just confess!*

Chet looked around the room. "What was that?" he asked. "Some kind of intercom? Do you have someone on the other side of the mirror?"

Carla and Caron looked at each other in confusion. Caron looked back at Chet, ignoring his outburst. "So someone brought her to the lake," he said. "Maybe they had a talk with her there, and things got heated."

"I don't know," Chet said, still looking at the mirror.

Alice kicked Carla's foot. *You do know, you piece of shit*, she thought. *Everything you say is a lie. You have absolutely no redeeming qualities. It's you who should be dead, not Shari. Shari deserved to live.*

Sweat was starting to develop on Chet's forehead. "Cut it out!" he yelled.

Caron's eyes narrowed. "What's going on Chet?" he asked. "I just made a comment about what might have happened down at the lake that night with Shari and the person she was there with."

It was you, Alice thought. *Just tell them it was you, and this could all be over. And we could all go home.*

"Who could it have been?" Carla asked. She had obviously noticed Chet's distress, and even if she didn't understand it, she was capitalizing on it. "Who would Shari have met at the lake, and then gotten in a fight with? Which, strangely enough, was on the night before your son went down to the police to tell them about your crimes? It's definitely a curious situation."

It was you, Chet. Just say it. Just say you packed up her stuff, put it in her car, and made it look like she was leaving you. But then you drove her to the lake, and you had it out with her and then you killed her. You killed her right then. And then what did you do? Push the car into the lake?

"Can't you hear that?" Chet called out. "Why are you letting her say that?" He tried to stand up, but the deputy pushed him back down in the seat. "This is abuse! Witness abuse! Prisoner abuse! I have rights!"

Caron looked him right in the eye. "Chet, I have no idea what you're talking about. We're just having a calm conversation here about what happened that night. What did happen that night, Chet? Do you know? Were you there to see what happened? Did someone do something to Shari that night? Did they get upset with her, and maybe hit her over the head with a rock, or strangle her and then dispose of the car and the body? Do you know who it was, Chet? Who was it, Chet? Give me a name, Chet. Then it will all be over."

It will never be over for you, Chet. You deserve whatever happens to you when they all figure out that it was you, that you killed Brad's mother. The mother that took care of him. I wouldn't fault Brad if he came in here and killed you himself. You are scum. Just tell them that you know that you are the scum of the earth and that it was you who killed Shari. They know it already anyway.

Chet put his hands on either side of his head. "Why can't you hear it?" he insisted. "It's so loud! But I can't see anyone talking! What's going on here! Make it stop!"

It will stop, Chet. It will stop for good. Once you tell them, the words will stop, and you'll never have to hear them again. Tell them. But tell them the truth. Tell them word for word what you did, and where she is. And then, you can rest. I promise.

Tears came to Chet's eyes. "Okay," he said in a resigned voice. "Okay. I'll tell you the truth. Then make it stop! I did it! I did all of it! She came home from work that day and she told me it was over. She said she was taking Brad, and they were getting out of town. I asked her why. I mean, she had dozens of reasons to leave me, but I needed to know which one it was. She said she knew about the old lady, the one with diabetes. She said that she couldn't live with me anymore, or subject Brad to me. She started to pack her bags. I told her that I didn't do anything, and that it wasn't my fault that the old lady died. She told me that I should let the police decide that. I knew it then. I knew she was gonna go to the police. I begged her not to. She said she had no choice. She couldn't live with herself if she knew that I was responsible for someone's death and she didn't tell. I begged her to wait. I told her that I'd help her leave, help her pack. I told her that I would get her set up at a motel, so she could be away from me that night. She could go get the kid from my ma's the next day, and they could leave. And then, when I was ready, I'd go to the police myself, turn myself in. But I asked her to wait, not to tell yet. She agreed. She said she'd leave town, and give me a chance to turn myself in. I thanked her. I told her that I was grateful. I told her that I needed her car for the night, because my friend had borrowed mine, so I could drive her to the motel with the stuff and drop her off. I'd pick her up the next day and bring her to my ma's to get the kid, and then we'd all say goodbye. And then, I'd turn myself in, after she was gone. She was actually happy that I'd agreed. She thought I'd get a fairer shake if I turned myself in. Less time on the inside. I helped her carry out her bags. We got in the car.

"I told her I wanted to go to Luna Lake, in Wisteria, where we used to go, you know, to park and stuff when she was still in high school. It was where I knocked her up with the kid. I said, you know, for old time's sake. She agreed. I think she was feeling a bit nostalgic, too, now that she knew we had a plan. So we went to the lake, and I parked under the big tree by the edge, and we looked out at the water. Then I asked her to walk with me. I-I already knew what I had to do. While she was putting on her jacket in the car, I got out, and I looked around. I found a rock. A medium-sized rock. I put it in my jacket pocket. Then when we started walking, and she was talking about the first time we had even gone there, and I did it. I hit her over the head with the rock. It didn't knock her out. She went down on the ground, and she turned over and looked at me, more angry than scared. Before she could speak, I jumped on her, pinned her down, and I hit her again. I hit her a few more times, and by the time I was done, she was . . . there was no way she was still alive. I panicked. I knew I had to shut her up, but I couldn't believe what I had just done."

Alice's foot was still. Chet was telling the truth. Every word of it was the truth.

"Then what did you do?" Detective Caron asked.

"Then . . . then I decided I had to hide what I did. I loaded her in the car. I put her in the driver's seat and buckled her in. I leaned her head against the steering wheel. Then I put the car in neutral. And then I rolled it down the bank until it went into the water. I stepped in the water, and I kept pushing it into the deeper water, until finally I came to a ledge, and I could feel it tip in. I got out of the water and watched the car sink. It took a few minutes, but finally, it was gone. Then I went back to the spot where I . . . did it, and I saw the blood. I did what I could to clean it up. I pretty much buried it. I knew it would rain soon, and the whole area would be cleaned, but I didn't want a hiker to see something. I-I walked back to the house later, about four miles. My feet got blistered. I was limping. When I got there, I took off my clothes outside, and I went right for the shower. When I got dressed, I took a garbage bag, and I put my clothes inside, and I drove to the alley behind the deserted strip mall. I dumped them out, and I burned them. It didn't take long. After I tossed the plastic bag in a dumpster two blocks away, I went back to the house, and I called my ma's house and asked her if she knew where Shar was."

He stopped to breathe. There was silence in the room.

"Two days later, the sheriff's deputies were at my door. I thought that they had found the car. But they were there to arrest me for the con and the old lady. I was actually relieved. I didn't know yet that the kid had ratted on me."

Alice was speechless. The truth had come out. It had been recorded, in video and audio. No one would ever see her say anything. No one would ever see the expression change on her face. All they would see was a man teetering very close to the edge of sanity, wracked with guilt over murdering the mother of his child and hiding the evidence. She allowed herself a small smile.

You did good, Chet, she thought.

After the officer made the arrest, and Detective Caron had radioed to dispatch officers to Luna Lake, Carla and Alice were reunited with Kaya and Melody.

"You were amazing," Kaya told Alice.

Alice shook her head. Her body felt numb. She felt dizzy. "What did I do?"

Kaya smiled. "You got into his head, Alice," she said. "You got to him. I could actually hear your voice inside his head. You scared him straight. He was on the brink of confessing to killing Amelia Earheart and the Lindburg baby! But he told the truth! He confessed. The truth is out there! You are Alice, finder of the truth!"

"How did I do that?" Alice asked quietly. "I have no idea how I did it. I was just so mad, and I felt like lashing out at him. I felt like I was screaming at him in my head. I had no idea that he would hear me! I didn't even know he was hearing me until he started talking back. I just couldn't take his lies anymore! Every time he lied, I got angrier and angrier. I had to do something!"

"And you did!" Kaya said. She hugged her friend. "You were the one to make it happen, Alice. It was you who made the truth come out. I was able to see his thoughts about the lake, and his other thoughts about that night, but then after Carla ran with those details, you pushed him over the edge."

Alice felt her eyes well up with tears. "I'm exhausted," she said. She sat down on a chair.

Carla looked at the deputy. "Can you see if you can get her some juice or something?" The deputy nodded and went to talk to a guard. Carla looked back at the young women. "We make a great team, the four of us, don't we?" she asked. "Two weeks ago, I never could have imagined I'd be where I am today, with the people I'm with. It feels righteous, you know? We're putting away a really bad guy, for a really long time. Yes, there has to be a trial, but even if Chet's lawyer goes for the insanity defense, I don't think it will hold. No psychologist would ever call this guy insane. If anything, his own conscience finally got the best of him. If he even has one at all. C'mon, let's check out of this place and go get some food."

Alice chugged down the orange juice the guard brought her. Instantly, she felt her energy return. Putting angry thoughts into a convict's head was exhausting. She would remember that for next time, if there ever was a next time. Right now, all she wanted to do was go home, strip off her clothes, and take a shower to wash this vile place off of her. And then, she wanted to call Tony and ask him to come over. Tony would make everything feel normal again.

18

THEY WERE SITTING AT A picnic table at the park in Florence. It was Alice, Kaya, Peter, and Dr. Blake—Dirigo. Alice had brought egg salad sandwiches, Peter and Kaya brought a six pack of Sprite, and Dr. Blake, a store-bought package of two-bite brownies. They sat and enjoyed the sunshine on their faces and necks as they ate. "So what do you think you'll decide to do?" Alice asked Kaya.

Kaya smiled at her friend and then wiped egg off her face with a napkin. "I think it's pretty clear what I'm gonna do," she answered. "I'm gonna take the job. I mean, when am I ever gonna get another offer like this from a district attorney's office? I mean, I know it's not gonna be glamorous or anything. I'll be a glorified research gofer, but that's okay. I know that Carla will let me help, the way she lets you help, Alice. I can do good things here, like you do. We can put away the bad guys, and make sure they throw away the key. Carla's right. Together, we make a really good team." She looked at her father. "I wish there was a place for you, too, Dad."

Peter shrugged as he reached for a tiny brownie. "I'll be okay," he said. "I have some solid leads in my own field. I mean, advertising may not be something that saves the world, but I'm good at it. The guys I used to coordinate radio commercials for are now doing the work in-house, and they're interested in talking to me. Everyone's gonna want to know where I've been for the last nine years. It's a long break. I'm gonna have to find a place that gives me a chance. I have a lot of good references. But for now . . ." He popped the brownie in his mouth and ate it in one bite. "I'll just keep working custodial downtown. They always need people. I know it's just temporary." He grabbed another brownie. "Speaking of advertising," he said, "this is false advertising. I don't need two bites to finish these off." He ate the second one and went back for one more.

"It takes me more than two bites," Alice said as she nibbled around the edges of her snack. "I like to savor it."

"You couldn't work at the D.A.'s office anyway, Dad," Kaya said. "You'd have to work with Miss Green and that would make things awkward if the two of you get hot and heavy."

Peter laughed. "Would you please stop calling her that? It's Melody. And yes, you're right. I'm taking her to a movie tonight. It's going well, and I'd hate to mess things up by working together. Plus, I don't think law enforcement is for me."

"I'm glad all of you are finding your place," Dr. Blake said. He was still working on his sandwich. He took a sip of his soda. "I'm going to continue with my work now that I'm not teaching anymore. I still have the use of my office, and the school resources." He turned to Alice. "I would really like to encourage you to go ahead with the testing we would like to do. I think that having a look at your brain would be instrumental in helping us figure out what's going on with all of you, and maybe how to recognize other people who we can help. Just imagine what it's like for others out there, not understanding what's happening to them, and having no one to talk to about it . . ."

"Wow, Rigo," Kaya said. "Laying on the guilt kind of thick there, aren't you?" She turned to Alice. "But he's right. We have a very small sample size so far with just me and Dad and Graham. Having your images would really help us understand if this is all part of the same big thing. I would love to know where all of this came from. Was it dormant for centuries, or even longer, and then something triggered it to start up again? I'm guessing there are a lot of people walking around with this anomaly, but they don't have any abilities, like Graham. So why us? Why not them?"

Alice could hear the logic in what they were telling her. "I know," she said. "I'm aware that the more information we have, the more we'll know. And especially after what happened at the prison last week. I have to wonder what else I'm capable of. I mean, the more time I spend with you, Kaya and Peter, the more all of us seem to be able to do. It's like we power each other up. What would happen if we met others like us? Would we learn to do even more things? Think of the good we could do in the world with a group of people with super skills!" She looked at Dr Blake. "Rigo," she said, "I'll talk to Tony about it. I'll consider it. Can I bring him with me if I do it? You know, for moral support? And because I've had my license taken away?"

Dr. Blake clapped his hands together. "Of course!" he said. "The more the merrier. I also need to have some control subjects for the research. I can scan his brain also. I'll take whatever help I can get. Grayson had his head examined for the cause."

Kaya laughed. "He really enjoyed it," she said. "It got him interested in what the brain can do. He's been taking books out of the library, and he's considering taking some classes at the community college in neurobiology. I might, too. You know, the more you know . . ."

Dr. Blake nodded. "I would like to talk more about what all of you are capable of doing these days," he said. "When I first met you, Kaya, you were able to hear voices coming from thoughts when you touched people."

"Right," Kaya said. "Now, I can read thoughts even when I'm not touching anyone. I can be about ten feet away, maybe more, and hear them. And they're not always voices anymore. Sometimes, I get images, like my dad does. I've been able to encapsulate thoughts from other people and, well, download them into my own head, and watch them like I'm watching a movie. And I can also project my own thoughts into other people's heads." She looked at Peter. "Dad taught me that one. I'm also getting better at feeling the emotion behind the words. But I haven't been able to read whether or not someone is telling the truth, like Alice, unless they're thinking about whether or not they are."

"What about you, Peter?"

Peter nodded. "All the things that Kaya said," he reported. "I haven't heard the thoughts as voices, but I don't think I need to. I get images or ideas in my head. I can push my thoughts, encapsulate thoughts, and I do pick up on the emotion."

"Very much alike," Dr. Blake said. He turned to Alice. "And you?"

"I started out just being able to tell if someone's being honest," she said. "It's a feeling. Like, a sensation in my body. It has different levels for different degrees of lies. When I was with Chet McHale, I was feeling shocks throughout my body. But when Tony little white lies to me to surprise me about something, it's more like a tingle in my stomach. But since I've met Peter and Kaya, things have really changed for me. Now, I can hear their thoughts. I haven't really tried to hear other people's thoughts, except for Kaya and Peter. Kaya and I have major conversations in our heads." She smiled affectionately at her friend. "We have a lot of fun together without anyone even knowing! I haven't even tried to read Tony's thoughts, and for sure I didn't try to hear Chet's thoughts. But maybe now that things are calming down, I'll try. But then there's this thought projection."

"That was pretty cool," Kaya said. She looked at her father. "You should have seen her, Dad. She was pumping all sorts of stuff into Chet's head. Not just words, but also emotion. Pure anger. Chet didn't know what hit him! I mean, I can share my thoughts with others, but I have never been able to do it to that extent. It was really powerful! Alice, you have to be sure to only use that power for good. You could really damage someone with those kinds of thoughts. *I* even thought I might start to confess things, and I hadn't even done anything!"

Alice was shocked by Kaya's words. She had no idea that she had come across so strong. The idea of damaging someone with her thoughts scared her. She would have to learn how to control that skill quickly. When she had done it with Chet, she hadn't even realized she was doing it. It was as if her thoughts had simply taken over. Yes, she would have to watch herself, and, like Kaya said, only use the skill when it was absolutely necessary. "I think there was another time that I did that," Alice said. "I think one time, I was feeling really emotional when I was talking to Tony, and I projected some of my thoughts to him. He just thought I was talking to him. I never had any idea that he heard them until he said the exact words back to me at a later time."

"That might not be such a bad thing," Kaya said, touching Alice's arm. "But it's good to know. You'll have to be much more cautious going forward if there are things you don't want him to know." She smiled. "But I don't think you have too much to worry about. I bet it will only be good stuff you end up sharing with him."

Dr. Blake grabbed a brownie and held it in his hand. "So much progress," he said. "So much change. Yes, I really do think that the three of you being together has helped you discover more of your abilities.

I just have to try to figure out how these skills applied to our ancient ancestors. We've talked about evolution, and how being able to communicate nonverbally might have been essential to survival. And yes, those who could throw their thoughts, or express danger, or even be forceful in their communication, were most likely to breed and pass on their genes. But why did these traits disappear over the centuries? And what made them resurface?"

He put the brownie down next to him on the table. "These are the questions we need to look into. And what do we do now that we know that these abilities exist? And what can I do, as a professional scientist, to help you to best utilize your skills? I have no special skills of my own. Nothing interesting has ever happened in my life."

At that moment, a crow swooped down from a large pine tree, landed on the table next to Dr. Blake, looked him in the eye, and picked up his brownie. Then, it flew away, carrying the brownie in its beak. Everyone stared after the bird as it landed back on a branch in the tree. It proceeded to eat the brownie. No one spoke. A minute later, the same crow made a beeline for the picnic table and landed in the exact same location. Again, it eyed the doctor, but this time, instead of taking a prize, it dropped one in front of the old professor, and then took off, flying over the tree and out of sight.

Dr. Blake looked in front of him and then picked up the item. "It's a ring," he said. He turned it over and looked closer. Alice took the magnifying glass out of her purse and handed it to him. He nodded his thanks and then examined the ring. "I don't believe this," he said quietly.

Kaya's forehead wrinkled. "What is it?" she asked, leaning closer.

Dr. Blake looked up and looked around, as if he had forgotten that anyone else was there with him. "This is a class ring," he said. "Harvard." He looked again with the magnifying glass. "1963." He looked up at Kaya. "You have young, strong eyes, my dear. Can you read this inscription on the inside?"

Kaya took the ring from Dr. Blake's hand and held it between her fingers. "It's initials," she said. She looked up, her shock showing on her face. "D.R.B."

Dr. Blake nodded as if he had expected that answer. "D.R.B.," he echoed. "Dirigo Rodney Blake. Class of 1963. Harvard University, Graduate School of Psychology. Well, that just goes to show you. You think there's nothing special about you, and then a crow you've never met before steals your brownie and delivers your class ring that you lost three thousand miles away forty years earlier to your picnic table in broad daylight." He took another brownie and popped it in his mouth. "I guess I was wrong. Maybe I am special after all."

Tony picked up Alice at the park and drove her to the police station. Dr. Blake had dropped Brad off before the meeting at the park so he could give his statement to the authorities. He was told that Brad should be ready to go by two o'clock. Alice was happy to take on the task of retrieving the young man. "It'll be so good to see him again," she said. "When we dropped him off with Rigo, we couldn't say much to him about what was going on. Now, even if I can't tell him about what Kaya and I did, at least I can be honest with him about what we were trying to do."

"That will be nice," Tony said. "I haven't really talked to him for a long time, but when I did, he would just ask me for money."

Alice nodded. "I know. He was pretty desperate back then. I'm hoping things are easier for him now."

"So he's just gonna go back to his apartment?" Tony asked.

Alice nodded. "It's got to be so hard for him, being there all alone, especially now that he knows his mom's not coming back. He doesn't have any other family, and he still needs to finish high school."

"Yeah," Tony said. "I mean, it's great that the judge let him stay in Florence on his own, but it's still no good for a guy his age to be left to his own devices. I mean, who looks out for him?"

"Everyone," Alice said. "Mrs. Katz charges him almost nothing for rent, and she cooks for him. And the other ladies in the neighborhood leave him food and stuff like toilet paper."

"But do any of them stay to eat with him?" Tony asked.

Alice stared out of the windshield at the blurry road ahead of her. "I . . . I don't know. I guess not. At least not very often. Maybe we can come by once a week to have dinner with him, or we can invite him over to eat with us."

"Or," Tony said, "we could ask him if he wants to come stay with us, at least until he's done with school."

Alice's mouth dropped open. "You're saying . . . you want Brad to come live with us, at your apartment, and then at our house when it's ready?"

Tony nodded. "That's exactly what I'm saying. I mean, the guy needs much more than he's getting. His father's in prison, and he'll probably never get out now. His mom's dead. He's seventeen. He needs someone. Maybe two someones. He needs someone to care for him."

Alice considered his words. "Someone . . ." she started, "who will always remember his eyes."

Tony pulled up in front of the police station. He turned off the car engine and turned to Alice. "Alice, it's the right thing to do. We can offer it to him, and if he says no, we know that we tried. But if he says yes, just think of the difference it will make to him." He paused. "And us."

"I wasn't planning on moving in with you until I had a schedule of when the work would start on the house," Alice said. "I'm not even close to that point yet." She grabbed Tony's arm. "Tony, is this a ploy to get me to move in even sooner?"

Tony laughed. "No," he said. Alice paid attention. Tony wasn't lying. He was just telling a half-truth. "I mean, that occurred to me, but only after I thought of the idea of offering him a place. It's just a happy side effect of the plan."

Alice turned back to the windshield. She could see figures coming in and out of the police station door, but she couldn't see the features of their faces. She watched the blurry people move like bugs down the walkway and onto the sidewalk. Some got into cars, others stopped to chat with their fellow officers.

"I think we should do it," she said. She turned back to Tony. "Yes. Let's do it!" She laughed. "Let's have our first child together!"

Tony laughed. "Well, this is not exactly how I imagined the process, but I'll take it. There's no guarantee he'll say yes, so we can't get our hopes up, Al. We just offer, and see what he says."

Alice nodded. "Okay," she said. She opened her door. "Can you come get me?" she asked. "This is a busy road, and things aren't entirely in focus right now."

Tony nodded, got out of the car, and came around to get her. He took her arm, and together, they walked into the police station. They approached the desk and announced why they were there.

Ten minutes later, Brad appeared in the lobby. "Hey, Alice," he said solemnly.

Earlier, Alice had no idea what she would do when she first saw Brad. But now, that question was answered. She went right to him and encircled him in her arms. Brad was inches taller than her, but he held her back, resting his chin on her shoulder. After several seconds, Alice pulled away and took Brad's hand. "I'm so sorry, Brad." She didn't even have to say why.

Brad nodded. "I knew," he said. "I hoped I was wrong, but I knew I wasn't." He walked over to Tony and shook his hand. "Good to see you, man," he said. "Thank you guys for coming to get me. I could have walked home, you know."

"But it's your homecoming," Alice said. "We wanted to be here, to greet you. Let's go outside and sit down for a few minutes to catch up."

They walked outside to the sidewalk. They found themselves in front of the town's frozen yogurt store, and then inside, making their own self-serve yogurt sundaes. Back outside, they sat at a round table in the shade of an elm tree. "Thanks for bringing me out to Rigo's house," Brad said. "Dude's cool. He does Wii bowling. He gets really into it. He doesn't like to cook much, so we ordered delivery a lot. I think I gained twenty pounds in two weeks."

"You needed it," Alice said. She looked at Tony, and he nodded. It was on her to start the conversation as the one who knew Brad the best. "Brad, we wanted to talk to you about something."

Brad looked up from his yogurt. "I'm not in trouble, am I? That's exactly what my teachers say to me when I've done something wrong, like the wrong homework or something. Or slept through a whole day of classes." He grinned mischievously.

Alice laughed. "No, nothing like that. It's just, well, Tony and I have been talking. We're gonna be moving in together soon while our house is getting updated."

"What?" Brad asked, confused. "Our house? You two are, what, together or something? I thought you guys were just friends!"

Alice and Tony looked at each other. "We were," Tony explained. "But we were together in the past, in high school. We were pretty hot and heavy until Alice went away to college and I stayed here. But now, we've decided to get back together, and we're pretty sure it's a done deal. So we're fixing up Alice's house to make it ours, and in the meantime, Alice will be staying in my apartment, with me." He looked back at Alice. He smiled. "Our apartment."

Brad watched Alice blush. "Cool," he said. "You guys look great together. So what does all this have to do with what you want to talk about? Do you need help moving? If I help, you legally have to provide me with beer, you know. No free child labor."

Tony smiled. "No," he said. "We don't need your help with moving."

"We might," Alice interjected.

Tony thought about it. "Well, yeah," he said. "Maybe. But what we're trying to say, and doing a very poor job of, is that we would like you to come and live with us, at the apartment, and then at the house when it's ready. It's a big house, lots of room."

Brad's mouth fell open. "What?" he asked. "What the hell? I mean, seriously? You want me to live with you? Why?"

Tony shrugged. "I don't know, man. Maybe we're just not sure we'll, you know, be able to be alone with each other and stuff. Like, it will be easier to adjust to it if we have another person there. And it would only be until you finish school."

"Oh," Brad said. He stared into his froyo. "I mean, it's not a stupid idea. I could pay you rent and stuff. And I'm guessing you guys will be eating dinner and stuff, like, every day. Do you have a big-screen TV?"

Tony nodded. "Pretty big," he said. "And I have the Xbox 360, and the new Madden."

"Huh," Brad said. "I have the PS3. I've got some good games, too. I guess we could hook them both up. I have a TV, too, but it's not that big. You guys have good Wi-Fi?"

"Pretty good," Tony said. "And I have dish for cable. Every channel. Movies and sports."

Brad nodded. "Okay, I'll help you guys out. When should I move in?"

Later, after Tony and Alice had dropped Brad off at his apartment to start to decide what to keep and what to throw in the Dumpster, they went back to Alice's still-intact house.

"I've never seen a true dude talk before in real life," Alice said, amazement in her voice. "You guys basically made all of Brad's life decisions based on electronics and Wi-Fi. And what was all that about him helping us so we could adjust to living together?"

Tony beamed. "Good stuff, huh? I kind of made him feel like he was helping us, instead of the other way around. He knows very well why we want him to move in with us, but he'd never admit that he needed us, or anyone else. I gave him a chance to be able to say yes, but not to admit any weakness."

Alice threw her arms around Tony. "That's obviously your super-power," she said. She kissed him gently on the lips.

Tony held Alice close. "I still can't believe that I'm standing in your house, holding you in my arms," he said. "I was honestly afraid this was never going to happen again."

"Really?" Alice asked, pulling away far enough to look into his eyes. "You really didn't trust that I'd come to my senses eventually?"

Tony shrugged. "I hoped you would," he said. "But sometimes, you can hope for things, and you still don't get them. But I held on to my hope. And it paid off." He kissed her again. "Tell me about your meeting with Kaya and the guys."

They sat down on the couch and Alice recalled all of the details of the picnic in the park, up to and including the visit from the crow. "No way," Tony said, shaking his head. "No. It couldn't be his ring. What the hell? Uh uh. There must be some guy from Wisteria who was in his class who had the same initials. Right?" He looked desperately at Alice. "Please tell me that this is all just a huge coincidence."

Alice bit her top lip. "It's all a big coincidence," she said. "Just a co-incidental crow in a coincidental park, with a coincidental ring. Yeah. I'll buy that. Nothing special about it." She rolled her eyes. "I don't know what happened, Tony, but I saw it with my own two dysfunctional eyes. Kaya and Peter saw it, too. And the ring? It fit Rigo perfectly, like it had been fitted just for him. What do you think it means?"

Tony was still shaking his head. "Don't ask me," he said. "I mean, I'm still trying to come to terms that I have a psychic crime-fighting girlfriend with her own band of merry misfits. But now an old profes-sor crow whisperer? I think my head might explode."

Alice laughed. "I don't think Rigo's a crow whisperer," she said. "I think it's an omen, or a sign of some sort. Something to let him know that he's a part of this, not just an observer. He's one of the merry misfits, just like me, Kaya, and Peter. And who knows who else. And it convinced me. I'm going out to Palmetto next week to do the fMRI. I need to. I need to know what connects me to this group, and what makes us tick. And Rigo wants you to come, too. He wants to have images of brains to compare ours to, and I also need you with me, for my ride and my support. Will you do it?"

"You're not planning to go on my birthday, are you? Because I really don't want to spend my whole day driving back and forth to Palmetto on my birthday."

Alice smiled. "No, it won't be your birthday," she promised. "We'll go before your birthday. Remember, Emilie's coming home for both of your birthdays. I plan on spending as much time with her as I can while she's here. I need to make sure there's no question that she'll be coming back when she finishes school next year. And she and I have a lot to talk about. I was thinking of having a party for your birthday on the weekend."

"That would be fun," Tony said. "Who would we invite?"

"I was thinking Kaya and Grayson, Peter and Melody, Carla and Kaylie and Tasha, Graham and Gina and Mason, and anyone else you'd want to be there."

Tony thought about it. "With that group," he thought, "I'd better not invite anyone else. There's gonna be a lot of psychic energy in the air. Might not be safe for normal mortals."

Alice laughed. "You might be right," she said. "So I'll send out an e-vite for next Saturday night. We can keep it low key. Finger food, drinks, and cake."

Tony nodded. "Let's try to go to bed early," he suggested. "Tomorrow morning, I'd like to start getting my place ready for you and Brad to move in. And maybe you can start packing."

Alice looked around her living room and smiled. "I can't wait."

19

"WELCOME," ALICE SAID, AS SHE opened the door to find Graham and Gina, who was carrying baby Mason in a baby sling. "Come in. Everyone else is here already. Can I get you some drinks?"

Gina's eyes got large. "Do you have wine?" she asked excitedly. "I'm gonna pump and dump tonight. I can have a glass of wine. I have tons of milk in the freezer."

"That's a bit too much information," Kaya said, coming over to hug her brother and sister-in-law. "But it's nice to know there are options." She grimaced. "I'm stuck with Sprite. No caffeine, no artificial sweeteners, no alcohol." She made a face. "No fun."

Gina laughed. "Welcome to motherhood," she teased. "But it will be worth it the first time you lay eyes on your tiny baby." She let Kaya lead her to the kitchen to get her drink.

"Thanks for inviting us," Graham said to Alice. "I love your house."

Alice wrinkled her nose. "It's a bit retro," she said. "Maybe seventies style will come around again, but I'm not willing to wait. They're drawing up a plan to update everything, and the work should start within a month. I'm so excited!"

"How are things going over at Tony's place?" Graham asked.

"Pretty good so far," Alice said. "Brad's back there with Pony to-night. They're getting along great. Brad's settling in. It didn't take him very long. But there's a sadness there that's gonna be hard for him to get through. He has this tough exterior, but inside, he's just this little boy that misses his mom. I'm hoping that Tony and I can help him. At least we can make him feel loved and cared for."

"It's a great thing you're doing," Graham said warmly.

"I think I heard my name over here," Tony said, taking his place by Alice's side and putting his arm around her back. "How's it going, Graham? Things going okay with your research?"

Alice slowly detached herself from the conversation and started to wander around the room. She stopped in front of Dr. Blake and Peter, who were chatting on the couch. "Can I get you guys another drink?" she asked.

Dr. Blake looked up at her and smiled. "No thank you, Alice," he said. "I was just telling Peter about your test results. Why don't you join us?" He scooted over to make room, and Alice sat down. "I'm assuming it was okay to fill Peter in?"

Alice nodded. "Of course," she said. "We're all in this together. I just assumed we would all be privy to all of the information." She looked at Peter. "It was pretty amazing. It was actually fun. I kind of regret waiting so long to have the fMRI. It was nothing like the eye tests that I've had."

Dr. Blake chuckled. "No," he said. "No lasers to your retinas. Just hook you up, expose you to stimuli, and see how you react. And your reactions were just what we expected." He turned to Peter. "Her anomaly is almost identical to the ones that you and Kaya have. There were some slight variations during the reactions. I'm assuming this means that there is a difference in strength for different skills that each of you possess. But that might change as you learn more and your skills strengthen. I'd like to repeat the testing every six months to monitor for changes."

Alice smiled. "I have the knob," she said smugly. Then she laughed. "We need to come up with a better term than that. Did you know that knob only has one meaning in Great Britain? And it's not the one we use to describe the device that opens doors. Yeah. It's the other defi-nition. I guess we just need to make sure we're not talking about this stuff in front of a Brit!"

"I wonder what they call their anomaly," Peter said.

Dr. Blake shrugged. "I wish I knew if they called it anything," he said. "I would love to know if there are other researchers out there in the world right now who are studying the same phenomena. I would expect they would be using the utmost discretion, like I am. I would certainly appreciate an opportunity to collaborate with my peers about this, but at this point, that's not an option. Maybe someday we'll find a way to figure out who has the anomaly, and therefore be able to find out if they have anyone who is helping them, the way I hope that I'm helping all of you."

"You've been a great help," Kaya said, walking over with a glass of red wine and handing it to Alice. "Here, drink this," she said with a grin. "It's your medicine. It's good for you." She took a gulp of her Sprite and then belched. "Oh, excuse me," she said.

Carla and Kaylie wandered over with Tasha. They sat on the floor, spread out a blanket, covered it with toys, and sat their daughter on it. Carla let out a sigh. "Please let her just sit here for a few minutes so we can rest," she begged. "Since she's been crawling, we've both been exhausted with babyproofing and chasing her around. As soon as she hits the floor, she's off." She watched the baby closely. "She seems to be ready for a rest. Thank God. I am, too." She picked up a glass of wine from the coffee table and took a swig. "This is my glass, isn't it?" She looked around. "You know, I just don't give a shit." She took another gulp.

"Your house is so classic," Kaylie told Alice. "I love the windows. And the moldings. I hope you're going to keep them when you remodel."

Alice nodded. "I'm keeping most of the structure. Tony insisted. Plus, I think the original flourishes add to the value of the house. The aesthetic value. I think that's what my parents liked about the house when they first looked at it. It was built in the 1920s, when they used to build really solid houses."

"It will be nice when it's brought into the 2000s, though," Tony said, sitting down next to Alice, leading to everyone scurrying over a few more inches.

Alice took his hand. "Tony has some really great ideas. Bamboo floors. Those will be nice, and they're really sustainable. Bamboo grows back loads faster than wood."

"And I'm really looking forward to the breakfast bar," Tony said. "I have a waffle maker. I think I'll be making a lot more waffles once I have the room and people to make them for."

Melody wandered over from the food table, and Peter pulled her down on his lap. She giggled. Kaya rolled her eyes, and Alice smiled. "What's everyone talking about?" Melody asked.

"The house," Tony told her. "We came up with a plan with our contractor, and it's looking pretty good. They're gonna start with all the structural stuff, including tearing down the wall to build the breakfast bar, and then building the master bedroom and bath. That's my favorite part." He put his arm around Alice's shoulders.

"Once all that is done," Alice continued, "we get to do the fun part, picking out tile and wallpaper, and countertops and stuff. Tony will get to do most of the choosing, but I'll have a say, too. Even if it gets to the point where I can't see what's in the house, I'll still know what's there, and I don't want to be totally embarrassed!" She smiled to let her friends know that she wasn't feeling sad or asking for sympathy. Tony reached over and kissed the side of her head.

There were footsteps on the stairway, and Emilie entered the room. "Hey," she said to the group. "Sorry I was gone so long. Apparently my cat escaped, and the cat sitter was freaking out. I talked her down, and she found him in the backyard, sleeping in the milkweed patch. It's where he always goes when he gets out. Then I had to coach her on how to catch him without scaring him away." She looked at the coffee table. "Did someone drink my wine?"

Alice jumped up. "I'll get you another one."

"I'll come with you," Emilie offered.

They went into the kitchen, and Alice got a bottle of white wine out of the refrigerator. "We get to start a new bottle," she told her best friend. "Would you like to do the honors?"

Emilie smiled. She loved to use a corkscrew. "Of course," she said. She peeled off the paper and started to insert the tool. "Are you having a good time?"

Alice grinned. "I should be asking you that," she said. "It's your birthday party. I hope you liked the necklace."

Emilie pulled the necklace out from under her tank top. She fingered the charm. "A tiny computer? What's not to love? I'll never take it off! And I loved the CD that Tony gave me. Offspring! That guy's a kick."

Alice laughed. "He is indeed."

Emilie sat down on a kitchen chair. "So things went okay for the two of you, once you talked? I mean, it looks like things are going very well."

"Things are amazing," Alice said, sitting down next to her. "Living with him and Brad has been so great. You know, there are the obvious great things about living together, but I guess also I didn't realize how much I was missing out on with my sight until I started to get more support. Tony was right. He's really helping me, and it doesn't feel like I'm losing myself because of it."

Emilie put her hand over Alice's. "I knew it would be great," she said softly. "The two of you have always belonged together. You just had to find your way back to each other. I'm just sorry that you lost so many years."

"I don't look at it that way," Alice said. "I think those years were useful for us. It helped us figure out what we wanted. And it just so happened that what we wanted was each other. So yeah, everything happens for a reason."

Tony came into the kitchen. "Are you coming back out?" he asked Alice. "I miss you." He turned to his twin. "You too, of course."

"Of course," Emilie said, rolling her eyes.

"I think it's time for cake," Alice said. "Why don't the two of you go back in there, and I'll bring it out. Tony, introduce Em to the people who came in while she was on the phone upstairs. Go."

After her boyfriend and best friend left, Alice searched for the matches. She had forgotten how small a matchbook could be. She ran her hands through her junk drawer and used her sense of touch. Eventually, her fingers found what they sought. She lit the candles on the giant two-layer chocolate cake and started out toward the dining room, singing the Happy Birthday song. Everyone joined in while Tony and Emilie sat next to each other in awkward embarrassment. They took turns blowing out candles, and everyone clapped.

After the cake was cut and served, Alice and Tony returned to the couch with their plates. "What did you wish for?" Alice asked Tony.

Tony grinned. "If I tell you my wish, it won't come true. But I will tell you this: it has already partially come true, so I'm pretty hopeful."

"What do you think Emilie wished for?"

"I have no idea," Tony said. "I know something that she has been wishing for, for a long time, and that has come true, too." He kissed Alice's cheek.

"Hey, you guys," Kaya said, sitting on a recliner with her cake. "I wanted to ask you something. Those of you who have, well, you know. The knob." Everyone laughed. "No, really. Since we're all here, would you mind if we tried something? I was wondering after the whole thing at the prison, where I could read Chet's thoughts while Alice was putting thoughts in his head, if maybe there was more that we could do. You know, like, can more than one of us communicate at the same time? So, like, Alice and Dad, can we all have a conversation together, at the same time, inside our heads?"

Peter shrugged. "It's an interesting thought," he said. "I could see how that could be beneficial, if we were trying to do something." He laughed. "I get a picture in my head of us trying to infiltrate a criminal compound and using our skills instead of walkie-talkies or earpieces. I bet we could."

Alice nodded. "I'd be willing to give it a try."

Grayson looked up. "Kaya, I'm starting to get concerned about all of this," he said softly. "I mean, I understand you wanting to know what you can do and all, but sometimes you seem exhausted after you do things like this. You're already dealing with feeling sick all the time."

Kaya smiled at her husband warmly. "Grayson, it will be fine," she said. "This is just like a party game. I get tired when it's serious, or when I overdo it. Alice does, too, and Dad, I think. I promise you, if it feels like I'm getting tired, I'll stop." Grayson looked at her for a few seconds and then nodded once. "Okay," she said to the group. "I'll start." She closed her eyes.

A few seconds passed, and then Alice felt a tingle in her head. Then, words appeared in her brain. *If you can hear me, lift your left hand.* Alice lifted her left hand and then glanced at Peter. He was lifting his left hand, too. He looked at Alice and they both smiled.

"Let me try," Alice said. She closed her eyes. She tried to send a message. *Snap your fingers if you hear this.* Nothing happened. "Could you not hear me?"

Peter shook his head. "I couldn't," he said. "Could you, Ky?" Kaya shook her head.

Dr. Blake's hand went up. "Sharing thoughts is a new skill for Alice," he said. "When the two of you first started sharing thoughts, you had to touch in some way. Maybe with new skills, you need to have touch at first until it gets stronger. Why don't you all try holding hands and see if that helps."

Alice shrugged. "I'm willing to give it a try." She got up and moved to the middle of the floor and sat down. Kaya and Peter sat with her in a small circle. "Okay, here I go." *If you can hear me, say the month of your birthday out loud.*

Two voices out loud.

"April."

"December."

Kaya dropped hands and clapped. "It worked!" she exclaimed. "We both heard you. Let's see if we can have a conversation."

They reached for each other's hands.

Tony looks so happy, Kaya thought. *And so do you, Alice. The two of you are so great together!*

It's true, Peter thought. *I caught some of his thoughts by accident earlier. He was talking to Grayson, but he was thinking about you and how much he loves being with you and having Brad there.*

Alice blushed. *Thank you, you guys*, she thought. *It's great for me, too. I never thought that things could be so good! I always wanted to be able to—*

Help . . .

A small voice came through. Kaya dropped Peter and Alice's hands. "What was that?" she asked.

"What was what?" Grayson asked, concerned in his voice. "Are you okay, Kaya?"

Kaya nodded. "I heard something while Alice was sending out her thoughts. Did the two of you hear it, too?"

Alice nodded. "I thought I heard someone say 'help,' but I thought I was imagining it. Was it one of you, or did we pick up on someone else in the room? Did anyone here think the word help?"

Everyone shook their heads. "Sometimes I think 'help,'" Kaylie said. "But it's usually when I'm knee-deep in poop and a screaming baby. But not now."

Peter shook his head. "That was weird," he said. "I could barely hear it. Should we try again? Let's hold hands again and see if we hear anything else." They all grabbed hands. *Anything?* he thought.

The two women shook their heads. *Let's give it a minute*, Kaya thought. *Maybe it's intermittent. Let's try to concentrate on hearing it, and maybe—*

Help me!

Alice kept hold of Peter and Kaya's hands but shook her head. "There it is again!" she said. "Very soft. I could barely make it out. But it sounded like 'help me' this time. It sounds vaguely female."

"We need to figure out how to make it louder and see if we can talk back to it."

Dr. Blake put his hand to his head in thought. "I'm not sure how to amplify the sound," he said. He turned to Graham. "Do you have any ideas?"

Graham considered it. "The three of you get stronger together, and holding hands makes you even stronger." He looked at his own hands. "I have the knob. Maybe I can help." He stood and went to join the circle. He sat between his father and his sister, and they all grabbed hands. "Now what do I do?" he asked.

"Just concentrate," Peter instructed. "Focus on the voices."

"It seemed like the voice came when we were all communicating," Alice said. "Let's share thoughts. We can try to include Graham."

Graham, can you hear us? Kaya thought in her head.

Graham nodded. *Just like I can when we do this alone. Can you all hear me?*

I can hear you, Alice thought. *Peter?*

Loud and clear, came Peter's answer. *Is there someone else out there?*

I'm here, a voice came back. *But I don't know what's happening. Is this real? Am I going crazy?*

I can hear you, Kaya said. *I can hear you really well now. What's your name?*

I'm Thea, the voice said. *What's going on? Why are you in my head?*

It's okay, Alice thought softly. *You're not going crazy. We're not just voices. We're real people. We're all together. We're sitting in a circle, holding hands.*

Is it a seance? Thea thought. *Because I don't think I'm dead. I can't be dead.*

Kaya laughed in her mind. *No,* she thought. *It's not a seance. It's a birthday party. We were talking to each other, using our minds, and somehow, we heard you. You must be nearby.*

How are you hearing me? Thea asked.

We all have a difference in our brains, Peter explained. *It's a long story. We've all had it for years, usually since our teen years. At least that's when we started to notice that we were different.*

Yes! Thea's thoughts said. *I was sixteen. I noticed it then. But it wasn't until later . . .*

What? Alice asked. *What wasn't until later?*

That others started to notice, Thea continued.

How? Peter asked. *What did they see? What is it you can do? We all have different skills, but we think that we can all learn each other's skills eventually. What is your skill, Thea?*

It's when I touch people, Thea thought.

What happens when you touch people? Alice asked.

It's—oh, I have to go.

No, wait, Kaya insisted. *Don't go. Tell us more. What is it you can do?*

There was a hesitation. *He's calling me. I have to go, now.*

Who's calling you? Peter asked.

Really. I have to go. I don't want anything bad to happen. But I know you're out there now. That actually helps.

We want to help you, Thea, Alice said. *We heard you crying for help. What do you need help with? Thea, where are you? How can we help you?*

I'm in Wheeler, Thea answered. *Oh no, he sounds mad. I have to go. Thank you so much. Goodbye.*

Wait! Thea!

There was no reply. The four of them tried to reach Thea for five more minutes, but she was gone. Finally, they dropped their hands.

"What happened?" Dr. Blake asked. "You were off in your own world for a long time. Did you reach the person?"

Graham nodded. "We did," he said. "Her name is Thea, and she's in Wheeler. She sounds like she's in some kind of trouble."

"What kind of trouble?" Carla asked. "Wheeler is our jurisdiction. Maybe we can help her in some kind of way."

"She didn't say," Peter told her. "She said that *he* was calling her, and *he* sounded angry. Maybe some kind of domestic abuse? She seemed scared of him, whoever he is."

"Maybe we can try to find her," Melody suggested. "Her name is Thea and she lives in Wheeler. That can't be too hard using the internet."

"Let's try," Tony said. He got up and went into the kitchen. He came back with his laptop computer. "I'll try to do a Google search." He typed in Thea and Wheeler in their state. "There are lots of them," he said. "How do we narrow it down?"

"She sounded like she was about our age," Alice said. "Mid-twenties maybe. Maybe married? I don't know. Maybe there are records of the Wheeler High yearbook? We can narrow it down to the 1990s."

"That's a great idea, Al," Tony said, giving her a smile. "I'll see if I can find anything on the Wheeler High website. This might take a minute or so."

"Hmm," Dr. Blake said quietly.

Kaya looked at him. "Hmm, what?" she asked.

"I wonder if Thea might be short for something, a nickname. You know, like Theodora or something."

Tony nodded. "That's a good point. I've never heard that name before. It might come from a different name,"

"Hmm," Alice said.

Kaya looked at her, exasperation in her eyes. "What now?"

"I wonder if we can do a Google search for the name Thea," she said. "Maybe we can find out what it's short for, and see if any of those names might hold a clue."

Dr. Blake's brows rose. "Yes," he said. "I'm learning to suspend belief these days. My name means 'guide,' and that's kind of the role I've taken on in this group. *Alice* means 'truth.'"

"*Kaya* means 'pot,'" Kaya said with a smirk.

"It also means 'wise child,'" Peter said. Everyone looked at him. "I looked it up after the conversation we had a few weeks ago, Kaya," he explained. "I remember you said it means 'the sea' in Hawaiian, and I wanted to see if there were other meanings. Wise child. It makes a lot of sense. The wise child knows all."

"What about Peter?" Alice asked. "Any special meaning?"

Peter shrugged. "It's often used as slang for penis." He laughed.

Kaya pretended to vomit. "Dad, you changed when you were away," she said. Then she laughed.

"It means 'rock' or 'stone,'" Tony said, looking up from his computer. "I mean, it's a stretch, but you're the oldest one of the band of merry misfits, excluding Dr. Blake, but he doesn't have the knob." He laughed. "Maybe we should change the name from knob to Peter!" Everyone laughed.

"Look up Thea," Alice instructed.

Tony typed for a few moments and then shook his head. "It means 'goddess,' or 'gift of God.' I don't see how that could fit in here unless she's an angel or something."

"It's possible that the gifts could be God-given," Grayson said. "I mean, we don't know enough about God to know how the concept works. Maybe the knob is a gift from God, or it was when people were first created, or developed from one-celled organisms."

"Possibly," Tony said. "But there are some other names here that Thea might come from, which is what I was going to look up in the first place. Here it says Althea, Mathea, and Dorothea. It could also be Timothea or Theodora."

"See what they all mean," Carla said, leaning in closer from anticipation.

Tony fussed with the keys. "Timothea is another God one," he said. "Theodora is 'gift of God.' I'm seeing a trend here. Maybe it's the root -thea, like theism. Dorothea is 'gift of God,' too. I'm guessing Mathea will be the same thing. Let's see. Yup. Bingo. Give that man a cigar. That just leaves Althea. Any guesses?"

"I'm guessing gift from God!" Kaylie yelled out.

Tap tap tap. "Althea," Tony said. "Here it is. Oh." He paused, looking at the screen. "Oh my. It's not gift of God. It is definitely not gift of God."

"What is it then?" Alice asked impatiently.

Tony looked up at the group. "It means 'with healing power.'"

There was a prolonged silence. Finally, Peter spoke. "I think we found our girl."

Tony started pounding on the keys again. "Bam! I've got it! Althea Bright, Wheeler High, class of 1994. And I have a picture from the yearbook." He turned the computer for everyone to see. "She's cute."

Alice glared at him, then looked at the computer. Then she shrugged. "Yeah, she is," she said grudgingly. Althea looked to be petite, with curly, bouncy brown hair and brown eyes. She had round cheeks and a friendly smile. The blurb under her picture thanked many friends and teachers, as well as her mother and someone named Benny. Then there was a quote from Yoko Ono: "Healing yourself is connected with healing others."

Kaya read the quote out loud. Then she shook her head. "This is a sign," she said. "It's pointing us right to this woman, this Thea. She needs us. We need to find out where she is right now. She's in some sort of trouble. And I have a feeling it has something to do with the things she's capable of doing. We have to help her."

"Yes," Alice said. "We have to find her. We have to help her." She turned to look at Peter.

Peter nodded. "We have to help her," he agreed. He put out his hand. Kaya put her hand on top of his, and then Alice added hers. "She needs us," Peter went on. "And we are going to help her, no matter what it takes."

Acknowledgments

I would like to thank those of you who have taken a chance on a new author and read my books, especially those of you that read one, then sought out others! That means the world to me. I have two superfans, and I never thought something like that would happen. And they aren't even people I've met!

As always thank you to Jai Design for all of the hard work you have done for me on my covers and marketing my books, Nicole Frail for making me look good with my grammar and spelling, and Milana Gilligan for taking one of the best pictures I've ever had of myself! I will use it for every book, ever! Thanks to illustrator and tattoo artist Vivian McKay for bringing Alice to life on the cover!

Thank you to Chris and Bobbie, Delilah and Leya, for being there with me bright and early every Sunday morning so we can get to work. You ladies are my inspiration!

Thank you to my alpha Jonathan and my beta Clint. You guys are the best. Thanks also to Robert for reading all of my books and not hating them.

And, of course, thank you Al and Tory for putting up with me. Not to mention the cats.

About the Author

Debby Meltzer Quick has been writing for fun since age twelve. Growing up in Massachusetts, she became a huge fan of Boston sports, especially the Red Sox and the Patriots, and she aspired to be a sports reporter. Instead, she became a social worker. She is an avid reader of fiction and lover of puzzles and anything chocolate. She lives in Portland, Oregon, with her husband, daughter, two cats, and one rabbit. Debby has completed three book series, two of which have books currently published. Look for more books in the Anomaly and McKinney High Class of 1986, as well as a stand-alone novel, coming in 2025.

DON'T MISS THE NEXT INSTALLMENT IN

A HEALING TOUCH

BOOK 3

1

"I WANT TO GET A CAT."

Grayson was rubbing cocoa butter on his wife's slightly protruding stomach while she lay on her back on the bed, her tank top hiked up to her enlarged breasts. Grayson tried to keep his focus on Kaya's stomach. She was purring like a cat, so it was not a huge shock that Kaya was thinking of felines. "Okay," Grayson said. He was not averse to getting a pet, and if it made Kaya happy, all the better.

Kaya lifted her head slightly. "Are you serious?" she asked, a smile curling onto the edge of her lips.

Grayson nodded. "I mean, if we get a kitten now, we'll be able to get it used to living here, and it'll mellow out before the baby comes."

"No," Kaya said. "I mean a cat. A full grown cat. One that you get at the shelter. One that someone dumped off at the shelter because they didn't want it anymore. I want that cat."

Grayson laughed. Of course Kaya wanted that cat. She wanted to help the cat, to give it a home where it could be loved and cared for,

for the rest of its days. "I'm okay with that," he said. "What kind of cat would you want if you had a choice?"

Kaya reached up to her head, which was being held up by a firm pillow. "I like ragdolls," she said. "They kinda go limp when you pick them up. But I don't think we'll find any of those in the shelter. I bet we'll end up with a tabby cat or one of those tuxedo cats. I don't really care. Oh, it would be really good to get one of those six-toed cats! I heard they came over here on the *Mayflower*!"

That would be cool," Grayson said. He scooped more cocoa butter onto his fingers and applied it to his wife's taut skin.

Kaya made a face. "Are you just placating me?" she asked. "Is it one of those, 'anything Kaya wants, Kaya gets' situations? I mean, do you really want a cat?"

"I do," Grayson said, feeling the slickness of Kaya's belly skin on the tips of his fingers. "I really want a cat."

Kaya reached down and trapped Grayson's hand under hers. "Stop," she said. "You don't get to rub my belly until I know the truth. Can I try? Please?"

Grayson knew what Kaya was asking. He hesitated. "You know I think it's awesome, all this stuff you can do with your mind," he said, "but I don't feel comfortable with you taking on more of it while you're pregnant. I'm worried you'll wear yourself out."

Kaya smirked. "So trying to tell if you're telling the truth will wear me out more than the activity that you're fantasizing about right now?"

Grayson glared at his wife. "I told you that you need to let me know before you run around inside of my brain," he said. "It's an unfair advantage. I can't read *your* thoughts."

Kaya laughed. "I don't need to pick your brain to know what you want," she said. "You've been rubbing my stomach for over fifteen minutes. You keep rubbing lower and lower. You show no signs of getting bored, and your pupils are as big as dishes. Your body gives you away, my dear."

Grayson shook his head. "So I'm a hot-blooded human man that has urges to make love to my wife. Call the press!"

Kaya rolled onto her side, and she laughed. "I'm a hot-blooded human woman," she said. "I've just entered the second trimester of my pregnancy, and I stopped vomiting over a week ago. How do *my* pupils look?"

Grayson looked into her eyes. "Kinda dishy," he said with a grin.

Kaya looked at him with satisfaction. "Okay then," she said. "We're on the same page. But first, I'm going to test to see whether you want a cat. Get off me."

Grayson reluctantly hopped to the side as Kaya sat up. "I'll get to get back on you after this though, right?" he asked. "You're not gonna get mad at me if for some reason this goes wrong and you can't tell if I'm telling you the truth, even if I say I am?"

Kaya tilted her head. "I promise," she said. "Okay. So, sit criss-cross-applesauce, and I'll face you."

"That's cross-legged, right?"

Kaya laughed. "I thought you'd be up on all my cheerleader lingo by now. But yes. Okay. Now, take my hands. Empty your mind as best as you can." Kaya closed her eyes. "Now close your eyes. Focus on just you and me. Stop squeezing my hand like that! Hey, wipe that smile off of your face! Okay, so now, I'm gonna ask you a question. Do you, Grayson Pike, want to get a cat?" She opened one eye and looked at him.

Grayson kept his eyes closed although he knew that Kaya was watching him. "I want you to have a cat," he said.

Kaya dropped both of his hands. "That's not what I asked you, and you know it!" She took his hands again. She closed her eyes. "Okay, I'm going to ask you again. This time, answer the question. Grayson, do you, yourself, exclusive from my wishes, want to get a cat?"

"I do," Grayson said.

Kaya sat still for several seconds, still holding Grayson's hands, her eyes closed. "Nothing," she said. "I can't read anything. Does that mean that you're telling the truth, or that it isn't working? Hold on a sec." She dropped Grayson's hands, but kept her eyes closed, focusing.

"What are you doing?" Grayson asked.

"I'm contacting Alice," she said. "I'm sending her a message, asking her what I should do."

Grayson shook his head. "You're doing it again," he said. "You're overdoing it with your skills. We don't know enough about these long-distance thoughts yet. Just because you could read that woman in Wheeler the other day—"

"Thea," Kaya said, eyes still closed.

"Thea," Grayson echoed. "It took four of you to be able to communicate with her. It's too much for just one person."

Kaya opened one eye. "Grayson, I've been doing all this stuff since I was fourteen. I know what I'm doing. This isn't going to hurt me, or the baby."

"You could just call her, like a normal person."

Kaya laughed. "What did you just accuse me of not being? A normal person? That's hysterical! Oh, she's here. Hold on." Seconds went by. "She says I need to ask you something, and you should lie. Duh. Of course. Okay, I thanked her. I said goodbye. Okay. Let's try this again." She took his hands. She closed her eyes. "Okay, husband of mine, lie to me, baby. Do you want me or not? Tell me, Grayson, do you want my body?"

Grayson felt hot. "You want me to lie?" he asked, his heart accelerating. "Do I want your body? Okay. Here I go. No, Kaya. I don't want your body. Your body repulses me to no end. You are not desirable at all to me. Now, go! Away from me!"

Kaya fell back as if jolted by an electrical shock. Grayson startled. "Are you okay?" he asked.

Kaya sat up, laughing. "Oh my God!" she exclaimed. "Wow! So that was a whopper of a lie, Grayson! If that lie had been any more clear, you might have electrocuted me! But it worked! I did it!" She threw her arms around his neck. "I'm a living, breathing lie detector test!" She kissed him on the mouth.

Grayson grinned. "We're getting a cat!" he said. Then, he gently laid her down on the bed on her back. "And now my reward for telling the truth . . ."

Kaya held out her arm. "You don't get rewarded for telling the truth," she told him. "You're expected to tell the truth. But *I* get rewarded for being able to tell when you're telling the truth. So take off your pants!"

Grayson smiled, his pupils as large as frying pans. "Yes ma'am, Mrs. Pike. Your wish is my command."

"What was that all about?" Tony asked. He was lying naked and sleepily on the bed the two of them shared in his apartment. Since Alice had moved in, it had been *their* apartment while they waited for Alice's, well, *their*, house to be remodeled. So for now, it was Tony, Alice, and Brad, their teenage border, in the small two-bedroom apartment in Florence, along with a large white dog named Pony.

"That was Kaya," Alice said.

Tony laughed. "Alice, it's not like sending messages by your thoughts is a phone call. Of course it was Kaya. The only other person it could have been was Peter, and I would feel a bit put out if Kaya's psychic father was sending you private messages at night, right after you and I made love."

Alice looked amused. "Yeah, I guess we need to come up with a whole new language for what Kaya and I can do. I mean, we can't set up a voicemail or anything." She looked down. "I wish we could, though. We've tried to reach Thea several times since we talked to her in our minds a couple of weeks ago, and she never answers us. I don't know if she can't hear us, or if she's just ignoring us."

"Maybe she thinks it's all in her head and she's going crazy," Tony suggested. "I mean, that's what happened to Kaya when she first started hearing thoughts. She thought they were voices."

Alice nodded. "I don't know. I hope not. That would be so scary for her. But anyway, back to Kaya. She's practicing her truth-or-lie skill on Grayson. She's a really good student. She's picking up on the skill really easily. I wish it was that easy for me to read other people's thoughts, like she and Peter do. But it will come in time." She rolled back over into Tony's strong arms. "But it looks like Kaya and Grayson are getting a cat. Grayson was truthful about wanting one."

Tony burst out laughing. "Grayson would do anything for Kaya," he said. "She didn't believe him that he was okay with getting a cat? You know, I would bet that Grayson would be the only one that could fool Kaya about telling the truth. He wants her to be happy so badly, that even if he was allergic to cats, and hated the very ground they padded upon, he would want that cat more than anything so he could see the smile on Kaya's face. So he'd be telling the truth in that respect."

Alice smiled. "Is that what you do for me?" she asked. "Like, when we were choosing paint colors for the bedrooms and bathrooms, you wanted me to be happy so badly that if you were lying, I'd never be able to tell?"

Tony shrugged. "I wouldn't say *that*," he said. "I mean, you have fantastic taste. We have similar tastes. I'm not surprised that I liked the stuff you picked out."

Alice looked into his eyes. "There was a small lie in there," she said. "Just a tiny one, though. I remember when we were in high school and you always told me you thought I looked beautiful. I think that you *did* think that, more or less, but there was a time or two when I could tell you wished I hadn't worn something, or done my hair and makeup a certain way. The very first time I felt the sensation I feel when someone tells a lie near me was when we went shopping at the mall and I tried on that orange dress for homecoming. I remember you telling me that everything looked beautiful on me, but suddenly I felt a wave of nausea. It was enough for me to associate that dress with feeling bad. I didn't realize what it was that I was feeling until later."

Tony was staring at the ceiling, thinking back. "I remember that," he said. "I . . . yeah, I really didn't like that dress. Orange was *not* your color!"

Alice laughed. "Thanks for your honesty now!"

Tony brushed her hair back from her face. "Now you be honest with me," he said softly. "You haven't said anything about what happened yesterday. Talk to me about it."

Alice looked at him. "A lot of things happened yesterday," she said. "I went to court with Carla, and I sat in on an interview with Melody. I ate a portabella burger for lunch. It was messy. I walked Pony—"

"Alice," Tony whispered. "Please. Talk to me."

Alice closed her eyes. "It's hard to talk about," she said. "If I don't talk about it, it's possible that it was a fluke, that it won't happen."

"Alice," Tony said again.

Alice sighed loudly. "I couldn't see Pony's face," she said. A tear dripped from the corner of one of her eyes. "Okay? I looked right at his face, but it was like he had no eyes. Just a big, gray blob. It went away after a minute or so, but it happened. It's getting worse, Tony." Both eyes were tearing up now.

Tony pulled her into his arms and held her tight, allowing her to cry onto his bare chest. "Alice," he said. "I'm so sorry. I know you thought you had more time before things progressed. But maybe it's just temporary. I mean, I'm not saying that it's not going to get worse, but maybe it's still going slowly. Maybe . . ."

"I don't know," Alice said weakly. "I just don't know. But I don't want it to happen again. What happens when I can't see *your* face anymore, Tony? Brad's face? Our house? What if I get worse before the house is done, or . . ." Her tears continued. "Before we have a baby, and our second baby, and . . ." She started to sob. "I don't want to be blind, Tony!"

Tony tried to hold her closer, even closer. "I know, baby, I know," he whispered. "I know. I don't want that for you either. That's why—"

"I know," Alice said. "That's why you wanted us to move in together. I was reluctant at first, but now I know. I have to do things now, before it's too late. I have to have my seeing life while I can still see. I need . . . I need to go to the support groups. I need to go to the Commission For the Blind and get prepared. And I need . . ." She looked up at Tony. "I need to have our babies."

Tony pressed his forehead against hers. "Is that really what you want?" he asked. "I mean, do you want to do that now? I mean, not tonight. Or maybe tonight?"

Alice laughed through her tears. "Oh, sweetie," she said. "Not tonight, okay? I mean, it's not even possible tonight. I'm not ovulating. But yes, soon. I just can't wait much longer. I need . . . I need to have the memories, in my head, before it's all gone. I don't want my baby to have a gray blur for a face in my mind. I wouldn't be able to stand it, Tony."

Tony continued to cradle her in his arms, rocking back and forth. "Okay," he said. "Okay. Tomorrow, we'll make a list of the things you want to do. Places you want to see, people you want to visit. We'll make a complete list of everything you need to see before you can't see anymore. And we'll put having babies on that list." He laughed. "Can you imagine that list? When we come to the baby one, when we do it, we can check it off!"

Alice laughed. "I can't wait to check that off," she said. "But there's one other thing we have to put on our list."

Tony looked into her eyes. "Whatever it is, we'll put it on." His eyes were questioning.

Alice nodded. "I think that you and I, well, we're gonna need to get married. And soon."